THE GROUND BENEATH US

A NOVEL

RACHEL ALLORD

This is a work of fiction. Names, characters, places, and incidents either are the product of the author's imagination or are used fictitiously, and any resemblances to actual persons, living or dead, businesses, companies, events, or locales are entirely coincidental.

Copyright © 2015 Rachel Allord
All rights reserved. No part of this book may be reproduced in any form, or by any electronic or mechanical means, including information storage and retrieval systems, without permission in writing from the author, except by a reviewer, who may quote brief passages in a review. Any members of educational institutions wishing to photocopy part or all of the work for classroom use, or publishers who would like to obtain permission to include the work in an anthology, should send their inquiries to Rachel Allord via rachelallord.com
Two Birds Books
ISBN: 0692554238
ISBN-13: 9780692554234

To Doug,

For taking my hand and walking beside me.

ACKNOWLEDGMENTS

A sincere thank you to those who offered their expertise on topics ranging from running marathons to growing cranberries: DeDe Gibbs, Shari Hanneman, Darren Babcock, and Jacki Pfaff. A special thanks to Kent Youngstrom who not only supplied me with a vivid glimpse into the world of art and design, but also gave me a couple of lines to boot.

My gratitude goes out to those who read various stages of this manuscript: Ann Brunner for enthusiastically reading early, half-baked chapters and final proofing, Dawn Brandt for letting me know I was on the right track, Roxanne and Lily Mesyk, for generous feedback, and Tori Schultz for fresh perspective and insight. A heartfelt thank you to Angie and Jeff Nyquist and Whitney Swenson for being brave and for your willingness to help with the artistic process. I'm indebted to my readers, friends, and family members: thank you for your love, encouragement, and prayers. Elijah and Maylie, I love you both like crazy and I'm so tickled to be your mom.

Sometimes a cliché says it best: Doug Allord, I couldn't have done this without you. Your encouragement, attention to detail, artistry, tech-savviness, and commitment to read draft after draft leave me humbled and grateful. I love you and I'm honored to spend my life by your side.

1

Maggie and I argue all the time, but never before have those words come out of her mouth. They pierce me quick and unexpected, the sting of a wasp. I stand at the back door, immobilized, and watch her stroll down the driveway. She doesn't turn around, doesn't cast a glance over her shoulder to gauge my reaction. She doesn't know I heard, I realize. Only the eyes of the white pony on my daughter's hot pink backpack stare at me in silent condemnation. Once she reaches the sideway she breaks into a run, closing the distance between herself and her brother.

I turn and head back into my house. Retreat to the kitchen, which is no retreat at all. Last night, after returning home from his out-of-town construction site, John dumped his three-day supply of Tupperware containers on the counter. Add to that the bowl of hardening leftover pancake batter and gluey plates. At Maggie's request, I made the kids pancakes this morning.

I made the girl pancakes.

I swipe the assortment of Tupperware into the sink and start running hot water. A sticky note pressed against the side of the refrigerator catches my eye. My husband's version of a text. I shut off the water and grab the note.

H,

Get receipts to Bob.

J

Bob. Our taxman. It's April 4th.

My throat tightens. These words mark John's first to me since he returned home. Not *how are you?* or *I'll pick up a pizza tonight.* Only this hasty imperative to get receipts to Bob. Why does it always fall to me? And why did he get to go out with friends last night instead of coming home to help with taxes, or kids, or anything? I look at the note again. He didn't even bother writing my name.

I crumple the square of paper in my fist.

I pace to the far window, to the sun-drenched spot that often registers ten degrees warmer than the rest of the house, especially on brilliant January mornings. I tilt my face to the light, the sun warm as a freshly laundered towel on my skin. The angelic beams of morning light beckon through the glass. *Come away.* Come away from sassy daughters and insensitive husbands and catastrophic kitchens.

This isn't the first time I've felt the urge to run away, but I've always talked myself out of it. Not today. Today I will obey the sun. Pretend I don't have tax receipts to find. Pretend I didn't just have a screaming match with my seven-year-old. Pretend I don't have thirty unread work emails waiting for me in my inbox or twenty extra pounds to shed. Besides, when the sun shows up in April in Wisconsin you're a fool not to chase it. And I'm already in my sweatpants so it must be fate.

"Bernice!"

My Irish Setter trots in. I dig out her leash from the shoe bin and snap it on.

"We're running away."

Before I talk myself out of it, we're out the door and my feet are slapping pavement. The cadence proves satisfying. With my ponytail swinging in the wind and Bernice trotting next to me, I'm someone else. I'm invincible, unshakable. And then, seconds later, I feel like death. I'm Bigfoot in sweatpants.

What the hell was I thinking? I chase the kids around our backyard. That's it. Four blocks hardly constitutes running away.

Sanctuary lies a few blocks ahead so I lurch onward. I run a block, walk a block. Jog half a block, stagger half a block. By the time I stumble up the front steps to Annalisa's house and rap on her rounded turquoise door, I'm huffing like the Big Bad Wolf.

No answer. I pound again, sending the yellow floral wreath trembling. She has to be home. How can she not be home when I'm dying on her doorstep? Glimpsing no sign of life through the front window, I head around to the back. The van's gone and my throat is on fire. I crank the spigot, cup my hands, and lap like a dog.

I can't go home. Not yet.

Still panting, my eyes land on what might be my salvation. A converted outhouse is hardly an ideal refuge but right now it's all I've got. According to Annalisa, the previous homeowners had the thing moved from the lot of a long-ago family owned restaurant and turned it into a garden shed. When Annalisa and Marco bought the house, they transformed it into a haven for their boys.

Ignoring the NO GIRLS ALLOWED decree carved into the doorframe, I nudge open the door. My children have been inside countless times but I've only ever peeked in.

A hammock saddled with a sleeping bag hangs from the ceiling by two metal hooks. Nerf guns line the wall. A makeshift shelf holds a flashlight, a paperback edition of Captain Underpants, an assortment of whittled sticks, and a metal coffee can with a lid.

This could work. I could stay here. As long as I'm able to break into Annalisa's kitchen not twenty feet away and as long as the month of April doesn't go bi-polar.

Bernice, prone to anxiety on ordinary days, refuses to follow me in. "Get in here, you big chicken." She does and sniffs all four corners before lying down on the planked floor. I ease down next to her and bury my hand in her auburn fur.

I did it. I ran. Ran away. Sure, it was less than a mile and I've landed in an abandoned outhouse opposite a dangling spider, but a victory is a victory.

"Now what, girl?"

She eyes me in trepidation.

Even as Maggie and I were locked in battle I knew I'd eventually end up at Annalisa's. Not here specifically but in her kitchen, where I'd pour out my frustrations as she poured coffee and consolation.

I reach for the coffee can. Unable to glimpse what's beyond the opaque lid, I give the thing a shake. Nothing hisses. Tentatively, I remove the cover. Candy. Or at least discarded wrappers. I riffle through the plastic chrysalises until my fingers hit a fun sized Butterfinger. I'm about to tear into it but stop myself. Have I sunk so low? Runaway to interloper to candy thief? Sighing, I drop it back into the metal can and snap on the lid. I lean my head against the wall and try not to think about what people used to do here a hundred years ago.

It could be worse. I could be home delving into a carton of cookies and cream. Or ransacking my medicine cabinet for prescription pills. At least running—or my feeble attempt—benefits my thighs. The hammock is calling and I'm about to pull off my shoes when I hear the familiar hum of Annalisa's van. The engine ceases. A door opens and shuts. Bernice stiffens and barks. I shush her but she yaps again, apparently claiming this territory as her own.

I hear footsteps now and I consider calling out. Would that give Annalisa —assuming it is Annalisa— reassurance or a heart attack?

As if she's picked up a familiar scent, Bernice's tail starts up. I'm about to shout, "It's only me" when the door flings open.

Annalisa stands there, eyes wide, two-year-old Jackson straddling her hip. Jackson laughs when he sees me. "Holly?" Annalisa says.

"Surprise!"

"What are you doing here?"

"Sorry. You weren't home," I say, as if that should explain everything.

"I was at school, turning in receipts for PTO. Is everything alright?"

She puts Jackson down and he runs to me. I close my eyes and take a whiff of his curls. He smells like a bakery. "I ran away."

Annalisa steps over the threshold. "You ran away?"

"Can I live here?"

"Sure?" She draws out the word, one thin eyebrow raised. "Can I get you a glass of water first? You look kind of..."

"Out of shape?"

"Out of breath. Your cheeks are red."

"That's because of the running part."

"So you're serious. You ran?"

"Seven whole blocks. And then I needed to pass out so I thought I'd do that in your kitchen but you weren't home. So Bernice and I landed here, thought we could camp here for the day, or maybe the week, because I'm kind of done with the wife and mom thing. I'll pay you rent. I won't be any trouble. I just need some food and water and maybe a big shoe because that spider in the corner hasn't taken her eyes off of me."

Annalisa tilts her head. "Why don't you come inside? I have coffee."

I spring to my feet. "Okay."

Annalisa's kitchen could be the set for a cooking show. Last summer she and Marco remodeled it so beautifully that if it were my kitchen I'd never cook because I wouldn't want to mess it up. It's not spacious—none of the rooms in her 1920's bungalow are—but the shades of blue and grey and white make you want to linger, breathe deeply, bend yourself into a yoga pose. Her entire house could be a case study for color therapy. For as pretty as it is, her house bears evidence of life. Pine floorboards showcase scuff marks. The coffee table features water rings. Today I notice a few orange marker flecks on the whitewashed baseboards in one kitchen corner. I drop into one of her padded kitchen chairs and exhale.

Jackson thrusts a half eaten animal cracker at me.

"Thanks buddy. I'll save this for later." I tuck it into my pocket.

Annalisa hands me a glass of water. "I didn't know you were thinking about taking up running again."

Again. She's one of the few who remembers I used to run track, a lifetime ago, in high school.

"I wasn't." I gulp my water.

Annalisa's gray-for-the-moment eyes remain fixed on me. She's wearing a white shirt but if she were to change into a sapphire or emerald blouse, her irises would do the same. She's part chameleon, part pixie.

She announces that Thomas the Tank Engine is on and Jackson flies from the room. "Have you cooled down enough to want coffee?" she asks.

I nod, mostly wanting to wrap my hands around comfort.

Annalisa doctors hers and hands mine to me black then sits across from me at the table. "So you just woke up this morning and thought, today I'm going to run?"

"Run away. You're not getting this. I ran away. From home. Want to join me?"

"In the play fort? No thanks."

"We could pool our money and hightail it to Minnesota. Track down some good lefse. Hit the Mall of America and max out our credit cards."

"Tempting, but Jackson has a well baby appointment at eleven thirty."

"Dream killer."

"Rough morning?"

I close my eyes for a second, wishing I could rewind the morning. "Where do I start."

She waits.

"Guess what she said? Maggie? Guess what she said on her way out the door? I hate you. My seven-year-old. Said it three times as a matter of fact. I hate you I hate you I hate you."

Annalisa's thin shoulders slump. "Ouch."

"She doesn't know I heard. She's seven and she hates me."

"What happened?"

I gaze at Jackson, lying on his tummy in the next room crashing magnetic trains together—toys that used to belong to my Ben. Something twists inside of me. I wish my babies were still babies. "She made a lunchbox."

"Oh. That's bad?"

"You should have seen it. She found this old ratty shoebox and colored it and made a handle and put all of her food inside, in this stinky old shoebox, and insisted on taking it to school. I told her no, it wouldn't last the walk over. It'd fall apart." I peer into my coffee and consider ending the narrative there.

"And then she told you she hated you?"

"No. She found packing tape and made the seams stronger and I still said no. I told her she had a lunchbox, a lunchbox she picked out in the fall, and we were going to be late and she was wasting time and that thing looked ridiculous."

Annalisa cringes.

"So she had a meltdown," I continue. "We both did. I dumped all her food back into her real lunchbox and crammed it in her backpack. On her way out she slammed the back door so hard the key shelf fell down. I went after her, ready to tell her to come back inside and try that again. That's when I heard her. She didn't scream it. Just stated it. Like a simple fact."

Annalisa gives me a weary smile. "I'm sorry."

In my mind I see her, my little Magpie, storming down the driveway. Ignorant of the fact that I overheard her battle cry. Then it hits me. Has she voiced these words before? Released such venom on the way to school other mornings? I drop my face into my hands. "I'm a terrible mother."

I feel Annalisa's hand rest on my head. "You're not. We're all terrible some mornings. She didn't mean it, you know. She doesn't hate you. She was just angry."

"But she did mean it," I say, lifting my head. "In that moment she meant it. That girl knows my buttons. She knew we were running late. She knew we didn't have time to fool around. It's like she wanted to make trouble."

Annalisa nods and gazes out the window. With her faintly freckled ski-slope nose and fair, almost translucent skin, she possesses a fairy-like quality. Someday she will be eighty years old and still look like a girl. Her ash blonde curls are piled and bound on the top of her head. Judging from her attire, I'm guessing she's already tackled her morning yoga session, which she has no business doing since she wears a size nothing. She faces me again. "She probably spent a lot of time on it."

"All morning. And yes," I add before she does, "I know. I should have said something nice. I get it. But we were running late. I didn't have time." I drop my head once more. "Of course I had time to tell her it looked ridiculous."

"You can make this right."

"You think I should have let her take it to school?" My defenses are on the rise.

"No, not necessarily. But telling her it looked ridiculous..." She shrugs her shoulders.

"Was mean. I know."

"Did John say anything?"

"John had already left for work. John didn't even see the kids this morning. John was supposed to be home for dinner last night after being gone for three days on site in Crandon, but John decided to go out with the boys instead and didn't get in until after eleven. But guess what? John left me a note."

"A love note?"

I laugh. "Oh Anna. How I love your naïveté. We're talking about my husband, not yours. No, not unless you call a post-it telling me to get our receipts together for our taxman a love note. Our accountant calls him but for some reason, just like everything else, it's my responsibility. Yet another reason why I ran away." I pause in my diatribe to take a sip of coffee.

Annalisa rests her pointed chin in her hand and gazes out the window. "I've fantasized about running away. To some beautiful brownstone apartment that doesn't have a single Lego on the floor. Where the toilet seat stays down." She turns her attention back on me. "Maggie doesn't hate you. She was angry. She's strong and creative. Like her mother."

Jackson ambles over and asks for juice. Annalisa gets up and assembles a sippy cup. "Are we still on for Friday night?"

"Wouldn't miss it. I'll bring taco dip. Is Laura coming?"

"I hope so. She needs to, I think."

The mere thought of Laura shrinks the events of my morning down to size. "I'll give her a call and offer to pick her up," I promise.

After rinsing my coffee cup and placing it in Annalisa's dishwasher, I head down the hall to make a pit stop.

When I catch my reflection in the bathroom mirror, I see that my face is glowing. Wisps of dark, damp hair curl alongside my cheeks. Inspired, I peek under the hem of my shirt. Still doughy and white. I tug out my disheveled ponytail and quickly assemble my mane into a braid that falls just above my bra strap.

When I return to the kitchen, Jackson wraps himself around my legs. I scoop him up and nibble his cheeks while he chortles. "This child," I say when I set him down, "is going to break hearts. Can't imagine if you'd had that elusive girl instead."

Annalisa smiles. "I can't either."

I look out the window and sigh at the play fort.

"Would you like to stay?" she asks.

"Yes, but my kitchen desperately needs me. But thanks. It's nice to know it's here."

She follows me outside and waves me off. I untie Bernice and we set off at a brisk walk.

On impulse, I take Cherry Street home. The chatter of the birds and the hint of things yearning to bloom and the breeze against my cheek calm me. My kitchen has been dirty before. Maggie loved me yesterday. John and I will muddle through taxes. I can do this. My walk turns to a jog and my jog to a run.

Some vault in my memory unhinges and the voice of my high school track coach wafts out: Pay attention to your breathing. Concentrate on your stride. Tuck in those chicken wings! I elongate my stride and straighten my back so my head's no longer jutting forward. I breathe in and out, steady and regular. *Click*. I remember how to run.

I pass the kids' school. Is Maggie sitting there with a lump in her throat, all because of me? Make things right, Annalisa advised. But how? I'll stumble upon the answer, I'm convinced, if my feet keep slapping the pavement. If I run hard enough, fast enough, far enough, I'll run smack dab into the solution.

Maggie is proficient at presenting me with problems. Seven and a half years ago she entered the world red-faced and screaming and some days it seems little has changed. Ben, my first born, did little to prepare me.

I'm wheezing now and someone's jabbed a poker into my side. I look down at my feet. Mercifully, my shoe's untied. I drop the leash and crouch down. Bernice barks and bolts.

"Bernice!"

She's galloping through the front yard of a ranch house across the street. I catch sight of a rabbit tail before it disappears into a hedge that separates the house from the neighbor's. I dig out Jackson's half eaten animal cracker from my pocket, hold it out, and jog across the street. "Ber-neeese. Come here, girl. Treat!"

She doesn't even look up, the prospect of fresh rabbit apparently more enticing. "Bernice. Get over here. *Now.*"

I inch closer, ready to lunge for the leash. She dashes. "Stupid, stupid dog!"

A high-pitched whistle pierces the air. Bernice's head snaps up, as does mine. I turn and see a man standing on the front stoop of the ranch house, waving something in the air. Bacon, I think.

Bernice watches him trying, it seems, to decide.

"Here girl!" He walks down the steps and tears the strip of bacon in two and tosses half of it in the direction of my insubordinate dog. Bernice trots over, sniffs and gobbles. The man picks up the end of her leash. "Good girl," he says, and feeds her the rest. "Good girl."

I jog over, my cheeks hot. "Thank you. Sorry."

"No worries. What kind of dog?"

"An old, disobedient dog."

He laughs.

"An Irish Setter."

"She's a pretty girl." He hands me the end of the leash. Traces of red—paint? Blood? Marinara sauce?—stain his fingernails. He's wearing white socks with no shoes, as if he glimpsed my dilemma from his window and ran straight out to help.

"She saw a rabbit," I explain. "Maybe that's how I can get her to run faster."

"You're a runner?"

The moment of truth. "Yes." How ridiculously confident I sound! Now that I've declared it to the world, or at least to this man with floppy golden brown hair who I suddenly recognize from the kids' school, does that make it true? "You're a Hoover Elementary parent, right? I think I've seen you around."

"My daughter Ava is in first grade. You have kids there?"

"Ben's in fourth and Maggie's in second."

"You'll have to steer me toward the right teachers," he says and smiles.

"Who does Ava have?"

"Mrs. Thompson."

"Strict but effective. How is Ava doing with her?"

He exhales. "Well this has been a rough year for Ava, starting in a new school and all, but she's doing okay. Mrs. Thompson said she hardly said a word in class until after Christmas. She kind of depends on the other girls to do the talking for her."

"She should meet my Maggie. She loves talking for other people. She's either going to be a lawyer or a ventriloquist."

He grins. "Maybe they've already met."

"Maybe."

"Seth Caldwell," he says, extending his hand.

"Holly Lewis." I shake his hand and tip my head toward Bernice. "And The News."

His grin widens, the corners of his eyes crinkling behind his Clark Kent glasses.

"I'm kidding," I say. "That's Bernice."

"I don't think I've ever met a Bernice."

"She's named after my aunt and she's sorry for all the commotion she caused today. The dog I mean, not my aunt."

He laughs. "Are you always this droll?"

My heart does a peculiar little flip-flop. "Only when I've been humiliated by my very bad dog."

He gives Bernice a pat on the head. "Oh, she's a good girl. I'm glad Bernice dashed over today—the dog, not your aunt. It gave me the chance to meet you both."

"Thanks for sacrificing a piece of bacon on our behalf. I suppose we should continue our run, right girl?" I begin to walk backward down his driveway, pulling Bernice who's straining at the leash, hopeful for more bacon.

"So are you training for anything?"

"Escaping," I blurt before thinking. "Actually, I'm new to this running thing. I ran track in high school but that was back when people used walkmans."

"The Jigsaw Race is in a couple of months. Good cause, good place to start."

"Oh, so you run?"

He nods and squares his shoulders.

"I see," I say nodding. "You're one of those real runners, right? Marathons and all that?"

"You make it sound like an accusation."

"You marathon runners are in a class all by yourselves. I'm just trying to make it around the block."

He shrugs. "You gotta start somewhere."

"Yes and now it's time I finish. Thanks again."

"See you around Holly Lewis and The News."

I cast him a smile. I jog to the end of his driveway and turn right, both hopeful and fearful he's watching me. When I reach the intersection and cross over I glance his way. He waves and I wave back and then manage to run all the way back to my schoolhouse shaped home. For a full five minutes, I sit at the picnic table in the backyard with my head between my legs and try not to throw-up.

After showering, I find Maggie's shoebox-turned-lunchbox and examine her handiwork. A marker-drawn family of four smiles on one side of the box, their little brown stick arms linked together. A pink heart floats between the tallest figure with dotted yellow hair, John, and the next tallest figure with long brown hair, me. Even Bernice made it into the scene. Although she's purple and slightly cross-eyed.

On the other side of the box, *Maggie's Lunch* is written in curlicues, her signature smiley face dotting the *i*. A slice of pepperoni pizza next to what I deem to be a chocolate milkshake adorns one end. I turn it over to examine the other side. The string of words scrawled in purple marker shatters me: *I Love My Mom.*

John walks in minutes after the kids get home from school. As soon as she sees him, Maggie springs to her feet and runs, her straight blonde hair swaying. She leaps into his arms. "How long are you home for this time, Daddy?" she asks.

"Maggie, my back," He sets her down. "For the weekend. I don't need to be on site until Monday."

"What are you building next?"

"A swimming pool."

Maggie's jaw drops. "You get to dig out a swimming pool? I want to go! Can I go, Daddy? Can I?"

"You have school, Magpie." He moves past her and gives Ben's hair a tousle. Bernice, who's been anxiously clicking around the wood floor, noses her way in. I'm standing with an armload of folders and school-papers, all of which seem to require my signature, and give him something like a wave.

Our children represent an intriguing fusion of both John and me: Ben inherited my thick dark hair and John's cool blue eyes while Maggie acquired John's virtually yellow hair and my mahogany eyes. Although against the backdrop of her fair skin and hair, Maggie's eyes appear to be more striking, particularly when she rages.

John sets his lunch cooler on the table and heads to the kitchen while Ben trails after him, lamenting about the upcoming presidential wax museum at school. "And I have to be Ronald Reagan," he concludes.

"Jelly beans," John says, his head in the fridge.

"Jelly beans?"

"Reagan liked Jelly beans."

"He did? Can we get some?"

John emerges and opens a Leinenkugel. "Sure. Ask Mom." He gives me a smile on his way to the family room where he drops into the recliner and clicks on the TV.

I stand there, waiting, but no question comes my way. I head to the kitchen to start the potatoes. Some time later I ask Ben to set the table.

"Who's coming over?" he wants to know.

"No one. But your dad's home."

"Why is there a tablecloth?"

"Because."

"What's that?" He's pointing to the center of the table.

"A centerpiece. Your sister made it."

"It's a shoebox. Why is it on the table?"

This child is going to work for the IRS. "Because I want it there, okay? Enough questions."

He gives me an unconvinced look and heads to the silverware drawer.

When Maggie bounds into the room she notices the table decoration and halts. I go to her, brush a strand of hair from her face. "Maggie. I love the lunchbox you made. It's beautiful and I wanted Daddy and Ben to see it too."

Her dark eyes penetrate mine. She's standing so still, her mouth a thin, unreadable line. I fear the battle will rage on. But all of a sudden she throws her skinny arms around my neck. I run my hand down her hair, the tight ball of fear unraveling inside of me.

Later that night, when I climb into bed next to John, he drops the newspaper he's been reading and presses against me, his hands wandering.

I stiffen. "Not tonight."

He flops on his back. "Not much of a welcome home."

"I could say the same thing. You're the one who chose to go out with the boys last night."

"I needed to unwind."

"You can't unwind here?"

That's what he's trying to do here, his look tells me.

I roll my eyes and reach for my hand lotion. "You know, you could at least ask about my day before climbing on top of me."

He's quiet for a while. "How was your day?" His voice holds sincerity and for some reason this only feeds my anger. Too little too late.

There is much I could say. I could tell him about the screaming match I had with Maggie, how I ran away and moved into an outhouse. I could tell him about the math paper I found in Ben's backpack, the one with *Needs Work* written across the top in red ink. I could tell him I didn't get the tax receipts to Bob, maybe he can take care of that. I could tell him about the chirping birds and Annalisa's advice and how the voice of my high school track coach popped into my head. I could tell him how Bernice ran away, how a man rescued me with bacon. A man with white socks and mysterious traces of red on his fingers and warm hazel eyes. A man who laughed at my stupid jokes and called me—what was the word—? Droll.

I tell John none of this. I only roll to my side and tuck my chin under the sheet. "Fine. My day was fine."

2

It rains all Saturday.

In the evening, when the kids are literally climbing the walls, their sweaty bare feet pressed against the inside of door frames, John tells me he doesn't want to go to Annalisa's and Marco's.

"I've already made the taco dip," I tell him. "And I need a night out."

He doesn't look up from the TV. "Playing Monopoly with six kids running around is a night out?"

"Yes. Today, yes. See how easy you have it?"

"We could just send the kids"

"You're hilarious." I find the remote and click off the TV. "Magpie," I say, tugging on my daughter's pant leg as I pass under her, "get down. Get your shoes on." She thuds to the floor.

John sits there, watching the blank screen. "Besides," I tell him, "we haven't seen Laura in forever. Let's go for Laura's sake."

I've pulled out the big guns. No argument can stand against Laura. John gets up and shuffles over to his shoes.

Minutes later, Marco welcomes us inside and holds the taco dip while I shrug out of my coat.

"No Laura?" Annalisa asks as I follow her into the kitchen.

"I called and texted, but she never got back to me. I was hoping she'd already be here."

Annalisa scoops decaf into a coffee filter. "I haven't seen her in weeks. I can't remember the last time I saw her in church and she doesn't return many of my messages either. I just don't want her to feel alone."

"She's made it through the first year," I say helplessly.

"Yes, but maybe it's just starting to sink in."

After locating Annalisa's big blue bowl, I open the bag of chips I bought and dump them in. "She has until seven-thirty. If she's not here by then we'll pop in."

"You think so?"

"Yes. I'm worried, you're worried. It's time to intervene." We grab food and drinks and join the men in the dining room.

The Monopoly board sits unfolded and waiting on the table. Marco has claimed the tiny chrome car and John divvies out pastel colored bills. Within minutes our pawns set off around the square even though the true game doesn't begin until we start bartering for properties. Then we're cutthroat. Anything goes. Once, in exchange for weeklong possession of Annalisa's dangle jade earrings, I handed over Park Place. Marco changed the oil in John's truck, John drove Marco to the airport, and Annalisa even cleaned out my fridge—all for these little pieces of cardstock. Leftover cake, babysitting services, driveway shoveling, it's all been ante on the table.

Currently Marco is pining for my Reading Railroad. Ordinarily, his Italian accent is slight to nonexistent but right now he's laying it on thick, taunting me with his—in his words—legendary ravioli recipe. The man's a charlatan. The man doesn't cook. His recipe, no doubt, begins and ends with a box of pasta and a jar of Ragu. I shut him down and pass the dice to John. There's a soft knock on the door and Laura and TJ walk in.

Annalisa jumps up. "Laura! It's so good to see you. We were hoping you'd come, TJ. Everyone's waiting for you in the den."

She helps him out of his coat and he tromps down the hall to join the other kids.

Laura absently fluffs her bangs, glancing in our direction without making actual eye contact. "Sorry I'm late." She takes the vacant chair on the other side of John.

Marco hands her the stack of money we've optimistically prepared and I slide over the tiny iron—her favorite—and Annalisa gives her the deeds to States and Virginia Avenue. "It's only fair," she says.

"No," Laura says. "That's not fair. I'll start off with nothing like everyone else."

"Don't be silly," Annalisa says. "Take the purples."

Laura glowers at her iron.

"Have you eaten yet?" I ask. "Taco dip?"

"Decaf?" Annalisa offers. "Brownies?"

Laura picks up the purple properties. "I'm not hungry, thanks."

I nudge John to roll. He does and ends up in jail. I roll, move my boot, pay John twenty-two dollars in rent, and hand the dice to Marco. He takes second place in a beauty pageant. "How's TJ doing these days?" I ask.

Laura shrugs. "Fine."

Annalisa rolls, acquires Connecticut, and hands the dice to Laura.

Laura stares at the freckled cubes in her hands as if she's never seen them before, then cups her hands together and shakes. She shakes and shakes, her hands pumping up and down, her face vacant. After what seems like forever, she opens her hands and the dice clatter to the table. A ten, but the iron stays put. "This is such a pointless game," she says, staring at the dice. "To go around this square. Buying, selling, trying to stay out of jail. Paying taxes. I pay taxes in real life. And a mortgage. And utility bills. Why would I want to do it here, as a game? What kind of sick person thought up this game?"

Annalisa looks like she might cry. "We can play something else…"

Laura shakes her head. "No, of course not. We always play Monopoly. I don't want to ruin the fun."

"It is kind of silly," Annalisa says.

Laura props her elbows on the table and rubs her face with her palms. "Please stop being nice."

"We have Taboo," Marco says. "Or Balderdash."

Laura shakes her head. "You're doing it again. All of you. You're all being too nice. It's weird. Like you're afraid I'm going to fall apart, as if I'm made of glass." Her chin quivers. "I just really hate this… stupid… game."

Annalisa scoots her chair closer to Laura and puts her arms around her. "Oh, sweetie."

"I shouldn't have come. I'm sorry—" She stands but Annalisa clasps her wrist and gently pulls her to her seat.

Laura fiddles with her small silver iron, pushing it back and forth on the table as if it's flattening a teeny shirt.

"Did something…. happen today?" I venture.

"It's T-ball season."

I glance at Annalisa but she looks to be as in the dark as I am.

"Remember when Jake signed TJ up for T-ball last year?" Laura says. "He bought him a new little mitt and a ball. TJ still talks about it, how they practiced throwing and catching in the backyard, how Jake taught him the 'Peanuts and Cracker Jack' song. And then of course TJ didn't do T-ball." She excavates a tissue from her pocket, swipes her nose, and stuffs it back. "Today was show and tell. One of his friends brought in his baseball glove and told the kids all about starting T-ball. TJ threw a chair across the room. His teacher took him to the guidance counselor and I picked him up and took him home. Where he threw another chair. A stool, actually."

She drops the iron and shoves her hands into the front pocket of Jake's old Green Bay Packer sweatshirt. The elastic around one of the wrists is exposed and the drawstring to the hood is missing. "It's not getting easier," she says. "It's like we've been in survival mode this past year. Making it through, one day at a time. We can do it. We can survive. But so what? Why would we want to?"

"Oh Laura," Annalisa says.

"I'm not going to slash my wrists or anything. But it just feels like, what's the point? So we're surviving. Big deal. If it wasn't for TJ... I don't know. Maybe I would be asking you to check me in."

Annalisa's eyes are brimming. I'm biting my lip since I figure one of us needs to hold it together. Marco and John sit in reverential silence, powerless to do much for the widow of their dead friend. Although over the past year, they've done plenty. Between the two of them they've replaced the belt on Laura's dryer, unclogged drains, hauled furniture in and out of her house, and changed the oil on the van. All chivalrous deeds that add up to little compared to the void Jake left.

We've tried to go on, the five of us. A few months after Jake's death, we attempted a cookout in my backyard, which seemed like a good idea at the time. Something relatively normal. Simple. Something we all enjoyed *before*. Maybe it was too soon or maybe we were trying too hard. Laura was stirring a bowl of barbecue sauce when she fell into John, her sobs so sudden and virulent she would have certainly fallen to her knees if he hadn't been there to catch her. She collapsed into him. The metal bowl clanked to the ground, the sauce splattered across the patio like blood. Annalisa and I took over, held her under the elbows and led her inside, away from the children.

John did the right thing of course, the only thing he could do. Even so, as I watched my husband hold another woman, a weeping one at that, something strong and urgent and somewhat monstrous in its intensity rose up inside of me. Even now, as John sits beside sniffling Laura, I wish, for her sake, he'd offer a hand on her shoulder. A quick hug. And at the same time, I hope he doesn't.

I get up to find Kleenex. When I return to the table, I motion for John to switch seats so Annalisa and I can flank our friend like we've done countless times before. We offer few words. What do you say to a thirty-seven year old woman whose husband one day drops over dead from a brain aneurysm?

"You're doing such a good job, Laura," Annalisa murmurs after a while. "You're working. You're taking great care of TJ. Your strength has amazed us all."

"Well I'm tired of being strong. I never asked to be strong… " And her chin begins to quake again.

"You don't have to be strong for us," I say.

Laura laughs a little and blows her nose. "Clearly, I know."

Annalisa leans in closer to Laura, her forehead now touching the side of Laura's head. "Give Laura strength, God. Give her peace, give her joy."

Annalisa prays as if The Almighty himself has been standing here all along. And she doesn't always cap her invocations with "Amen" so you're never quite sure if she's done.

"Laura," Marco says, "let me take TJ to T-ball."

Laura shakes her head. "You have your own boys. I'm not going to burden you with that."

"You're talking crazy. It would be an honor. Lucas has been saying he wants to try T-ball anyway."

"He really has," Annalisa adds.

Laura smiles. "I'll ask him. Thank you."

"And I'm picking you up for church on Sunday," Annalisa says. "You haven't been for a while."

"Okay, fine. I guess we need to go."

I stare at my pretend money, dreading to hear Annalisa's next words: that she's picking me up for church as well. I haven't been to her and Laura's church in forever. Not since Christmas. Thankfully Maggie stomps in. She's bored, she says. The boys are making farting sounds with their armpits.

Annalisa holds out her hand. "Hang with us, Magpie. I think we're done here anyway. Can I braid your hair?"

My daughter's face brightens. She positions herself in front of Annalisa who's already combing her fingers through Maggie's hair and asking if she wants French braids or a waterfall.

Marco tells John he wants to show him his circular saw in the basement. As he's getting up from the table, John catches my eye and smiles. I smile back. We're both here. We don't have a brokenhearted child who's throwing chairs across the room.

Annalisa's small fingers work quickly. As she twists and turns Maggie's hair, she tells her how kids used to tease her about her hair when she was a little girl, how she used to pray for straight smooth hair just like this. "I like your hair," Maggie pronounces. "It's like you have a pet lamb on top of your head."

I momentarily shut my eyes. "*Maggie.*"

Laura laughs long and hard, the sound of it worth my daughter's bluntness. Annalisa winks at me and agrees, her hair is rather like lamb's wool. She finishes the braid. We have no ponytail band, so Laura loosens the scrunchie holding back her own drab hair and secures it around my daughter's braid.

When John drives us home an hour later, the kids doze in the backseat. The rain, now a drizzle, falls softly on our windshield. The wipers gently, patiently carry the drops away.

"Poor kid," John murmurs.

"They're doing okay. They're making it." Yet this statement only seems to underscore Laura's words.

"Maybe I'll take him camping this summer, with me and Ben."

"TJ? He'd probably like that."

"He's six now, right? He probably doesn't remember when all of us went a couple of years ago."

Maggie makes a snoring sound from the backseat.

John turns on to our street. "Jake caught this Muskie. A big one. He showed TJ how to clean the thing, how to hold the knife, talked him through the whole thing. I thought TJ was too young. But now… it's almost like…" The words hang between us.

"Like he knew it was his chance to teach his son how to clean a fish," I finish.

He glances at me. "Yeah."

We pull into the driveway. This memory that's been rattling around in my husband's mind for who knows how long is a gift. I rest my hand on his leg. He shuts off the engine then slides his hand into my hair, starting at the base of my neck, and rakes his fingers down through my mane. When he reaches the end he gently tugs.

"I think you should take TJ camping," I tell him.

"Me too," Ben says from the backseat.

I turn and glimpse my sleepy-eyed son, his sister, mouth open, snuggled up against him. In the rearview mirror John grins at Ben. For a moment I wish we could linger inside this still, quiet van, snug and shielded from the rain coming down around us.

3

Stars now dot the squares on my kitchen calendar. Each time I go for a run, I draw one in the appropriate day box. By the end of April, I count ten red stars, enough, I reason, to reward myself with a new pair of running shoes with electric blue laces.

By the middle of May I'm down eight pounds. What's more miraculous is that I can run a half of a mile without stopping, an accomplishment that prompts me to set a weight loss goal. I actually write down a number and tuck the scrap of paper behind my driver's license. My own little secret. Not even known to Annalisa or John.

I'd be lying if I said I loved to run. Most days I hate it. But I do love how loose my jeans feel and I have developed a serious affinity for the birds that gossip to each other like lifelong neighbors. And my new shoes, how I love my new shoes.

Today is golden, perfect for a run. Nevertheless I have been tethered to my computer like a slave, revamping the website for *Pleasant Dental*. By two o'clock the screen jumps and wavers, either due to the hours I've spent in front of it or the gallons of coffee I've poured down my throat. With the sun showing off like it is, the task at hand suddenly borders on cruel and unusual punishment. I holler for Bernice and lace up.

We make our way to our underwhelming yet supposedly historic downtown—a hodgepodge of restaurants, bars, hair salons, and specialty shops. I stop at Leman Park to catch my breath and let Bernice bark at the ducks. Then we head over to Hoover Elementary. As soon as we reach the flagpole, Bernice flops on her side in the grass, her stomach swiftly rising and falling. Should I have checked with the vet? Subjected her to some kind of physical to make sure her old body can tolerate such activity? I plant my palms against the flagpole and stretch my legs.

"Holly Lewis and The News."

I spot Seth and straighten. "Hey there!"

He's eating an apple and walks over to us. Bernice suddenly comes back to life. "No bacon today, girl," he tells her before turning to me. "Training for anything yet? This isn't the first time I've caught you running, you know."

"So how is it that I never see you running?"

"You're not up early enough." He crunches into his apple.

"Aren't we smug. How early is early?"

"Six."

I go back to stretching. "Show off."

"It's what works when I have Ava."

"So she's a hard sleeper, your Ava?"

"I don't leave her by herself. My eighty-year-old saint of a neighbor comes over just in case. She sits on the couch and does something with yarn. Sometimes she brings muffins."

"I'd get up that early for muffins."

"You've got it. If I ever see you running that early you can have one."

He finishes his apple and pitches the core in the trashcan next to the front door. He's wearing an unbuttoned plaid shirt over a white, fitted t-shirt that bears various stains of what can only be paint. "Can I ask, what is it that you do?"

He grins, swallows, and says, "I'm still trying to figure that out. Some days I paint. Some days I pound wood. Some days I reupholster furniture."

"You're an artist."

He shrugs. "Trying to be." He reaches into the back pocket of his jeans and extracts a business card, a token which seems incongruent with the rest of him. "Just in case you ever need barstools or anything. I make some pretty mean bar stools with reclaimed wood and steel."

I take the card. *Caldwell Studio* is stamped across the middle in Euphemia font. "Thanks. Have you done any projects I'd know about?"

"Most of what I do ends up in people's homes or online. But maybe you've seen The *Journey of a Caterpillar* mural in the public library?"

"You're the caterpillar mural man? We love the caterpillar mural!" I study his card again, zeroing in on his website address. "So business is good?"

He shrugs. "Business is… unpredictable."

The bell rings. Within seconds, kids flock around us. A small girl sporting lopsided pigtails wraps herself around Seth's legs. "Peanut! How was school?" She looks up at me with giant hazel eyes, much like her dad's. "Ava, this is Mrs.—" He looks to me.

"Just Holly."

"This is just Holly."

Without warning Maggie barrels into me, crushing my foot. "Ouch, honey. That hurt."

She thrusts a neon green sheet of paper at me. "Book Fair next week, Mom. We have to bring in all of our old books. No rips, tears, or stains," she says, listing the criteria on her fingers.

"Well alrighty, we'll do that." I turn her around by the shoulders. "Maggie, this is Ava and Ava's dad. Ava is in the first grade. Maybe you've seen her around?"

Maggie cocks her head. "I've seen you. You sit on the ladybug at recess all by yourself."

"Maggie!" My reproach is automatic although I don't think she meant to be hurtful. "Well now that you've met Ava you can go over and say hi."

Two tiny indentations appear between Maggie's eyes as she considers this. "Okay. Wanna come over to my house and play?"

I give Seth an apologetic look. With Maggie, it's all or nothing.

Ava tucks herself behind Seth. "Thanks Maggie," he says. "Maybe some other time."

"But we have popsicles," she throws out, confident that this will change everything.

Ben appears, dragging his backpack behind him, and Seth and I play another round of introductions before we all start walking home. Maggie darts back and forth like a puppy, running up ahead then back to Ava, taunting her to play, to chase her, to do something other than grip Seth's hand. Ben trails us with Bernice.

I hold up Seth's business card. "So who does your website?"

"My website?"

"Yes. Who designed it, who maintains it, who handles search engine optimization?"

"I'm not sure what that last one is but that would be me."

"That's a big job."

"I guess. I probably don't pay enough attention to it."

I sigh in exaggeration. "If I only had a business card on hand."

"Why? What do you do?"

"Funny you should ask."

He smirks. "Let me guess. Websites?"

"Wow, you're good. And I'm good at what I do. You'd be amazed at what kind of business a proper site can generate."

"You're probably too good for me to afford."

"Probably not. I'm part time so my rates are lower than my competitors. Besides, I have a pretty good track record of improving my client's' business so, in the end, maybe you can't afford *not* to hire me."

He chuckles. "Next you'll be telling me you have popsicles. Tell you what. Take a look my site and tell me what you think. Send me a proposal if you want. Who knows? Maybe I do need you."

Maggie, who's been holding a one-way conversation with Ava this whole time, announces that she and Ava are going to meet at the ladybug during recess tomorrow. I tell her that's a fabulous idea. Before we part ways, Seth crouches down and Ava hops on his back.

When our house comes into view, Maggie breaks into a sprint. I wait for Ben and Bernice to catch up with me.

"Who was that man?" Ben asks.

I ruffle his hair. "I told you, silly. Seth. Ava's dad. How was your day?"

He shrugs.

"How are you feeling about the wax museum?"

"Mom, we need jelly beans."

"I'll get them tomorrow. I promise."

"When's dad coming home?"

"Tomorrow."

"Why can't Dad get a job here? Why does he always have to go away for jobs?"

"Because that's the way it works, you know that. With construction you have to go where the work is."

He sighs.

"Tomorrow," I promise. "He'll be home tomorrow. In time to see you as Ronald Reagan."

"Tomorrow, tomorrow, tomorrow." He stoops to pick up a pinecone and throws it at a tree. He misses and runs ahead with Bernice.

That evening, after the kids are in bed, I force myself to finish one more page of *Pleasant Dental,* the prospect of viewing Seth's site my dangling carrot. After thirty minutes of work, I plug in his address. Up pops a professional quality photo of him. I click around. Other than the actual photographs of himself and his projects, it's bland and poorly worded, entirely too formal for the laid back, walk-out-in-your-socks kind of vibe Seth emits. Already my mind is spinning with possibilities.

I close my eyes. Seth. Seth and his rumpled clothing and easy grin. Seth munching an apple on school grounds and crouching down so his daughter can climb on his back. Relaxed. Causal. Hip, but in an effortless way. His site should reflect these qualities. Right now, except for the pictures, it reflects the opposite: Formal. Tedious. Blah and blah.

My cell phone rings. John's picture flashes across my screen. "Hey, how was your day?" I ask when I pick up.

"Slow. We're behind schedule. The shipment was late and it's pushed everything back."

"Oh no. You'll be home tomorrow night though, right? For Ben's thing?" I click on *Shop Art* and take a look at the bar stools Seth was telling me about. They're striking. If I had room for them in my kitchen I'd want them.

"What thing?"

"The wax museum. Remember? He's only been talking about it for days."

"That's tomorrow?"

"Yes, John. That's tomorrow."

He pauses and I know exactly where we're headed "Can you tape it for me?"

I sigh. "Are you kidding me?"

"Holly, what do you want me to do? Quit my job?"

"Right. That's what this is about. Me wanting you to quit your job."

"Well what do you want me to do then?"

"I want you to keep your promises."

"I didn't promise him anything."

"You *told* him you'd be there. That's a *promise*. Can't you tell Jeff no? Tell him your son has an important school event and you promised to be there. Tell him you have to leave early."

"No. I can't. Jeff is my *boss*."

"And Ben is your *son*."

"Fine, Holly. You get a full time job. You start working twelve hour days instead of poking around on the computer all day—"

"*Poking around on the computer all day?*"

"Do you think I *like* missing the kids' events? Do you think I *like* being away from home so much?"

I'm silent for a beat. "I don't know. Do you?"

He hangs up.

I squeeze my phone in the palm of my hand, tempted to chuck it across the room. But then I'd wake the kids, if they're not awake already, and I'd have to explain to my son—who's freaked out about this event as it is—that his dad can't make it. Even though he promised.

No, John's not going to get off that easily. Not this time. Tomorrow, John can call Ben and tell him himself.

I release my hair from the clip that's binding it and let it tumble over my shoulders. My cursor hovers over Seth's photograph, the best thing about this dreary site. Arms crossed, he's leaning against a rustic wood door, smiling somewhat precociously. He's not wearing his glasses and the combination of the grain of the wood behind him and ethereal light of either dusk or dawn brings out the amber flecks in his eyes. I zero in on his left hand. No ring. Even without seeing this picture I already knew; several things he said today confirmed his single-dad status.

What happened with Ava's mom? What I really want to know is, who did the leaving? Seth most likely, because what woman in her right mind would leave a guy who turns reclaimed wood into beautiful furniture and gives his daughter piggyback rides?

An hour later I climb into bed yet sleep doesn't come. My mind races from thing one to thing two, much like Maggie running back and forth on our walk home today. I roll over on my stomach. I press John's pillow to my head. I toss my pillow on the floor. But my mind doesn't stop. Seth. John. Seth. John.

How can John do this again? How many events will John miss before he realizes what it's doing to Ben? And Seth. What happened with him and Ava's mom? What went wrong? In my striving for sleep my thoughts grow frenzied and bits and pieces of today's conversations churn together. Muffins and Popsicles. Websites and barstools.

At one in the morning I give up and pad to my desk. Might as well put my racing mind to good use. I fire up my computer and begin working on a proposal to convince Seth how much his sad little site needs me.

4

Ben turns out to be the cutest little Ronald Reagan ever. He fills the pockets of John's black suit coat with jellybeans and hands them out to anyone who stops to listen to his dutifully memorized, entirely monotone speech. I've heard it at least a dozen times. John heard it too, over the phone, after he told Ben he had miss the event. Judging from appearances, Ben handled the news well, although I did pick up on a slight catch in his voice, a faint hitch when he said *It's okay, Dad.*

At what age, I wonder, do children lose their capacity to forgive so freely? When do they start keeping score like the rest of us?

Antonio is masquerading as William Taft, his trousers and shirt bulging with pillows and rolled up towels. By the time Maggie and I weave our way over to him in the packed cafeteria the poor kid is sweating like a Mississippi lawyer. Traces of black eyeliner smudge his upper lip where a mustache used to be.

After recording both boys' speeches, I sweep my phone across the room to capture the presidential chaos. "Let's step out for some air," Annalisa suggests, coming alongside me with Jackson incarcerated in the stroller. Marco offers to take Maggie and Lucas to Jimmy Carter for a bag of peanuts. Annalisa and I step outside, the evening air a blast of refreshment. I ask if she's heard from Laura.

Annalisa hands Jackson a box of raisins. "You haven't talked to her lately?"

"No. Why? What's going on?"

"I should probably let her tell you."

"Tell me what?"

She waves her hand in front of her. "Nothing."

"Annalisa, you're bursting at the seams like your little William Taft. Spill."

"Maybe you should give Laura a call."

"I will but right now you need to tell me *what's going on*."

"Okay fine," she says. "But maybe act surprised when you talk to her." She clasps her hands together and smiles. "Laura's met someone."

Her words are a snowball in my face. "Met someone? You mean like a man?"

"Of course like a man."

"Who?"

"Remember when she went to that May festival thing at her mom's church? The one way out in the country? That's where she met him. Phil. His name is Phil Lancaster."

"*Phil?* That's an old man name. How old is he?"

"I don't know. Not *old*."

"How do you know?"

"Because she would have mentioned it if he were eighty."

"So you haven't met him?"

"Not yet."

"Has he ever been married before?"

"How should I know?"

"Because you *talked* to her."

"I didn't think I needed to interrogate her."

"Anna, we should be looking out for her. She's completely vulnerable. What if she's throwing herself at the first guy who looks her way?"

"Give her a little more credit."

"What does he do, this Phil? Flip burgers? Deliver pizzas? Or does he live in his parent's basement?"

Annalisa glares at me. "He's a cranberry grower, Holly. A hardworking cranberry grower. A grown man who doesn't live in his parents' basement because he owns his *own marsh*."

"Oh."

"So I think he's doing pretty well for himself."

"So he's a rich snob."

She turns the stroller around and walks away.

"I'm sorry," I say catching up to her. "I'll stop. I'm just worried about Laura. This is all so fast."

We make our way to the flagpole and sit on the cement base. A mom exits the building clutching a screaming toddler in one hand and a girl dressed up like Teddy Roosevelt, I think, in the other.

Annalisa crosses her arms around her chest. "I don't even know if they're serious or anything. They've only been on two dates."

"Two? Already?"

She groans.

One after another, as if I'm watching clips from home movies, memories of Laura and Jake flicker through my mind: slurping watermelon on my deck on the Fourth of July with the kids running around. Toasting in the New Year at Annalisa's. All of us meeting at the apple orchard, Laura and Jake swinging TJ between their arms. "It's only been a year," I say. "Isn't that too soon? Aren't there rules about this?"

"I don't know. And like I said, this may turn out to be nothing. Laura sounded so happy on the phone. *Happy*. I didn't feel like firing questions at her. Maybe I should have but I just wanted to let her be happy."

"Maybe that's why she called you and not me."

"Maybe."

I inhale slowly, letting the cool air travel deep inside of me before releasing it through my mouth—an exercise I've perfected since taking up running. "What if she's so lonely she's desperate? What if this Phil guy is all wrong for her and TJ but she can't see it?"

"Keep in mind she is a grown up."

"We need to meet him."

She studies her fingernails for a moment. "He and Laura are coming for dinner on Sunday. I was thinking about inviting you but now I don't know…"

"I'll be good."

"You'll put him on the hot seat."

"I won't. I promise. I'll be nice. Cross my heart and stick my finger in my eye and all of that. Please invite me."

She sighs. "Fine. Sunday at six. Does that work for John?"

"Yes, and even if it doesn't he'll be there. He owes me."

"I'm sure he'd rather be here," she insists. "The guy works hard."

"Yes and I do too. Reagan costumes don't just come together by magic you know."

"Neither do Taft costumes."

"But Marco's *here*."

As if on cue, Marco appears with Maggie and the boys, their cheeks sweaty and flushed. Ben and Antonio have shed their costumes and are clutching bulging grocery sacks. From the stroller, Jackson hollers and tosses his Sippy cup to the ground. Annalisa bends to retrieve it, her lavender top slipping from her shoulder to reveal a teal colored bra strap. When Annalisa straightens, Marco rights her shirt and murmurs something in her ear. Probably in Italian. But I don't need to hear a word to pick up on the gist: those kids are going to bed early. Annalisa promises to call me tomorrow to firm up plans for Sunday and we part ways.

As the kids and I walk home, I put my hand on Ben's shoulder. "You were a great Ronald Reagan."

"I wish Dad could have been there."

"I know. Me too. But we can show him the video."

"Whatever." He pops a jellybean into his mouth.

My heart sinks. Maybe the scorekeeping has already begun.

If Phil Lancaster happened to be wearing boots, I believe he'd be shaking in them. He's wearing brown loafers and an uneasy expression when he steps through Annalisa's door on Sunday evening. Laura makes introductions while Phil grins uncomfortably and shakes hands. His face is ruddy to the point of shininess and his hair is poorly cut. His build is slight—nothing like burly Jake—but he's wiry and, I'd guess, strong. I wouldn't categorize him as attractive, but he's not the worst looking man I've ever laid eyes on either. Overall he's rather nondescript. Forgettable. Plain. Which, to be fair, is an accurate description of Laura.

Although tonight she's glowing like a firefly, prettier than I've seen her in a year. And lo and behold her hair has been liberated from its customary scrunchie and falls just to her shoulders. I think she even straightened it and is that a hint of lip-gloss I see?

While the men head to the family room, Annalisa, Laura, and I linger in the entryway. "He's nervous," Laura mouths.

"Poor guy," Annalisa whispers. "I hope he knows he's not on trial here."

"Yes he is," I say. Annalisa gives me a little shove.

We join the men where Phil is giving the history of the Lancaster cranberry bog. It's been in his family for three generations, he explains, and although it's by no means the largest bog in the area, it does yield abundant produce. Laura nestles next to him, watching him as if he's explaining quantum physics.

"When does harvest take place?" Marco asks Phil.

"Late September through October," Phil says.

"Wet or dry harvest?" John asks. I look at him, surprised. I had no idea he knew anything about cranberry bogs.

"Wet. I only know one grower that does a dry harvest."

"Philip is a big supplier for Ocean Spray," Laura informs us.

"Did you know Wisconsin produces more cranberries than any other state in the country? I never did until now. Cranberries are such a beautiful crop and Phil has a beautiful piece of land."

Phil smiles at her. "Harvest is quite a sight, when we flood the beds."

"Flood the beds?" Marco asks. "I thought they grew in water?"

"They grow on vines. We flood the beds when the berries are ripe and then use water reels to stir up the water until the berries detach and float to the surface. Makes for an easier harvest."

After a few more minutes of rural Wisconsin history, Annalisa ushers us to the dining room. John catches my eye and grins. *He's all right*, his expression says.

I frown. It's way too early. All we know is that the guy gathers floating berries for a national juice company and doesn't pay much for his haircuts. As our group figures out who's sitting where around the table, I tell Annalisa I'll get the kids started in the kitchen.

They're all outside, tearing around the backyard. Before I round them up, I stand on the deck and observe little TJ. He shows no signs of distress over the fact that his mom brought over a strange man. Right now he looks happy, chasing Maggie around the play fort with a Nerf gun.

I holler it's time to eat and the kids come running. While they're washing up in the bathroom, I dish up lasagna, clumps of salad, and a breadstick. Then I pour water and place extra napkins on the table.

"I like him," Annalisa whispers when she comes in for the second lasagna.

I half nod, half shrug.

She's stands in the doorway, lasagna in hand, and looks at me questioningly. I smile, grab the salad bowl, and brush past her. Why am I the only one who's being cautious with all of this?

And am I the only one who sees flashes of Jake while we eat? Jake and his hearty laugh and flannel shirts. Jake who could squash this guy like a beetle, like a *cranberry*, if he wanted to?

But Jake wouldn't want to I realize as the conversation continues. Even though Jake and Phil seem to be, at first appraisal, polar opposites—big, small, loud, quiet, gregarious, reserved—they share a similar trait that, at least in part, wins me over: unpretentiousness. Jake wouldn't dislike Phil. Quite the contrary. He'd probably be asking him when he wanted to go fishing.

The kids trickle into the dining room, asking for dessert. Annalisa shoos them out and promises cake and ice cream later. TJ lingers beside Laura and eventually climbs into her lap. He's holding a matchbox car and zooms it around the dishes. At one point Laura tells him to stop, to play with it on the floor, but he stays put.

The conversation turns to politics and I feel myself check out. All of a sudden, Laura's glass tips over. Wine splashes across the table. Laura promptly rights the glass and Annalisa and I grab whatever napkins we can and start blotting. The sleeve of Phil's beige oxford shirt is now stained crimson.

"Timothy Jacob," Laura says, "next time I say stop, *stop.*"

TJ freezes where he stands, his face impassive. He's still holding the toy car.

"It was an accident," Phil says.

Marco hands Annalisa a roll of paper towel. "No worries," she singsongs, unrolling long white sheets and laying them across the table.

As I stack dishes, I see Phil gently nudge TJ with his elbow. "I didn't like this shirt that much anyway." TJ looks up at him and seems to start breathing again.

Phil catches me watching him.

I smile and rip off a fresh paper towel to wipe off the butter dish. One point Phil.

Later that evening John and I sit staring at some oversensationalized news story about a wife who goes missing on an Alaskan cruise. I ask him what he thought of Phil.

"Seemed nice. Normal."

"Too normal, maybe."

"What do you mean?"

"Didn't he seem a little stiff?"

"He was probably nervous," John says, still looking at the TV.

"It's just strange seeing Laura with anyone other than Jake."

"I give it a year. Or maybe less than a year."

"Until they break up?"

"No, until they get married."

I laugh. "What? Are you crazy? That's too fast. Way too fast."

"Laura seems eager."

"No kidding," I say. "It was like watching sixteen-year-olds on a date."

"Must be nice," he says, staring at the TV.

"What's that supposed to mean?"

He stands up and heads to the kitchen.

"What are you trying to say?" I call after him.

He returns with a bag of chips and plops back on the couch. "Nothing. Just that Laura gave Phil a lot of attention. Like she always gave Jake a lot of attention."

"And you don't? Get attention? Is that it?"

He props his feet on the coffee table and bites down on a chip.

I watch him for a minute but he doesn't answer. Finally, I cross my arms and stare at the screen. But I can't anymore. I can't sit next to this man who thinks he's the only one in this marriage who's not getting his needs met. Poor, poor John.

I stand up and start gathering newspapers and mail scattered throughout the room. I head to the kitchen, shove all the papers I'm holding into the recycling bin, and hope I haven't missed any bank statements or bills that are, of course, my responsibility.

"Maybe," I say, returning to the family room, "if you pitched in once in awhile I'd have *time* to give you attention."

"Right," he mutters. He sits there, eating his chips, letting crumbs fall over the couch.

I storm to the hall closet. Yank out the vacuum cleaner. Roll it into the living room and plant it in front of the TV. "The couch is going to need some attention," I tell him. "And the floor. In fact there are a lot of things around here, including *people*, who could use some attention."

Whether he retorts or apologizes, I have no idea. I don't stick around long enough to find out.

5

The following week Maggie begs to have Ava over for a play date. "She's *practically* my new best friend," she pleads.

Practically is her latest favorite word. Right after *scat*, thanks to Ben and a science article he brought home describing how scientists learn about the environment based on poop. The kids giggled over the pictures for an hour.

I study Maggie, parental intuition telling me that what she likes about Ava is her mute submission. "You don't boss her around, do you?"

"Mom, she *likes* it when I boss her around."

"No one likes to be bossed around. Not really. Not for long."

"I *don't* boss her around."

She plays to win, but I can play too. I know a golden opportunity when I see it. If she cleans her room, I tell her, including dusting and taking care of the socks and wrappers and whatever else is lurking under the bed, she can call Ava. An hour later, Maggie takes my hand and leads me to her room. Finding no hidden piles, I kiss her forehead and hand her my phone.

After school the next day the girls burst through the door, nab a bag of corn chips, and close themselves in Maggie's room. I stand in the hallway, listening for sounds of tyranny. I only hear giggling. This is Ava's first time over so just to be sure, I rap on the door and peek in. "You two doing all right?"

Maggie glares at me from a mountain of stuffed animals. Ava smiles, clutching Maggie's striped tiger, and doesn't look the least bit victimized. I close the door.

A couple of hours later, Seth is on my doorstep. "How'd it go?"

"Great," I tell him. "I think they're treating Barbie to a Caribbean cruise in the bathtub."

"Thanks for having her. She needed this."

"Anytime. Do you have her most days?"

"Yeah, during the school year. Now that the divorce is finalized and Tori moved in with the guy I'll have Ava more often."

I cobble the information together. Tori. Ava's mom. Seth's ex-wife. Who now lives with *the guy*. An affair, maybe?

"Oh," is all I can think to say.

"It's tricky. I never know if Tori's going to act her age or like some co-ed on spring break." He shakes his head. "Sorry. I've broken a cardinal single-parent rule: never bash your child's parent, no matter how much she may deserve it. I don't ever want Ava to think our problems have anything to do with her. It's just hard."

"Give yourself time," I offer.

"It's been two years since we split. Time isn't the magical cure-all it's purported to be."

His words remind me of Laura. "You're right, it's not. I guess it's what we say when we don't know what else to say, to show we care."

"Well, thanks for caring."

"By the way, I've been meaning to tell you, I checked out your website."

"And?"

"And... it provides information. But if I'm being honest, it's bland. It hardly does your art justice."

"Don't sugar coat it," he says.

"Seth, you clearly posses amazing artistic skill and your site should reflect that. It should be just as alluring and creative as your art. Frankly, I don't get the discrepancy."

He shrugs. "I'm not a techie guy. I'm hands-on with wood and paint and fabric, not computers. I knew I needed a site so I just paid a fee to get the thing up and running, just to have *something*."

"Yeah, well it shows."

"Ouch."

At times I push too far. I think I've pushed too far. "All I'm saying is I could make that little site of yours sing."

"Sing, huh?"

"What your site has going for it are the photographs of you and your work. But the text, the colors, the whole *vibe*... it's all wrong."

"You want to give me a whole new vibe."

"No, I want to give your site *your* vibe."

He shakes his head and grins. "So let's hear it then Holly Lewis and The News. How badly are you going to bleed me dry?"

"No one's going to bleed anyone dry. If you're okay with it, I'll write up a proposal with all the details."

The girls appear, drenched Barbies in hand. "Mom, can we cut their hair?" Maggie asks.

Last summer I scored a cardboard box full of dolls at a rummage sale for five bucks and gave Maggie carte blanche. She cut hair, painted fingernails, and administered tattoos. She even gave one baby-doll a bellybutton ring, an incident that kept me up at night. By now the dolls have been sufficiently used up and the one downside to the activity is I now have to be a vigilante regarding all of her other dolls, even the ones that set Grandma back a hundred dollars.

"No," I say to Maggie, "but I'll tell you what. Rummage sales are just starting so we'll go on a mission to rescue all the unwanted dolls we can find and you can give them all makeovers, okay?"

"Ava too?"

I look at Seth. "It's fine with me if Ava does makeovers with you."

"Your mom here is pretty cool. Some moms don't go for all of that avant-garde, free spirited play."

I shrug. "I do what I can."

Ava tugs on Seth's hand. He bends to her and she whispers in his ear. "I don't know," he says. "You ask."

Eyes downcast, Ava twists like a turnstile and says in just above a whisper, "Do you want to come to my house sometime?"

"Yes!" Maggie says. "Tomorrow!"

I place my hands on her shoulders so she'll stop bouncing. "How about you let them decide."

"How about we give you a call soon," Seth says.

Maggie hugs Ava rather roughly. "Later gator!" she calls as she runs down the hall.

Seth's halfway out the door when he turns around. "Send me that proposal, Holly Lewis."

I grin. "Will do."

From the front window, I watch them walk down the sidewalk, hand in hand.

"When's Dad coming home?" Ben's voice startles me. I turn and see him in the corner curled up with a blanket and his Kindle.

"Tonight." I begin to collect mail strewn along the coffee table.

"What's for supper?"

"Cheeseburgers."

"That's good. Dad likes cheeseburgers."

"We all like cheeseburgers."

"Dad *really* likes cheeseburgers."

"Fine. Dad likes cheeseburgers the most."

"Are you going to grill them? Dad likes them grilled."

I tear open the water bill. "I don't know Ben. Dad can do the grilling, if he gets here in time."

I head to the kitchen. If I get the patties formed and the salad made I can devote a few more minutes on Seth's' proposal.

Sleeping in is high on my list of favorite things to do. So on the first morning of summer break, when I drag myself out of bed at six-thirty, splash water on my face and tighten my Nikes, I feel as if I've crossed some invisible line, unceremoniously joined the big league, the real runners.

Newborn sunlight stretches across the sky and from somewhere above me, two finches catch up on gossip. The morning is cool but by the time I approach Hoover Elementary, where the playground sits desolate, I've worked myself into a sweat. I push myself to tackle three more blocks before slowing to a walk.

When I hit the main drag of Green Avenue, I turn around. I consider stopping at Annalisa's. Jackson is an early riser and I know if light glows from Annalisa's kitchen window, it's safe to drop by. We haven't discussed Phil in detail yet, although from her demeanor on Sunday night, she's already given him the stamp of approval.

I turn down Orchid Lane and spot another runner in the distance. As the gap between us closes, I realize it's Seth. We both wave and seconds later we're face to face.

"So you aren't all bluff," I say breathlessly. "You *do* run."

"Guess I owe you a muffin."

I nod and switch directions. "The kids are home. Got to fit it in early."

"I got your email," he says, not the least bit winded. "With the proposal. I'm intrigued. I mean I know you're right. My site is kind of blah and my art is kind of amazing."

"Site will be too. Amazing. If price okay." My exertion has reduced me to stilted caveman talk.

"I can swing it."

"Great..." *Huff puff.* "Will start..." *Pant pant.* "...next week."

"Perfect. By the way," Seth says after some time, "if you don't mind me saying so, you look like you've lost weight. You look good."

My cheeks grow warmer. "Thanks. Getting there."

"Where's Bernice?"

"Morning off."

We run on. It feels different today, running without Bernice's collar jingling beside me. Running next to another person. Before long the rhythm of our feet synchronize and somehow, as If I'm siphoning energy from him, I don't feel as weary as I did moments ago. I can keep going, I realize. Even my breathing—perhaps taking a cue from Seth's steady exhales—has settled down.

Birds trill overhead. Cars grumble blocks away. A dog barks in the distance. A sprinkler *tisk tisks* beside us. Above it all our feet drum against the ground and I feel a surge of contentment. This is exactly where I want to be. But just as quickly something else rushes over me, edges in and challenges this simple moment of pleasure. A contradiction. A quiet warning. It's crazy, Annalisa's house is nowhere in sight, but I picture her watching me—watching *us*—from her window. Watching and frowning. We're merely two people running side by side. Nothing wrong with that. Two people who met on the road by chance. Imaginary Annalisa needs to get off her high horse.

"Perfect morning," Seth says. "That sky. Like water color." His arm brushes against mine.

"Gorgeous." Imaginary Annalisa is crossing her arms now, scowling. "I better turn here."

"All right. Let me know when we should talk about the site."

"Next week?"

"The sooner the better. Catch you later Holly."

I turn and briefly shut my eyes. Give my head a firm shake. Then, as if I'm being chased, I pick up my pace, running faster and faster until I reach my driveway. I plant my hands on my thighs and lower my head, try to gain control of my breath and this exhilarating queasiness that's overtaken me. What am I? Thirteen?

Minutes later I enter the kitchen. John is fitting a filter into the coffee maker. "Out for a run?"

"Perfect morning for it." I get a glass of water. After a few gulps, I look at him. "I'm down ten pounds."

He glances at me. "That's good."

That's good? As in *it's about time?* Is he relieved I've lost weight? I refill my glass. "You know if you ever want to join me…"

His eyebrows plunge downward just like Ben's. "Running?"

"Yes."

He lets out a snort.

"Never mind." I'm grasping for a branch, a twig. Something. *Anything.* He doesn't see it.

"I don't run. You know that."

"Yep. I forgot." I find a pen and star today's square on the calendar. June is dotted with dentist appointments and kids activities and John's work schedule and nothing particularly fun. "We should do something this summer. We should go somewhere. Take a trip. Without the kids."

"We can't afford that."

"I'm not talking Hawaii. But we have airline miles. We should cash them in. We probably have enough for at least one round trip ticket. Let's go somewhere. Let's go out east. To Boston or something."

"Boston?"

"Or Seattle?"

"That's west."

"Wherever. Anywhere."

I wait for him to warm to the idea, or suggest another place, or at least dinner out. But he only watches the coffee drip into the pot. He doesn't see me out here on the edge, doesn't think to pull me to safety. He's unaware of what's stirring inside of me, doesn't know what I felt when I ran next to Seth. He doesn't feel the ground beneath us tremble and shift. He doesn't see any of this. He doesn't see *me*.

"We could get a movie tonight," he says, retrieving his favorite mug from the dishwasher. "That one about the baseball player looked good."

    I stare at him for a moment. "Sounds great."

    I walk away to take my shower.

6

The inside of Seth's garage takes me by surprise.

"My studio," he says, extending his arm.

I descend the unfinished wood steps that lead from his kitchen door to the garage, to a space that, at one time, used to be for oil changes but is now devoted to innovation and creativity. "Don't judge a garage by its door, I guess."

He grins. "Never."

Exposed light bulbs hang from the rafters at various levels shining over a paint-splattered cement floor. In the middle of the room sits a large work table filled with paint cans, paint tubes, cups holding various-sized brushes, paint soaked rags, spray bottles, candy bar wrappers, and soda cans. Part of me wants to grab a trash bag and start cleaning up; but the rest of me stands mesmerized by this buffet of imagination and chaos, a room ruled by possibilities. The girls play just inside the house, yet I feel worlds away.

Seth leads me to the worktable and clears off a spot. He motions for me to take a seat on what appears to be a refurbished barber's stool. I do and spin around, immediately regretting it. I'm here on business. Seth only smiles.

Maybe it's nonsense but whenever I meet with a client, or potential client, I harmonize my attire with who I perceive them to be. Last winter when I met with an independent tax accountant, I wore my black pinstripes and an oxford shirt. For *Playland Day Care*, I consulted in my sunny yellow dress and a chunky turquoise necklace. *I get you*, I want them to communicate. *I can deliver.* Today I'm in a sky blue peasant skirt and beaded sandals.

I retrieve my laptop from my bag and open it on the table, even though many of my questions have been answered simply by stepping in here. In preparation for this meeting, I've constructed three possible templates for Seth's site and show them to him one at a time. When I'm done pointing out the distinctiveness of each, I ask him which he likes best. He selects the third.

"That's my favorite too." I turn my laptop so it's facing me again. "Let me show you what I'm thinking for text."

I do some quick cutting and pasting. He gets up and stands over my shoulder, one hand propped on the counter. The scent of his aftershave reminds me of rain.

I clear my throat. "So here, on your homepage, I'd pair your name with this photo. Give your viewer an immediate taste of both you and your art."

He leans in closer. "Nice."

My hair, swept in a low side pony, hangs over my shoulder and I feel his breath on the back of my neck when he speaks. "Your homepage should encourage people to explore but it shouldn't reveal too much."

"That makes sense."

More warm breath on the back of my neck. I feel warm and queasy and kind of wonderful. I hop off the stool. "So, maybe you could give me a tour?"

"Oh. Well, this is kind of it."

"Could you explain some of what you're doing?"

"I can try."

I meander over to an easel with a canvas propped against it. "Is this one finished?"

He cocks his head, studying the piece. "Not sure. What do you think?"

"What do *I* think? I'm not the artist."

"Sure you are, in a way."

I turn my attention to the rivulets of colors cascading down the canvas. It looks like someone spilled a drink down the front but I like it. Yet it seems incomplete. "I don't think so."

"I don't think so either."

I smirk at him. "You're just saying that."

"No something's missing. Nothing huge. Nothing jarring, but something."

We stand there, examining the art. "So grab a paintbrush. Let me see you in action."

He laughs. "Doesn't really work like that."

"So how does it work?"

"I'll grab a paintbrush when the mood strikes. Probably later tonight when I crank up The Cure."

"And you'll just... start painting? Without really knowing how to finish it? Without knowing what it will look like in the end?"

He nods. "It's an energy thing. I just go with it. Let it carry me, the paint, my brush strokes, the mood, the music. Let it all take me wherever it's going to take me and be okay with that."

"That's so Zen. So transcendental."

"Maybe that's what I'll call this one. *Transcendental*."

I grin at him, uncertain if he's joking, and move on to a table with scraps of metal, some bent, some curled, some flat. "That's going in the lobby of Community Bank," he says. "Eventually."

I run my finger along one of the smooth pieces. "Did you always want to be an artist?"

"I think so, but for awhile I tried to push it down. I took a painting class in high school, just to get some easy credit or so I thought, and ended up loving it. My dad's pretty blue-collar, worked in a factory his entire life. He still doesn't really understand what I'm trying to do but at least he's stopped telling me about openings at the factory. I've had other jobs over the years—worked in a few restaurants, over-the-road trucking believe it or not—but the art always pulled me in. My 'mistress' is what my ex used to call it. How about you? How did you get into web design?"

"By accident. My friend Annalisa tried her hand at a home business. She created these personalized gift baskets with rolled up towels that looked like animals or flowers and whatnot and I put together a website for her. Found out I have a knack for it. She ended up getting a lot of traffic. Too much actually. She found out she was pregnant with her third and decided she didn't want a home business. So she let her business dry up."

"While yours took off."

"Not all at once, but yes. Annalisa referred me to a photographer friend of hers who referred me to a guy that owns a winery and referral by referral, business grew."

Seth rearranges the metal pieces on the table so they resemble a sun. "Starting your own business takes guts. As much as I love working solo, sometimes I almost wish I had a boss to kick my butt into gear. Or to tell me when to *stop* working and go home."

"Right. Because work *is* home."

"Exactly. If creativity strikes at midnight I might end up in the studio until dawn."

"So you operate on creative impulse?"

"Yes. Although I know how to hunker down and get to work, even if I don't feel like it. You?"

"Sometimes I get so sucked into a project I can't focus on anything else until I get it just right."

"It's some kind of high, isn't it?"

I nod. I continue my way around the studio and stop when I come to a torn apart loveseat in the corner. Pea-green fabric hangs from the thing like partially shed snakeskin, exposing foam cushions. "You reupholster too?"

He shrugs. "It pays the bills." He rummages through a metal shelf and extracts a bolster of cream-colored fabric flocked with yellow canaries and delicate branches. "Love birds," I say, gently touching the vintage-looking material. "For a love seat. Perfect."

"A friend of mine lugged this baby in," he says, thumping the back of the love seat. "Said he'd been promising his wife for years he'd have the thing redone. It's a surprise for their twenty-fifth wedding anniversary."

"Did he pick the fabric or did you?"

"I did."

"It's gorgeous," I tell him. "She'll love it. And she'll love that her husband is making good on an old promise."

"Yes. Isn't it romantic." He rolls his eyes and makes a face.

"What?"

"Welcome to my dark side. I'm happy for the guy, I really am, but he just went on and on about how much she's going to love it, how she's going to flip when she sees it, how he can't wait to give it to her on their anniversary..." He puts the fabric back on the shelf. "I'm just an old, bitter divorcé I guess."

"It's hard to be happy for others when..." I have no idea how to finish.

"When they have something you want? Yeah, it is." He stares at the tattered loveseat waiting to be made beautiful. "The thing is, I never planned on my marriage ending. Not like this. I thought I'd be that guy in fifteen years."

"Everyone wants a happily ever after."

"I guess we're all suckers then. Wanting something that probably doesn't exist."

I laugh a little. "You are jaded."

"Sorry. How did we get here?"

"The lovebirds."

"Right. Those happy little birds."

I have this absurd urge to take him by the hand and sit with him on the loveseat. Just sit together. Talk. My cheeks flush and I turn away. "Well," I say, taking a final look around the studio, "I think I have everything I need for now."

"Great. Maggie can stay if she wants."

"She'd love that." I make my way to the steps, my hand sliding across the railing as I ascend, until I feel his hand cover mine. Surprised, I stop and turn.

"Thanks," he says.

"Of course," I say brightly. "It's my job."

"No. For listening."

"You're welcome. And I'm sorry, Seth. Life's unfair."

He smiles and I feel myself sinking into those tiger-eyes. He removes his hand from mine but his fingertips are now just barely touching the inside of my wrist. Something in his look changes, intensifies. I'm plunging headfirst into a raging current and I hold my breath. How long, I wonder, can I hold my breath?

The chirp of my phone makes me jump. Climbing the rest of the steps, I dig in my bag and pull out my phone. It's a text from Annalisa. She wants to know if I can take the boys tomorrow.

Maggie and Ava are at the kitchen table cutting paper. I tell Maggie to get her things together.

"She can stay," Seth says.

"Oh, that's right."

Maggie whoops for joy.

I promise Seth I'll pick up Maggie in a couple of hours, hurry out the door to my van, start the engine and click off the radio.

I need silence. A chance to tidy up these manic thoughts before I get home. Figure out what just happened. Nothing, I'm sure. I'm being juvenile. Seth is a nice guy, an artist who probably didn't even realize he gripped my hand. I reset my mind to the day ahead, to dinner and John coming home tonight. But when I pull into my driveway, all I see is Seth and that loveseat, all those happy yellow birds free to fly wherever they wish.

The lounge chairs at the city pool might as well be made of gold, given how coveted they are. Once I asked the check-in counter girl why the city can't acquire more chairs. She smacked her gum and stared at me as if I had suggested they fill the pool with gin. On the upside, the chair shortage promotes punctuality, at least for me.

Five minutes before the pool opens, the kids and I, including Ava today, are unloading from the van. At one o'clock, when the doors open, I'm flip-flopping my way into the pool area. Since Annalisa is meeting us, I claim a row by the kiddy pool for Jackson's sake, using my tote and the kids' towels as stake. Then I spread my towel over the hot vinyl noodles of my chair, grab my magazine, and sit down.

Finally, at one-thirty, Antonio and Lucas emerge from the men's locker room. Moment's later, Annalisa exits on the women's side with Jackson in tow.

I remove my beach bag from the chair I've been saving. "Man do you owe me a Coke. Bet I could have sold this baby for ten bucks."

"Sorry." She looks sorry. Too sorry.

"I'm kidding. No big deal."

She secures Jackson's floaties and watches as him waddle to the kiddy pool. Then she unrolls her towel, arranges it and sits down. She shakes up a bottle of SPF 45 and squeezes white lines down her white legs. She begins rubbing furiously.

"What's wrong?" I ask.

"Is it really the worst thing in the world if your son burps at the table?"

"Not at my house."

"Which is worse, a kid burping or a grown man throwing a bowl?"

"Depends on the burp. And the bowl."

She glares at me.

"The bowl. Hands down, the bowl. What happened?"

"Marco came home for lunch and Antonio let out a few burps at the table. Marco told him to stop and some time later Antonio burped again. Maybe on accident, maybe on purpose, I don't know. Anyway, Marco stood up, grabbed Antonio's bowl, and threw it across the room, into the sink. *Threw* it. It shattered into a million pieces." She dots her nose with sun block. "A glass that happened to be sitting there broke too. He's such a hothead."

This is no newsflash to me. Over the years, I've witnessed Marco lose his cool more than a few times—Italian spewing, hands flying. His proneness to tantrums has always struck me as more comedic than anything but of course I don't live with him. I experience a sudden pang of alarm. "Annalisa, has Marco ever taken out his anger on you? Or the boys?"

She stops smearing lotion on her cheeks and looks at me. "Oh, no. You know him better than that, don't you?"

"I'm just checking."

"I mean, he slams doors, kicks walls, that kind of thing, but his outbursts have never been directed at us. Although he does scare me sometimes, when he gets like that. He's unreachable."

"Have you ever told him? That he scares you?"

"No."

"Don't you think you should?"

"I don't know. It's not that big of a deal, I guess."

"It *is* a big deal."

"He always apologizes afterward. He already called on his way back to work and left a message apologizing."

"Great. You still need to talk to him."

"Maybe. It's not only his crazy anger that scares me, it's what he's teaching the boys. To lash out, throw things, throw tantrums when you're angry? I mean how can we tell them to stop pitching fits if it's okay for their Dad?"

"Good point. Talk to him. Talk to him tonight, when he's not throwing dishes around."

She wrinkles her nose. "I don't know."

I love her but sometimes she's as weak as tea.

Jackson's laughter rings out from the kiddy pool. He and a little blonde boy are taking turns splashing each other. "It's not like his passion is always a bad thing," she adds, her lips tilting up at the corners. "Passion has its upsides, too."

"I'll take your word for it." I scan the pool for the kids. Ben's in the deep end and Maggie and Ava are in the shallow end practicing underwater handstands.

Annalisa tosses her sun block into her bag and takes out a magazine. "Sometimes I wonder what it'd be like to be married to an Even Steven."

"You mean like John?"

"Yeah, I guess."

"Oh it's a picnic." The girls are now taking turns jumping into the pool. "Sometimes I wished he'd smash a cereal bowl, liven things up a little."

She looks at me. "Are you guys okay?"

"We're fine. The grass is always greener, right?"

Annalisa glances around. Then she reaches into her bag and draws out two Twizzlers. She quickly drops one on my towel, next to my leg, then takes a bite of hers and conceals it inside of her magazine. Ever since one of the lifeguards confiscated our box of Milk Duds last summer, we've become more stealthy. The snack shack sells candy and sodas but who wants to stand in line with all of those dripping wet kids clamoring for overpriced candy? Besides, we don't want to run the risk of losing our chairs.

Annalisa huffs and throws a towel over her legs "I'm burning. Already! I didn't slather early enough. Meanwhile you already look like a sun goddess. So not fair."

"Says my size four friend."

"What are you talking about? You look great. How much have you lost?"

"Fifteen."

"Seriously? All that from just running?"

I look at her over the top of my sunglasses. "*Just* running? You think I magically float out of bed at the crack of dawn and glide down the street? Just Running. Running is hard work I'll have you know."

"Forgive me. Take away the *just*."

My phone chirps from the nest of towels beside me. It's a text from Seth letting me know he needs to pick up Ava earlier than expected. Tori is taking her somewhere. "That might not go over very well," I murmur as I type a response.

"What?" Annalisa asks.

"Maggie's friend needs to be picked up early."

"Who's she here with?"

I point to the girls who are now standing at the steps for the slide. "Ava."

Annalisa leans forward and squints at them. "The cutie in purple? I've seen her around school."

Maggie notices us watching and waves, then elbows Ava to wave too. Annalisa and I wave back.

We bask in silence for a while and I finish my *People* and swap Annalisa for her *Better Homes and Gardens*, even though all those pillowed sofas and repainted end tables leave me cranky. I've never had a knack for decorating. The boys come scouting for candy-bar money and Annalisa and I give each of our sons a dollar. No way would we trust them with the Twizzlers.

Minutes later, I spot Seth. I adjust the top of my suit, throw a towel over my thighs, and run my fingers through my hair. He's strolling along the pool, his hand blocking the sun from his eyes. I wave him over, fiddle with my straps again.

"Sorry I have to break up the party," he says when he reaches our chairs. "I forgot all about this."

"That's okay," I say. "They've had over an hour."

"Watch me Daddy!" Ava hollers from halfway up the steps of the slide.

We watch her spiral down then fight to keep her head above the water as she's thrust out at the end. Seth gives her a thumbs up.

I introduce Seth and Annalisa to each other. Afterwards, Seth begins throwing Ava's stuff into her bag. "So is it too soon to ask how it's coming along?" he asks.

"Ask me next week. But based on the changes I've already made, I think you're going to like it."

"Can't wait."

"Can't rush a good thing, Seth. It's an energy thing. I just need to go with the energy, let it take me wherever it's going to take me."

"What yahoo fed you that line?"

I laugh and swat him with my towel.

"By the way," he says, "I didn't see you at the Jigsaw Race."

"You're kidding? That's funny. Must have been too many people."

"Liar."

"Oh that's right. I forgot to sign up."

"You're out running almost every day anyway. Why not put a goal in front of yourself?"

"I do. It's called a shower. And an iced latte."

Ava scampers over and tugs on Seth's hand. "Did you see me, Daddy? Did you? Did you?"

"I did. You've gotten so brave!"

"She was scared," Maggie broadcasts. "But I told her to do it anyway. I *dared* her to."

I grin at my daughter. "You'll make quite the coach someday Magpie."

Ava beams. "And I *did* Daddy! Again and again and again!"

"That's my girl. Hey, guess what? We need to get you home because your mom's taking you to a movie, remember?"

"But I want to stay."

"Sorry, babe," he says and wraps a towel around her. "We gotta go."

Both girls begin to fuss. "Hey," I tell them, "we'll be back. We'll give Ava a call the next time we come here, okay?"

Seth tells Annalisa it was nice to meet her then turns to me. "Thanks for taking her Holly. And listen, the city 5k is coming up."

"Is this a dare?"

"Worked for Ava." He waves and they stroll away, Ava's feet leaving dark marks on the pavement.

I reach for my water bottle and take a sip, then turn back to my magazine.

"A client of yours?" Annalisa asks.

"Mm-hm. A brand new one."

"And the two of you… run together?"

"Oh, not really. I mean, we bump into each other every now and then."

From my periphery, I can tell Annalisa is watching him walk away. "He's attractive," she says.

"I guess."

"Come on. You can't tell me you haven't noticed."

"Fine. Sure. He's attractive. Have you ever made risotto? Can I rip out this recipe?"

"So you do. Think he's attractive."

I let the magazine drop to my thighs. "Yes, he's attractive. So what? Can I have this recipe or not?"

"It's yours." She opens *People* and props it in front of her face. "Take the whole magazine if you want."

I look at her. "What?"

"Nothing. Forget it."

"Forget what?"

"Nothing. Really."

"Annalisa. Spit it out for once."

She drops the magazine. "It's just that…" She shakes her head.

"What? I'm not supposed to take on clients who happen to be attractive?"

"No, of course not."

"Then what?"

"You seemed to be… flirting."

"Flirting? I wasn't flirting."

"You kind of were."

"I was talking to a *client*."

"You swatted him with your *towel*."

"It's called building rapport!"

"Just forget it. I knew you'd get angry."

"A man and a woman joke around together? What century do you live in?" I turn the risotto page so vehemently it tears.

For a minute or so, we rip through our magazine pages in

silence. Then Annalisa stands up and peels off her cover-up up in one fluid movement. She makes her way to the diving board, trots up the steps, raises her arms above her head, and slips headfirst into the water, creating a tiny ring behind her. Then she front crawls the length of the pool and climbs out at the ladder. She returns to her chair, ringlets dripping, and pats her face with her polka dot towel. She doesn't look at me as she secures it around her waist and slides back into her chair.

She's just abandoned her toddler in the kiddy pool, does she realize that? Sure, I'm right here, as are several attentive lifeguards, but still. Who is she to point fingers?

We stare at our magazines, stare at the pool, and the sun beats down. She's donned her holier than thou hat and she doesn't even realize it.

Finally, after I've watched Maggie zip down the slide three more times, Annalisa sighs. "I'm sorry. Maybe I'm overreacting. I don't know… after everything with Marco… I just feel all worked up."

I push my sunglasses to the top of my head and look at her. "Maybe I was flirting. A little. But give me a break, that's harmless."

"He was flirting with you," she says.

"He was?"

She tips her chin down and gives me a parental look. "Just be careful."

I reposition my sunglasses. "I will."

But as I stare out into the sea of bobbing bodies, Laura's troubling words come back to me: *What's so great about surviving?* That's what my marriage feels like: survival. I'm operating out of habit, carrying out a decade old vow for the sake of… of what? Tradition? Expectation? There's no comparison to my situation and Laura's and yet, in my own way, I get it. She's right. Surviving for the sake of surviving is draining and meaningless. Running beside someone with the wind in your hair, however…

Being with someone who laughs at your jokes, who notices

you've lost weight and tells you you look good, someone whose eyes crinkle at the corners when he smiles and shares from his heart... That's a breath of fresh air. A surge of life. So why carry on the charade? Why merely survive? as Laura says. Why not let the house of cards fold and play a new game?

I scan the pool. That's why. My children. My two anchors pinning me to reality. Two beaming, beautiful faces that depend on me to keep up the pretense. My love for them stings my eyes but still I wonder. Are they enough? Should they be enough? Can they be the mortar to hold their parents together?

I can do it—just like Laura can survive—I can prop up my marriage, give it the semblance of life. Pull the strings and force the thing to move. Pretend it's alive. Feign life. But why?

Some things are beyond saving. Like the nearly dead plant that takes up space on my kitchen windowsill, a pathetic thing beyond resuscitation I senselessly water and talk to anyway, as if it'll make any difference. Aren't I only postponing the inevitable? No matter how much you talk or wish or hope or pray, dead things don't come back to life. Dead is dead.

Just ask Laura.

Annalisa pokes my leg with another Twizzler. I grab it and bite off an end, my eyes on the lifeguards, congratulating myself for fooling them all.

7

I peer into Marco's van and smile at the row of boys. Shoes kicked off, the van already smells like feet. Ben tries to squeeze past me and join them. "Bye Mom!"

I grab his arm and pull him close. "Not so fast." Sure, his friends are watching. No doubt they all got hugs, and probably kisses, from their moms too. I release my son and he scrambles away, smiling as he climbs in and joins Antonio, Lucas, and TJ.

Ben has been packed for this camping trip for a week. Phil squeezes Ben's sleeping bag into the already cramped van and then finds a spot for John's duffel. I was surprised to find out yesterday that Phil was tagging along. "It'll be tight but we'll make it work," he says.

I smile and shove my hands into the pockets of my brand new size eight shorts. Sleeping bag hoisted on his shoulder, John stands before me. "Have a good trip," I tell him.

"You and Magpie doing anything fun?"

I shrug. "She wants to go roller-skating. The girls and I might get together tomorrow night."

Phil takes the sleeping bag from him and disappears in the van.

John looks at me for a moment and lifts his hand. I wonder if he's going to rake his fingers through my hair, all the way to the ends, but he only takes off his baseball cap and wipes his brow. "See you in a couple of days," he says.

"See ya."

John climbs in the passenger seat, next to Marco. I watch the van back out of our driveway. Ben turns to wave, his face stretched in a grin, but John never glances my way.

The following night, Laura arrives at my house with a bottle of Pink Moscato and a mega sized bag of M&M's. Moments later Annalisa raps on my front door and enters bearing a deep pore mud mask and homemade hummus. They follow me to the kitchen.

"Where's Maggie tonight?" Laura asks as she rummages through my drawer for a corkscrew.

"Her friend Ava's house." I manage to avoid Annalisa's gaze. "What about TJ and Jackson?"

"At my mom's," Laura says.

"Babysitter," Annalisa says.

We vote on doing facials before watching whatever mindless romantic comedy Laura picked up on her way over. In my bathroom, I hand a hair band to Annalisa and unclip my hair. After brushing through the tangles, I twist it up and secure it on to of my head again.

"I don't think I've ever seen your hair so long," Laura says, her hair already pulled back in that infernal scrunchie. "It's gorgeous."

"Thanks. I usually have it pulled back in the summer."

Laura fluffs her bangs in the mirror and sighs. "Meanwhile I'm stuck with this frizz."

"Phil can't seem to take his eyes off of you," Annalisa says.

Laura grins. "You don't realize how nice it is to be noticed by a man until it's gone. And you don't realize how much you'll miss other things, too."

I raise my eyebrows. "Other things?"

"A year and a half is a long time. Enjoy your men, ladies. Frequently." She cackles and begins covering her forehead with the mud mask.

"How much did John pay you to say that?" I mutter.

"Why? How long has it been?"

"Laura!" Annalisa's cheeks grow pink.

Laura starts on her cheeks. "I thought this was a slumber party."

"Truth, dare, double dare, promise or repeat," I recite. "Haven't played that since eighth grade."

"Hopefully," Laura says, "it hasn't been as long for you as it has for me because if it has, you'd better drive yourself to that camp and climb into that tent and surprise your man."

I laugh. "John would have a heart attack and die on the spot—" I fall silent. My words. My clumsy, thoughtless words. "I'm sorry, Laura."

"Oh please. I understand hyperbole." She finishes up with her chin and passes it on to me.

I smear seaweed and mud and whatever else this gritty concoction contains on my face and try to remember the last time John and I *were* together. A month? Longer? John, no doubt, is keeping track. But who has time for that? Right now, the only intimate memory that surfaces to my mind is from years ago, when we dropped off the kids at John's parents and stayed at an inn up north for the weekend. We soaked in a double whirlpool and ate doughnuts in bed and rolled around on an Alpaca rug in front of a wood burning fire. Maggie was four, I remember. Not yet in school. Three years ago. Things were good between us three years ago.

"So things with Phil are going well?" I hear Annalisa ask.

"Very well," Laura says. "Things are going *very* well."

"Phil must be *doing* pretty well," I say. "Owning a marsh and all."

"Yes, his family has money," Laura says matter-of-factly. "But he doesn't parade it around. He's been to Haiti several times to help the orphanage that he basically funded single-handedly."

"Salt of the earth," I say.

"So when you say things are going well," Annalisa says, "how well do you mean?"

Laura smoothes her hair back with her hands. "We've talked about it."

I stare at her. "Marriage? Are you telling me you've talked about *marriage*?"

She lets out a wild laugh. "Holly, I'm thirty-eight. Philip's thirty-five. We're not teenagers."

"But you've known each other five minutes."

"Three months. We've known each other for *three months*. Three wonderful, amazing months."

You certainly sound like a teenager, I want to retort. "That's not enough time, is it?" I say instead. "To really know someone?"

"Who says it's not?"

I look at Annalisa, hoping she'll jump in. Back me up. Tell Laura she needs to deflate, float back to earth for a second and think about what she's saying. She's studying Laura thoughtfully and I can't decipher whose side she's on, if there are sides. "What about TJ?" she asks. "How's he doing with all of this?"

"He's doing okay. He's made it very clear on several occasions that Philip is not his dad. Philip gets it. His mom died of cancer when he was seventeen so he understands he can't force anything. He wants to be like a dad to TJ, but he knows TJ has to set the pace." She smiles. "That's one of the reasons I fell in love with him. I'm not saying our getting married would be problem free, especially for TJ, but we know to be realistic. We know that becoming a family would take time."

"Right," I say. "And you're jumping in pretty fast."

Laura snaps the lid shut to the facial mask. "Look. I didn't plan this. I didn't plan on meeting Philip and falling in love. Last year at this time, if you would have told me I'd be dating again, let alone thinking about *marrying* someone, I would have said you were crazy."

"Because it's too soon."

"Well maybe these past sixteen months have flown by for you, Holly, but not for me. They've dragged. They've felt like decades. But these last few months with Philip, I've felt alive again. And that doesn't mean I didn't love Jake—"

"I never said that," I interject. "I never even thought that."

"—because I *still* love Jake. I still miss him. But he's gone and he's not coming back and miracle of miracles, I fell in love with Philip and he's *here*. Maybe that doesn't make sense to you, how I can love both of them, but it does to me. I can't explain it."

She just did. She loves two men. One dead, one living. But can a rational woman like Laura fall for a man in three short months? Yes. Of course she can.

I sit down on the toilet lid. "I just don't want you to have any regrets."

"Listen, I know what it is to be married and I know what it is to be alone. Given the choice, if a good man like Philip wants to marry me, build a life with me and TJ, then I choose marriage. I've never been smart or beautiful, not like either of you, but I was a *good wife*. I *liked* being a wife. I know it sounds silly but I did the wife thing really well. And I'm probably not supposed to admit this kind of thing out loud but I liked depending on a man. I like that he fixed the car and I cooked and he worked full time and I took care of the house. Call me a simple housewife. That's what I am. Or was. Anyway, that's what I want to be. I love Philip. And TJ, in his own way, is beginning to love Philip. He's a *good* man. He loves me, and TJ. He loves God. He's not Jake but I don't *expect* him to be Jake. So I'm sorry Holly, if I'm not sticking to your timeline and you're not ready for me to move on with my life. I am. If Philip asked, I'd say yes."

Her blue eyes shine like pools against the green of the facial mask. How can I argue with such an appeal? I stand up. Brush back a clump of hair that's fallen across her brow. "You deserve to be happy, Laura. And I'm happy for you."

She hugs me and Annalisa hugs us both. When we untangle we notice we've left traces of green on each other's shirts.

"Okay then," I say. "Let's go pour that wine. Time to celebrate."

"He hasn't asked yet."

Tears erode Annalisa's mask. "But he *will*."

The next morning, gloriously alone, I sleep in until nine. I linger over the paper with a cup of coffee, check my email, dress in my running clothes, and at ten o'clock, step out the door with Bernice to fetch Maggie.

Be careful Annalisa admonished by the pool. Yet this morning I'm in a safe zone: I'm un-showered, wearing a barbecue stained t-shirt and no makeup, and armed with an old dog. So Seth and I converse easily. We joke around together. Banter. So what? That's what friends do. Like it or not, attraction exists between people. Innocent, unavoidable attraction is a fact of life, whether or not Annalisa wants to admit it. Moreover I am married and we are adults. Seth is my friend, my client. So be careful of what?

Ava opens the front door in an oversized t-shirt with *Bob's Plumbing* scrawled across the front and smiles in her bashful way.

Maggie appears and attempts to push me down the stoop. "Mom! You're too early."

"Well good morning to you too, Sunshine."

"We're making pancakes and they're not done."

Seth hollers to come in. I holler I've got the dog.

He comes around the corner, spatula in hand, wearing heather gray sweat pants and his glasses. His hair is all mashed up on one side. "Good. Bernice can clean up the splats on the floor. Time to flip," he says and disappears.

Maggie tugs at my hand. "Banana chocolate chip."

I look to Bernice but she offers no advice. Two kids, a dog, and we both look and smell like morning. Hardly the makings for romance.

Bernice and I follow the girls to the kitchen which looks like the *before* set for a cleaning product commercial. Flour is scattered across the countertops, discarded banana peels lay in heaps, drips of batter dot the floor much to Bernice's delight. "Atta girl," Seth says as she laps them up. He stacks pancakes on a plate which he hands to me. I carry it to the table and help the girls with the butter and syrup.

"Thanks," he says.

I smile and shrug. We're both parents. We're adults. He's my client and I'm married. He hands me a glass of juice and sets another plate at the table. "Get 'em while they're hot," he says to me.

"Oh, none for me."

"They're good, Mama!" Maggie manages through her full mouth. "No blueberries."

"You don't like blueberries?" Seth asks.

"Not in pancakes."

"Well these are without a doubt chocolate chip. The girls were in charge of adding the chips and I just don't know if they poured enough in."

The girls giggle. I sit down and slide a knife through a pancake. "So where's the pancake part?"

The girls roar.

Seth removes a mug from a rack on the wall. "Coffee will balance it out. Black?"

"Please."

"None of that fussy creamer stuff for you, huh."

"Not any more. I used to like flavored creamer when I first started drinking it until..." *Until I got married and my husband converted me to strong and black.* "Until I didn't."

"Makes sense." He hands me a steaming Tinker Bell mug then divvies out fresh pancakes. I can't remember the last time John set a plate of anything in front of me. I eat, sip my coffee, and take in the room while the girls chatter. The walls are grey but an enormous painting of a multi colored tomato—somewhat reminiscent of an Andy Warhol—covers most of one wall.

Seth sits down at the table. "By the way, I love it."

"Love what?"

"My website. At least what I've seen so far."

Two days ago I sent him a link, mainly to gauge if I was on the right track, like I do for all my clients. "Good. I wanted to make sure I was heading in the right direction."

"You are."

I take a sip of coffee. "It'll be under construction for a few more weeks yet."

"My daddy works construction," Maggie announces.

Seth cuts through his plateful. "Does he?"

"Yep. He's real strong."

"Not as strong as *my* daddy," Ava counters.

"Oh yeah? Can your daddy dig a whole *pool?*"

"Daddy had a little help digging the pool, Magpie," I say. "Finish up. I'll get your bag together. We need to get going." I stand and glance down the hall. First door on the right, Seth tells me.

Ava's loft bed resembles a castle which, I'd imagine, is all Seth's doing. The headboard is painted to look like a stone wall. Climbing roses and pink tulle shrouds the play space underneath the bed. I take a peek behind the veil and glimpse a heap of dolls and Maggie's suitcase. I pull it out, stuff in her clothes, and glance around for her toiletries. I spot her hairbrush on a bookshelf beside a heart-shaped frame of Ava and, presumably, Tori. I pick up the frame and study the woman.

Her chin-length, streaked blond hair falls flatteringly over one side of her forehead. She's looking straight at the camera and appears to be laughing, both hands planted on Ava's shoulders. Ava smiles up at her mom. It's a beautiful shot. Candid and natural. I can almost hear their laughter.

I replace the photograph and toss Maggie's brush into her suitcase.

As I exit Ava's room, I unintentionally glimpse the bedroom

across the hall. Seth's, I'd imagine. The comforter, a lumpy, rumpled ball, sits in the middle of the bed. A pair of jeans, a towel, and more than a couple socks lay scattered along the floor. But the headboard of the bed... I step closer to confirm what I think I'm seeing. The headboard is actually a ladder, tipped sideways and reinforced with shelves that hold books and a few art pieces. "That's the coolest thing," I murmur.

"What is?" Seth says, suddenly in the doorway.

"Oh. Sorry. I couldn't help noticing your ladder, I mean, headboard. I love it."

He reaches past me and flips on the light, evidently at ease with his mess. "Found that baby at an estate sale. It begged me to bring it home and revive it. Judging from the way it's hinged, I think it's from the 1920's."

"What a cool up-cycle."

"Tori hated it. Made her feel like she was sleeping in a barn, she'd say."

Based on the photograph of the cool looking blond, I'm not surprised. "I like it."

He smiles. "Me too."

We stand there for a moment, staring into his room, my hand gripping Maggie's suitcase. "Well," I say at last, turning to exit the room, "I'll help you clean up."

"No need."

But while he puts away food items, I carry dishes to the counter and wipe the table. Friends help each other clean up. "Thanks for having Maggie over. And for the pancakes."

He looks up from the sink. "You're welcome." He's about to reach for a towel but I assure him I can let myself out. I'm an adult, after all.

On the walk home Maggie rambles on and on, her little, wheeled suitcase making thumping sounds against the uneven sidewalk as she drags it behind her. I nod and pretend to listen.

We are friends, Seth and I, and that is all.

Later that evening as I work on Seth's site, moving and resizing photographs and tweaking text, I tell myself that the pancake breakfast was nothing. Because it *was* nothing. Just like the way he touched my hand in his studio the other day was nothing. Or the way he intently looks at me when he talks or listens to me is nothing. We're friends and friends do these things—share breakfast, touch hands, listen attentively—even if some people get all worked up about it. Some people may misconstrue these simple friendly niceties, view them with an eye of judgment. So the following day, when John returns from his camping trip and asks about my weekend, I don't bother telling him about Maggie's sleepover or the pancake breakfast. I don't mention any of it to Annalisa either because really, there's nothing to tell.

8

I also don't bother telling John about the crazy thing I'm thinking about doing. One Thursday morning, I just do it. Bernice lies at my feet, offering warmth and moral support as my fingers tremble their way through the online registration process. If I don't do it now, I keep telling myself, I never will. And today, the last day before I plummet into my forties, feels very much like a deadline.

That night after supper, I tell John. He's just refilled his water glass at the sink and holds the glass inches from his mouth. "A marathon?" he says.

"A *half* marathon."

"How long is that?"

"Thirteen miles."

He whistles.

"It's not until April. I have nine whole months to get ready. Sounds like I'm pregnant." I laugh, my nerves getting the best of me.

He takes a drink of his water. I start recapping the seasonings I sprinkled on the burgers before they hit the grill.

As much as John's drawn-out whistle irritates me, it epitomizes my own feelings about what I've done. All afternoon I've yo-yoed back and forth between feeling inspired and wondering if I've gone insane. Thirteen miles. So far, I haven't even run a consecutive six. Why didn't I commemorate my fortieth with a tattoo, or an eyebrow ring? Or by jumping out of a plane with a parachute? But death by running?

"So this running thing," John says. "it's not a phase?"

"Does it seem like a phase? I'm up and out the door by seven most mornings."

"But a marathon—"

"*Half* marathon."

"That's a big commitment."

I stare at the leftover plate of meat, two charred hot dogs I'll wrap up, store in the fridge, and throw away a week later. I open the drawer that holds the cling wrap. "So you don't think I can do it."

"It's a big undertaking."

"Thanks for your support."

"Holly, sometimes you start things you don't finish."

I turn to him. "Like what?"

"Like the sun porch. You started painting it in the spring and it's still not done. And that dress you were going to make Maggie for Easter. She's never worn it."

"That's so unfair. My sewing machine is crap."

"You're a starter, not a finisher."

My throat begins to tighten. "I finish plenty of things! I have dozens of clients who are thrilled with the work I do for them, for the jobs I've *finished*."

"Settle down."

"You're one to talk. You tell the kids you're going to do something and then you don't. You say you're going to be somewhere and then you're not, so don't lecture me about following through."

He dumps the bowl of watermelon rinds into the garbage, sets the bowl in the sink, and heads out of the room.

"See? You can't even finish this conversation."

No response.

I start after him and grab the back of his shirt. "*Hey*. I'm talking to you. I hate it when you run away from me when I'm talking to you. Stop running away."

"I'm not the one running."

I stare at him. "Is that supposed to be a joke?"

"Why? Is it funny?"

Maggie thrusts a Little Pony in my stomach. "Mama, I can't get this knot out."

I nudge her aside. "Why can't you just listen to me when I'm trying to talk to you about something important?"

"I did listen. And then I said you shouldn't do it because you don't finish things. Maybe *you* should listen to me."

"Mama," Maggie whines, "I can't get it out."

I'm clenching my hands so tightly my fingernails are piercing the insides of my palms. "Have you even noticed, John, that I've lost twenty pounds? That I've found a type of exercise that actually works for me? Why can't you just *support* me with this half marathon?"

"Because I don't think you should do it."

"You don't think I *can* do it."

He opens his mouth, about to say something, but closes it and shakes his head.

I'm on the verge of tears, hot, choking tears that will steal my words and render me powerless. I swallow them back. "You don't get it. You're not even *trying* to get it."

He picks up the newspaper. "You've bitten off more than you can chew."

I grab the paper out of his hands. Fling it to the floor. "You know what? Other people, lots of people, have noticed I've lost weight and have said I look good. Crazy that I should expect that from you. Why should I expect your support with any of this? You don't support me in anything else. You don't help. Ever. With anything. With the house or the kids or the bills—it's all on me.

Me, me, me. And I'm tired. I'm tired of being the one to hold everything together. I'm so tired of doing everything and I'm so tired of this marriage and I'm so tired of you *I could scream!*"

I am, I realize. Screaming. And Maggie is crying.

John fixes his gaze at me, his pupils tiny stones. "I'll make things easier for you then." He strides through the kitchen and out the back door. Seconds later, I hear his truck back out.

Lucky John. He can leave. Stomp off and drive away. Crank up the music and go wherever he pleases. Meanwhile, I have to stay. Remain in this house where the walls are closing in, crushing me into some distorted version of myself. I must stay and face these children whose eyes are full of fear. John can run away, but I can't.

"Where'd Dad go?" Ben asks from the family room. Bernice, in her apprehension, has curled into a tight ball beside him.

I gather up a stack of books and walk over to my desk. "How should I know?"

Maggie, whimpering, sticks her thumb in her mouth.

"Maggie, you're too old for that. Take your thumb out."

She cries louder.

Ben glares at me. "You made Dad leave."

"No, buddy, I did not. Dad left of his own free will." I set the stack down and rub my face with my hands until my vision turns blurry. "Both of you, get ready for bed. Brush your teeth."

"But it's only eight o'clock," Ben protests. "It's *summer*."

"*Get ready for bed!*" I've screamed the words. My throat feels raw. The looks on my children's faces…

Maggie wails. I clutch the back of my desk chair and close my eyes, swallowing back tears so rapidly I'm choking. When I open my eyes my children are still standing there, too frightened to move. "Tell you what," I say in an absurdly bright tone. "Get your pajamas on and you can read or play on your Kindles and have cookies in bed."

Maggie's eyes grow wide. "Cookies in bed?"

I hope it looks like I'm smiling; that's what I'm striving for. "Why not? We'll wash sheets tomorrow. They need it anyway."

They stand there, blinking for a second, then race to their bedrooms. I go to the kitchen to find these magical, cure-all cookies.

When I open my eyes the next morning I whisper to the ceiling, "I'm forty."

John never came to bed. It was close to midnight when I heard his truck pull into the driveway. I swing my legs out of bed and shimmy into shorts and a tank top. I've left my running shoes somewhere in the family room.

From where he's sleeping on the couch, John's snores reverberate through the house. I creep closer, spy my shoes under the coffee table, and nab them as quietly as I can. One of his fists lays unfurled next to his head, like an infant. In his sleep he looks younger, closer to the towheaded nineteen-year-old tech school student I fell in love with.

We met through my roommate. At first I hardly noticed him among our group that frequented parties and pizza joints but ultimately his quiet persona contrasted so starkly with the unrelenting sarcasm that abounds among eighteen-year-olds that it was impossible *not* to notice him. His shyness, ironically, made him stand out. He didn't need to be the center of attention and the way he took his time before answering a question appealed to me.

Now it drives me mad.

I study this man who, right now, seems like a stranger lying on my couch. If he were to wander into my life today, would I like him? Would he like me? What drew us together in the first place and why the hell did we think we could pull off this crazy thing called marriage?

He begins to stir and I tiptoe away. I grab the leash and Bernice and I steal out the back door.

I run a few blocks and turn on Cherry Street, too disheartened to even try to convince myself I don't know where I'm heading. I know exactly where I'm going and I know exactly who I hope to see. It doesn't take long. He's up ahead, his back to me. In an irrational moment of panic I almost call out *Don't you run away from me too!* I shout his name instead.

He turns around. Even from a block away, I sense he's smiling. He jogs toward me and I toward him.

"Good morning, Holly Lewis and The News." Bernice noses him. "No bacon today, girl."

"Guess what I've done?" I say after we start running again, side by side.

"You've finished my website."

I smile. "Not yet."

"What then?"

"I signed up for a half marathon."

He stops jogging and looks at me. "You *what?*"

I nod.

"You mean to tell me that after all this time I've been badgering you about signing up for something as minor as the Jigsaw Race you go and sign up for a half marathon?"

I feel as if I've been kicked. Blinking wildly, I begin to run.

"Holly! Wait up!" He easily catches up to me. "What? What's wrong?"

"You don't think I can do it," I say, breathless. "You think I'm crazy for trying."

He grips my forearm, pulling me to a stop. "Hang on. That's not what I meant. I'm just surprised."

"But I shouldn't have done it, right? I should have worked up to it. Signed up for a 5k first. It was totally stupid of me."

"No it wasn't. It was brave. Impulsive maybe, but brave."

I try to reign in my breath. I have to ask. Everything is hinged on his response. "Do you think I can do it?"

He smiles as if it's a ridiculous question. "Of course."

With no warning I burst into tears. The dam that's been holding back the flood for days disintegrates. Worst of all, I have nothing to mop my face, not even a long sleeve.

"Ah…" Seth says. "Wish I had a handkerchief to offer."

This remark, like a line pulled from Jane Austen, prompts me to laugh. I turn away from him and dab my dripping nose with the hem of my shirt. "I'm sorry," I say facing him again. "I guess I needed to hear someone say that."

We stand in the middle of the sidewalk, looking at each other. Across the street, a gray-haired lady waters her geraniums and I wonder, if it weren't for her, would Seth draw me into a hug? Like friends do at times?

Without a word, we start running again.

"Guess what else?" I say after a block.

"There's an else?"

I wait a moment, feeling self-conscious and juvenile. "I'm forty today."

"Happy birthday!"

"Thank you."

"So that explains it."

"What?"

"The half marathon. The crying."

I side shove him.

"Any big plans for the day?" he asks.

"Not that I know of."

"No big party?"

I let out a grunt. "I think I can safely cross that off my wish list. My husband's not one for parties. I'll be happy if he picks up a cake."

A Jack Russell Terrier yaps as we pass a fenced-in front yard.

"How about you?" I ask. "Have you crested that proverbial hill yet?"

"I'm forty-one."

"Good. You can talk me down the other side."

"Yeah, like I'm some kind expert. Have you seen my life? Don't look to me for help."

I stop running and face him. "But I need your help." My labored breathing makes me sound more desperate than I feel. "I do. I need to know how to train for this crazy marathon thing. Tell me what to do because, honestly…" I swallow hard. "I don't know if I *can* do it."

His gaze is steadfast. He places a hand on my shoulder. "You can do it, Holly. I know you can."

Something lifts inside of me. We continue to run.

That evening, John breaks our silence by telling me to get ready to go out. I suppose I should be some degree of happy—at least he remembered and made dinner plans—but right now the last thing I want to do is sit in a restaurant and glare at each other when we can be angry at home for free.

"Why don't we skip the whole charade," I suggest.

"I've already told the kids and we're picking up Annalisa and Marco at six."

I look up from the laundry I'm folding. "All of us? And all of the kids?"

John nods.

I grab a pair of his boxers. "Happy birthday to me."

"Just be ready, okay?"

"As in McDonald's ready or Chuck E. Cheese ready?"

"Something nice. That dress with the things around the neck," he says and leaves.

The dress with the things around the neck. Some men are born poets, words dripping from their lips like honey. Not John. Yet I know which one he's talking about. A navy a-line with a smattering of tiny rhinestones, or *things*, along the neckline. I bought it a month ago and it fits perfectly, hugs me just right around the waist and falls right above my knees. I zip myself into the dress and step into heels. *Heels*. This better be worth it.

Maggie bursts through my door wearing a long hot pink skirt and a yellow t-shirt with the words *One Cool Chick!* printed across in obnoxious bubble letters. "How beautiful you look, Mommy!" Her words tumble out so spontaneously I can't help but kiss her.

"Thank you Magpie."

So far I've received a pendant necklace from the kids, a card with a forty-dollar check inside from my mom, a phone call from my dad promising a gift is on its way, a card with a hefty Starbucks gift card from my mother-in-law, and unyielding silence from John.

And unwavering belief from Seth.

When Maggie and I step into the living room, Ben presents me with a bouquet of cream-colored roses with yellow-tinged tips. My favorite. "Happy birthday Mom."

I breathe in the scent of the flowers that mirror what I held on my wedding day and glance at John. He's fiddling with a button on his shirt. "Thank you," I say to Ben and head to the kitchen for a vase.

On the drive over to Annalisa's, John and I don't exchange a word. The kids, however, are bouncing like ping pong balls in the backseat. I tell them to calm down but Maggie only punctuates her bounces with monkey calls.

John pulls into Annalisa's driveway and tells Ben to go see if they're ready. Both kids scramble from the van.

I stare straight ahead, arms crossed. "I thought birthdays were about doing something the birthday person wants to do."

"Well you never know. You may actually have fun."

"With five kids? Right. The best restaurants hand out crayons at the door. Here's a crazy thought. You and I could have just gone out, by ourselves."

John rests his elbow on his opened window and stares at the house. "Like you would have liked that."

"At least we could have talked."

"Or argued."

"You don't know that. You don't know if we'd have argued."

"We're arguing right now."

"Fine. The kids can do all the talking. And Annalisa and Marco. We'll let them do the talking. We're just along for the ride. On *my* birthday."

In a small, still relatively sane corner of my mind, I know I am turning into a fourth grader, or worse, but John never apologized.

He never said another word about the half-marathon. Never offered the tiniest word of support or permission, not that I need it. Not that I'm waiting for his say-so to live my life.

Ben races across the lawn to us. "They want you to come in. They have a gift for you."

I sigh. "Seriously? Can't they give it to me at the restaurant?"

"They said it'd be easier to give it to you inside. Come on, Mom!"

As we make our way up Annalisa's cobbled front walk, my heel catches and John reaches for my arm. I don't give him the satisfaction. I can steady myself without him.

I push open Annalisa's front door, the sight of my mother causing me to gasp. What is she doing here? And all of these people...

"*Surprise!*" they shout.

I reach for John's arm.

9

John leads me into Annalisa's house, his hand steady beneath my trembling elbow. I grapple with the jumble of faces before me. So many, too many to absorb. I'm a blind person overwhelmed by sudden sight. There's Annalisa and Marco of course, standing beside my mother, and Laura and Phil, and a few clients who've become friends over the years. I spy our retired neighbors, and Ben's piano teacher, and a couple from Annalisa's church we've gotten to know... and everyone is looking at me expectantly.

"I am," I manage. "Surprised."

Laughter ripples through the room.

Annalisa scurries over, heels clicking along the floor, and throws her arms around me. "We did it! We surprised you!"

"Completely."

"Was it difficult getting her here, John?" she wants to know.

He shrugs. "We made it work."

I stare at him. He knew. All this time, he knew.

My mother draws me into a hug. "I can't believe you're here," I say in her ear. "When did you get in?"

"Yesterday. John picked me up from the airport and Annalisa

put me up for the night."

"I had no clue."

"That was the idea." Mom grabs my hands and holds me at arm's length. "Look at you! You've gotten so thin."

"She looks beautiful doesn't she?" Annalisa says.

"She does," my mother agrees, grinning up at John.

"She does," John echoes but only because it's his turn.

Annalisa's dining room table boasts a bounty of hors d'oeuvres—stuffed mushroom caps, bruschetta, cheese plates and dips. And there, on top of her bookshelf, is my life in photographs. Me as a baby. A pudgy kid. A self-conscious teenager. A beaming bride. A new mom. I chat with guest after guest, all of whom want to know the same thing: was I truly surprised? I'm not that good of an actor, I assure them.

Finally, after greeting everyone, I assemble a plate of food and drop on the couch beside Laura.

"You're always a step ahead of everyone," she says. "I didn't think we'd be able to pull this off."

"Well, you did."

"Annalisa can breathe now."

"So this was Annalisa's brainchild?"

"Who else?"

I glance across the room at John. Who else indeed?

"She sent out the email months ago," Laura goes on, "and none of us spilled the beans. Can you believe that? Not even me. Did John give any hints?"

I poke a cherry tomato with my fork. "Not a word."

"Wait till you see the picture Marco snapped when you first walked in."

I force a smile, wondering if the shot captures my anger or shock. "Can't wait."

Phil comes over and stands at one end of the couch, as stiff as a floor lamp. I feel a stab of pity. Does he feel as uncomfortable as he looks among this group of virtual strangers? "How are things on the bog, Phil?" I ask.

He nods. "Looking at a good harvest this year."

"Wonderful."

He pulls up a folding chair and sits down. "How's business for you?"

"Good, thanks." Seth pops to mind, his absence here among my friends and clients acute. Not that Annalisa would have invited him. I take a sip of wine.

"I've been meaning to call you," Phil says. "I'd like to talk to you about redoing my website for my cranberry marsh."

Tonight's surprises are unending. "Absolutely. I'll give you a call next week and we can set up an appointment."

He nods, his eyes darting to Laura's empty wine glass. He slips it out of her hand. "White?"

"Thank you. What a gentleman," she says, watching him walk away.

My eyes scan the room until they land on John. On one level, I've got to hand it to him. Picking up my mother from the airport. Not blurting out the truth in the heat of our bickering. Managing to get the kids to keep the secret. I wait until he looks my way then attempt a smile. He smiles back, in a closed-mouth, half-hearted kind of way. I finish my wine. If I hold this empty glass in the air, how long would it take, I wonder, for John to notice and refill it?

I get up and refill it myself.

When we get home, I strip Maggie's bed and find clean sheets. She's thrilled to campout on her brother's floor and promptly constructs a *Do Not Disturb* sign for her doorknob. From somewhere in the basement she procures a small bell so that my mother can ring if she needs anything.

"What a sweet little innkeeper," my mother says.

"Don't be surprised if you find a bill under your door tomorrow morning." I snap open the top sheet and let it float down on the bed, taking note of the single carry-on in the corner. "How long can you stay?"

"Tuesday. Although the weather's so awful right now I may

just move back to Wisconsin for good."

This is one of her standard lines, the moving back to Wisconsin bit, but she'll never follow through. I nod and tuck a pillow under my chin to shimmy it into a fresh case.

Annalisa, of course, had the good sense not to include my father on the guest list. He and Linda live a two-hours' drive away but we typically only connect on holidays when Dad hands John and me a glass of sherry and we endure painfully stilted chitchat. Of course Mom won't move back. She couldn't stand to be in the same state as Dad. Although selfishly, I often wish she would. If Annalisa gets hit with the flu, her mom swoops in and Laura's mom in Minnesota can drive over for weekends. She's independent, my mother. Admirably so. She's carved out a whole new life for herself on the Atlantic coast, filling her hours with friends and volunteer work and golf lessons. I'm proud of her, yet feeling left behind stings. Clearly I'm getting the short end of the Grandma stick.

I stifle a yawn. "Do you need anything else, Mom?"

"I don't think so." She smiles at me and sits down on the edge of the bed. "Did you have a good birthday, honey?"

"I was completely surprised. Especially by you."

She tilts her head. "But, did you have a good birthday?"

Maggie's bookshelf holds a mason jar crammed with seashells she and my mother collected on the beach. Pale lavender and peach spirals that once housed living organisms sit trapped and useless behind glass. I pick up the jar, give it a little shake. Nothing happens, of course. Anything that was once alive is long dead.

I replace the jar and turn to my mother. "Of course," I lie.

The following week Annalisa calls. "Drop everything and come over."

I'm in front of my computer, deep in a productive groove, a hard thing to come by these long summer days. I've picked up a new client, Seth's divorce lawyer, and for the past hour I've been clicking along with the design.

"Thirty minutes," I murmur when Annalisa takes a breath. "Can't stop."

"No, Holly. *Now*. She'll be here in ten."

"Who?"

"Who? *Laura*. Haven't you been listening?"

I force myself to turn away from the screen. "Okay, what's going on?"

"Laura is going to be at my house in ten minutes," Annalisa says evenly as if I'm in preschool. "And I don't know for sure but I think she has *news* and I think it's *news* you'll want to *hear* so come over so we can celebrate it *together*."

"You don't think…"

"Could be."

I save and close out. "Be right there."

The kids have been romping through the sprinkler and I toss towels at them before we hop in the van. At Annalisa's house I ask if her kids might want to run through the sprinkler since mine are already wet. Jackson is napping but she tells her older two to put on their trunks and go outside.

Annalisa paces the length of her living room, chewing her lip.

"Sit down," I tell her.

"Oh I hope. I hope, I hope."

"It might be nothing. She could be coming over to show us she's gotten her eyebrows waxed—"

"*Shhh*. She's coming."

Laura gives a quick rap on the door and lets herself in. I immediately search out her left hand, but the little sneak has tucked it behind her giant purse. She strolls over to the fireplace and admires Annalisa's new family photograph hanging above the mantle. "When did you have this taken?"

"A couple months ago," Annalisa says. "In June? May? I don't know."

"Even Jackson's smiling. Who took it?"

Hope brightens Annalisa's face. "Do you need a photographer?"

Laura shrugs. "Oh, you never know." She's a cat, toying with its prey, and enjoying every second. Someone needs to put Annalisa out of her misery.

"So Laura," I say. "What's new with you?"

"With me?"

"Yes. If you have something to tell us can you do it before Annalisa here passes out?"

Laura laughs. Then she throws out her left hand. Sunlight from the window catches a diamond.

Annalisa shrieks and runs to her. "I knew it! Oh, how wonderful!"

I give Laura a hug. "When did he ask?"

"Last night. We were walking by the fields at twilight, just the two of us, with the crickets chirping and the frogs calling and all of a sudden he got down on one knee and said, 'Will you do me the honor of becoming my wife?' Those were his words. The *honor*."

Annalisa clutches her heart. "Utterly romantic."

"It is, isn't it?" Laura says. "I never really pegged him as a romantic but last night..." she plops down on the couch, "last night was perfect. After I said yes, we sat down right there on the path and made out. I have a billion mosquito bites up and down my legs but it was worth it."

I sit down next to Laura and take her ringed hand. "It's gorgeous. Good job, Phil."

Annalisa settles herself on the other side of Laura, like we've done so many times before. Four short months ago, in Annalisa's dining room, we sat on either side of this woman while she fell apart. And now here she is, glowing and grinning and flashing a princess cut diamond wedding ring.

"So when's the wedding?" Annalisa asks.

"August nineteenth."

"You're kidding. You're waiting a whole year?"

Laura laughs at me. "*This* August nineteenth."

I do the math. "That's two weeks."

"Yep."

"So you don't want a wedding?" Annalisa asks.

"We'll have a wedding."

I stare at her. "In *two weeks*?"

"Yep."

"That's soon," Annalisa says. "How romantic!"

Am I hearing right? In this moment of joy I don't want to be the cloudburst on someone's parade, but this is lunacy. Two weeks isn't enough time to put together a wedding. Not even close. I tell them as much.

Laura shoos away my concerns with a wave of her hand. "Oh, we're not fancy. What do we really need? A place. A dress. A minister." She might as well be crafting a grocery list.

"But why the rush?" I want to know.

"Because we want to be *married*. The wedding is kind of secondary."

I stare at her.

"Look, Holly. Don't start. Philip and I had a big long talk with his pastor who has known him forever. Pastor Dan asked a lot of questions and we talked through lots of issues, but in the end he said yes, even though we're moving rather fast—"

"Major understatement," I insert.

"—he knows Philip is a man of integrity. He knows Philip isn't rushing into marriage and he's confident Philip understands what he's committing to. We'll get married on the marsh. I'll find a dress and I don't know," she says shrugging, "It'll just work. And you two will help me, right?"

"Of course," Annalisa says, grasping Laura's hands. "It'll be beautiful."

Laura turns to me. "Come on, Holly. I can't do this without you."

I shake my head at the pair of them. What choice do I have but to kiss common sense goodbye and join the madness? "You're out of your mind. But if you want a wedding in two weeks Laura,

then you'll get the prettiest wedding two weeks time can buy."
She beams. "I knew you'd be up for the challenge."

10

First things first, the girl needs a dress. The next day the three of us chip in for a babysitter, corral the kids at Annalisa's house, and head to the downtown bridal shop where we snag all the size ten dresses holding a hint of promise.

The first dress should have stayed on the hanger. Laura catches her reflection in the three-way mirror and grimaces. This is only the first dress, Annalisa and I remind her as we help her out of it. Not to worry, there are plenty more.

The second one is modern and strapless and all wrong.

"No way can I pull this off," Laura says, pressing the bodice of the gown to her chest. The saleslady chirps that strapless is all the rage and a good fitting can accomplish wonders. "Like make my bust bigger?" Laura snaps.

The saleslady forces a grin. She holds out another dress that, in my growing hunger, reminds me of a cream puff. Laura takes one look at the layers and shakes her head. Instead, we help her into a satin mermaid which seems to accentuate her shortness.

"None of these are working," Laura cries. "This body's not made for formalwear!"

Annalisa asks the sales lady to give us a minute. Laura collapses on the upholstered settee. "Tank top and peasant skirt. That's what I should stick with. And are you looking at these price tags?"

"When you picture yourself," I say, sitting next to her, "what kind of dress do you see?"

"I don't want a butt bow again."

"No one does. Not since we've left the nineties."

"Something simple but stylish," Laura continues. "Nothing too fussy. I just want Philip to see me and think, *wow*. I want to wow my husband on our wedding day. Is that so much to ask?"

"No," Annalisa assures her. "Of course not."

"I'm no supermodel, I know that. *Phil* knows that, but for one day, my wedding day, I just want to be That Girl."

"That Girl," I repeat.

"You know *That Girl* everyone looks at. That pretty girl. I want to look *pretty*."

Brow wrinkled and her lips pursed, Annalisa studies Laura. Annalisa can pair a plain white t-shirt and an old pair of jeans with just the right accessories to make an outfit sing. "We'll find you the right dress," she says, "but I don't think we'll find it here."

Laura's already tugging at the zipper. "Let's blow this joint."

To boost morale we stop for coffee. "How will you get invitations out in time?" I ask after we sit at an outside table.

"There's this crazy new thing called email," Laura says.

"You're going to email invitations?"

"Small and simple, Holly. Small and simple."

I take a sip of coffee. "And food?"

"We'll have plenty of cranberry wine, that's for sure. Some neighboring growers have had this long-standing deal. If Philip ever got married, they'd supply the wine."

"Wine is good," I say. "So is food."

Laura exhales. "Do we really have to feed everybody?"

"People usually expect it," I say.

"But we don't want gifts. We want to keep it small. We don't want to mess with a meal. Maybe just something snacky."

"So graham crackers and juice boxes?"

"No, fruit snacks and Kool-Aid. We'll have *something*, Holly. Cheese and crackers? A veggie tray? Who said weddings always have to be so done up? If we want it simple, why can't we keep it simple? Why have weddings turned into such a circus?"

"People need to know what to expect," I tell her. "They need to know if they should hit a drive thru before attending your ceremony."

"Fine. So help me. How do we let people know not to expect a dinner? Without sounding like a cheapskate?"

I sip my coffee and think. "What if you have the wedding in the evening, around sunset, with desserts and wine afterward? If you set the ceremony for say, seven-thirty, or eight o'clock, no one would expect a meal. And on your invitations—your emails—you could include a line that says 'wine and chocolate reception to follow'."

Laura raises her coffee cup. "Bravo."

"A sunset wedding would be lovely," Annalisa adds.

"Tell you what," I continue, in full project mode now, "let me take care of the desserts. My gift to you."

"No gifts!"

"Organizing desserts hardly qualifies as a gift. And Laura, a lot of people are going to *want* to give you something. I bet I could call half the people on your list and ask them to bring a dessert in lieu of a wedding gift and they'd be thrilled."

"You think so?"

"Absolutely."

"I'll help you make calls," Annalisa says. "And I'll make a raspberry torte."

"Perfect. We should ask a few people to bring fruit, balance it out." I turn to Laura. "And all of this is taking place outside?"

"Yes."

"What if it rains?"

"Then we'll get wet."

"You have to have a rain plan, even for a simple wedding. How big is this porch you've been going on and on about?"

"Big."

"Big enough to set up tables with food and drinks?"

"Yes."

"Good, at least the food will stay dry. I'll look into renting some kind of canopy or tent."

Annalisa claps her hands in excitement. "And we can string white lights and wildflowers along the porch. If you're okay with that, Laura."

Laura stares at us, her two best friends who've hijacked her no-fuss wedding in a matter of minutes. I brace myself for a moderate scolding. "You guys would do all of this for me?" she says softly.

I release my breath. "Of course."

"You're getting *married*," Annalisa adds. "But tell us if we're taking over too much."

"You can do anything you want. Make it sparkle. Whatever. You have my blessing. And save your receipts because we have the money, it's just that all these details aren't our thing. But if you two want to take over, great. You two focus on the details of the day, I'll start planning the details of the *night*. I need lingerie. Something crazy sexy since it's his first time."

I choke on my coffee. "His first time?"

Laura raises an eyebrow and smiles.

"Are you serious?" I whisper, leaning forward. "Phil's a virgin?"

She nods.

"How old did you say he was?"

"Thirty-five."

"No way."

"Geez Holly, you make him sound like an alien."

"Now I'm really worried for you. What's wrong with him?"

"Nothing's *wrong* with him! So would you feel better Holly, if he had slept with dozens of women?"

"Well, no. But has he been in any other relationships?"

"Two. But they didn't work out. He's never been engaged, and he made a commitment to wait until marriage. Honorable men still exist. How fun for me, right?" She throws back her head and laughs.

I lean back in my chair. "That's one way to look at it. No wonder this wedding is in two weeks."

"Like I've said, sixteen months is a *long* time."

"Someone needs to warn Phil about what experienced girls like you expect on their wedding night."

Laura cackles. "Oh, we'll figure it out."

Annalisa hides behind her coffee cup and eventually veers the conversation back to the topic of wedding dresses. I'm about to suggest we drive the forty minutes to a decent mall when Annalisa says, "What about that place?"

I follow her pointed finger to a building across the street. "The antique shop? For what, a girdle?"

"No Holly," Laura says. "A flour sack."

Annalisa stands and throws away her paper cup. "Come on. I have a good feeling about that place."

The inside of the shop smells like musty basement and perfumed candles but—with Annalisa at the helm—we charge through the store anyway. I pause to admire a salvaged stained glass window. Seth would be all over this.

Two sad clothing racks sit in the back corner. Annalisa begins flipping through vintage dresses, fingering fabric, examining buttons, and occasionally holding one up to Laura.

"So we're going for a Caroline Ingalls kind of look," I say.

Ignoring me, Annalisa selects three dresses. A cardigan wearing salesman appears and asks if we need any help.

Annalisa smiles. "A fitting room, please."

He shuffles to a corner of the store, opens a narrow door, and tugs on the string to the light bulb. "Sink's broken," he announces and leaves.

A mop and a bucket sit propped beside an aqua toilet that has presumably been sitting there since the sixties. Annalisa glances around, looks at the back of the door, and hangs the dresses on a protruding nail. "There's a mirror right outside," she tells Laura. "Try one on and come out."

Laura gapes. "You can't be serious."

Annalisa closes the door.

We wait beside a baby pram holding a porcelain doll that resembles Marilyn Manson. After a minute Annalisa raps on the door. "How are we doing?"

"*We* are not coming out. Dress number one was made for someone who doesn't eat."

"Just go on to the next one."

Some time later, Laura steps out wearing a champagne colored lacy thing.

"Hey," Annalisa says, circling Laura. "Not bad."

I agree.

Laura inspects herself in the mirror. "But it's not great, either. It's a little too country clubish, don't you think?"

She disappears into the bathroom again. I pull Annalisa aside. "What if they all bomb? That girl is getting married in *ten days*. We need to bite the bullet and take her to a real mall. No way can we let her walk down the aisle in a tank top and peasant skirt and that god-awful scrunchie. She'd do it too, you know." I've gestured so wildly I've tipped over the baby buggy. I set it upright, thankful to find Marilyn Manson intact.

After ample time has passed, Annalisa raps on the door. "Laura? You all right in there?"

I can just picture her, sitting on that dirty toilet lid, crying. First, we'll feed her lunch. Then we'll call the babysitter, convince her to stay longer, and drive to a civilized mall. "Laura, come on out," I coax. "It can't be that bad. I have a plan."

The door slowly creaks opens. Laura steps out wearing a shy smile and the sweetest dress I've ever seen.

It's ivory with short, gently pleated, sleeves. The soft, organza skirt falls becomingly at her calves and a wide sash cinches her waist. Tiny pearl buttons travel up the fitted bodice, opening into a flattering v-neck. It's lovely and timeless and perfect. I reach for the tag. Sixty dollars. Sixty beautiful dollars.

Annalisa steps closer, touches a sleeve. "Laura, it's perfect."

"Too feminine?"

"No," I say, "Annalisa's right. It is perfect. It's *wow*."

Annalisa motions for Laura to spin. She does, the skirt flaring out before drifting back into place. "All you need is a veil," Annalisa says. "One of those short ones from the same decade. Nineteen-forties, I think."

"And the right shoes," I add. "It's so Mary from *It's a Wonderful Life*."

Laura turns this way and that way, examining herself in the mirror. "But is it *me*?"

"Yes," I say to her reflection.

"Are you sure?"

"If you don't get this dress, I'm going to pitch a fit and Mr. Rogers over there is going to throw us out. Annalisa, tell her to get the dress."

"Get the dress. You have to get the dress. I can't imagine you wearing any other dress."

The shop owner comes over and gives Laura that unmistakable once-over look of approval. "I don't know what the occasion is but that's the dress you should be wearing."

I want to hug the old goat.

That evening during dinner, I mention that Laura found a dress. Maggie wants a full description and while I deliver it, John seems intensely interested in his green beans. After awhile I ask him about work. Fine, he says. He needs to get to the chiropractor again. When he obligatorily asks how work is for me, his eyes flit to the TV.

I've joined the ranks of pole dancers, I consider announcing. Would he even notice?

When I climb into bed, however, he notices. His hand slides

up the back of my t-shirt and the massage should feel good, but instead it feels invasive. Demanding.

Abruptly, I sit up and swing my legs over the side of the bed. "I think I heard Maggie."

"No you didn't."

He runs his fingers through the length of my hair. "What's wrong?"

"Nothing."

We have yet to discuss the birthday fight. I could dredge it up, now that time has cooled us both. But I don't want to, I realize. I don't care anymore. So he doesn't support me with the half marathon. So what? I don't need his support. I don't need him to believe in me and encourage me and reassure me that I can do it. Someone else has filled that role.

"What's going on?" he asks.

So much. So very, very much. "Just restless I guess."

"I know something that can help with that."

The seed of annoyance in the pit of my stomach grows into full-fledged disdain, hard and bitter, like a small stone. I can't sit here any longer. I have to get out of this room, get away from him so I can breathe. Without further explanation, I exit our bedroom and shut the door on my husband.

11

"Laura is going to hate us," Annalisa says as we drive to Laura's house.

"What kind of friends would we be," I tell her, "if we didn't intervene? Now's the time."

Now. Five days before the wedding. Annalisa and I have made all the arrangements for today, secured a sitter and booked the appointments. Laura expects us at her doorstep in a few minutes, but has no idea what's about to hit.

Laura opens her front door wearing a neon green t-shirt and that tired old scrunchie. My resolve thickens. "You're here to help me pack, right?" she asks.

I grin. "We're here to *help*."

"But not pack," Annalisa rushes on. "We're taking you somewhere."

"Where?"

I step inside. "The wedding is less than a week away. Your dress is all clean and ready and you found a beautiful veil."

"Right," she says impatiently. "So now I need to finish packing."

"You need to do something else, too." I gently tug on her scrunchie.

She ducks out of reach. "What are you talking about? Annalisa, what is she talking about?"

"Today is you're luck day," I announce. "Today is your very own makeover day."

She stares at me. "No, it's not."

"Surprise!" Annalisa says from behind my shoulder.

"No. Don't say surprise. I hate surprises."

"You'll love this one," I assure her.

"You're the bride," Annalisa says. "Don't you want to get your hair done?"

"No."

"Why not?" I demand.

"I got it cut a few weeks ago. It's fine."

I place my hands on her shoulders. "This is your wedding we're talking about. It's not the time to settle for *fine*. You told us you wanted to be That Girl and *That Girl* does not wear scrunchies."

"I wasn't going to wear one on my wedding day."

"That Girl never wears a scrunchie. Ever."

She honestly looks wounded. "What's wrong with my scrunchie?"

"Laura, I'm speaking to you as your friend. I can't let it go on any longer. It's time to say goodbye to scrunchie."

"You're beautiful," Annalisa jumps in, "just the way you are, but wouldn't it be fun to do something a little different for your wedding? Maybe try a new cut with a few highlights?"

"I've never colored my hair."

"Right," I say, "so how do you know you won't like it unless you try it? You might love it. Besides, you said you'd let us do whatever we want to make the wedding pretty, remember?"

"The porch. I was talking about the porch, not me."

I shake her shoulders. "You're the *bride*. You're more important than the porch. You should steal the whole show. And listen, we're not talking about bleaching you blonde. We're talking about something subtle. A hint of eye makeup…"

"I wear mascara," Laura says indignantly.

I throw my hands in the air and let Annalisa take over.

"Remember what you told us in the dressing room?" Annalisa says. "How you want to wow Phil when you walk down the aisle? We want to help you do that, to wow him."

She's folding; I can visibly see it. Slowly, I move my hand to her hair. No sudden moves. I tug her scrunchie until her frizzy, nondescript hair falls every which way. "Trust us," I say, shoving the elastic cloth into my jeans pocket. "You won't be sorry."

She pats her wiry hair. "Nothing extreme?"

"We promise," Annalisa says.

I raise my right hand.

"Fine," Laura says. "Do what you want with me. But I swear if you take me in for a Brazilian bikini wax I'm calling this whole thing off."

Before she has a chance to change her mind, we whisk her away to Annalisa's hairdresser. Annalisa and the stylist prattle on about honey gold and mahogany brown and high-gloss serum and volume boosting layers. Laura's eyes ping-pong between the two of them as if they're arranging a kidney transplant. I back her into the chair and thrust a magazine at her. "Did you hear about that dog that pulled a kid from a lake? Here. Page fourteen."

Soon Laura's head is sprouting foil. While she's processing, the stylist swivels her around so she's not facing the mirror and pulls out a tackle box sized makeup kit.

"Natural and glowing," Annalisa instructs. "Nothing heavy."

"You've got great lips," the stylist tells Laura.

"I do?"

"Some women pay big money for that full, heart-shaped pout. You gotta let me put a little color on them. And how do you feel about getting your eyebrows waxed? Just clean them up a bit, nothing drastic."

Laura closes her eyes. "Lord have mercy."

The stylist pats her shoulder. "You're in good hands."

Annalisa and I hold Laura's hands during the eyebrow wax and murmur approval when the foil is removed. After Laura is dried and styled, the stylist adds a few last minute makeup touch-ups then grips the back of Laura's chair. "Ready or not, here comes the bride." She spins the chair around.

Annalisa and I watch Laura's reaction in the mirror.

"Who is that?" she finally whispers.

"You," Annalisa says. "The bride."

Keeping her eyes glued to the mirror, Laura slowly turns her head from side to side. "It is me. A better me."

"An *enhanced* you," the stylist says.

"It's the wow version of you," I say. "Phil's going to love it."

Laura lets out her breath. "Yeah, I think he will." She pulls her bangs foreword then brushes them to the side again, her eyes never leaving the mirror. "I think I just need a moment to get used to it but yeah, I think I love it. Man oh man, what would Jake say?"

I freeze.

"Jake?" the stylists asks with a little laugh. "I thought you were going on and on about a Philip?"

The three of us don't utter a word. The stylist quickly gathers her bowls and brushes and excuses herself to go clean up.

"Probably sounds weird to you," Laura says, "that I'd think of him right now."

Annalisa and I shrug. Who are we to say anything? Our husbands didn't die.

"You were married for eleven years," Annalisa says. "It's only normal, I'm sure."

I take a step closer to Laura. "You are sure though, right? I mean, you're not having second thoughts—"

"No. I'm really not. It's just that, sometimes, I can't *help* but think of Jake and wonder what he'd think about all of this. Especially when I'm with you two."

Annalisa squeezes Laura's shoulder. "You're safe with us, honey. You can talk about him. We can handle it."

"Thanks," Laura says, facing the mirror again. "And thanks for this. You were right. Happy? Can I get my scrunchie back now?"

I grin at her. Little does she know I shoved it in the trashcan on our way into the salon. "Not a chance."

We grab an early lunch then head home to relieve Jana the Babysitter who has managed to persuade all the kids to chalk the driveway. Annalisa rounds up her three and asks if Ben can spend the night. I'm quick to give my consent, especially since Maggie has a sleepover birthday party at friend's house tonight as well. Ben whoops and darts inside for his toothbrush. Before she drives off, Annalisa says she'll check with a local gardener about picking up flowers for the wedding and promises to give me a call tomorrow morning.

Maggie keeps chalking, her leg coated in pink and purple chalk dust. She shows me the eight-tiered wedding cake she's drawn for Laura and asks me to help her with the flowers. I crouch down and add a yellow daisy to the top of the cake. The *ding-ding* from a bicycle bell causes me to raise my head and I spy Ava, a block away, riding a two-wheeler. Seth runs next to her, clutching the back of the bike. Maggie notices them, springs to her feet, and hollers hello. Ava slams on her brakes. Seth nearly topples headfirst over her.

I sprint to the end of my driveway. "Are you alright?"

"Ava, you can't do that," Seth scolds. "You're going to break Daddy's neck."

"Sorry." Ava hops off her bike and joins Maggie.

"No one told me how hard this learning to ride a two wheeler thing would be. My back can't take much more of this. She's almost eight. She should have mastered this by now."

"Try a hill."

"What?"

"Let her coast down a small hill. Like the one by the school. She'll learn to balance on her own."

"I'll give it a try."

"Okay now you're turn. I need help."

"Shoot."

"The half. What do I do? Where do I start? How much should I be running each day? Why didn't you talk me out of this?"

"Take it easy. You gotta break it down. Don't think of it as a half marathon, think of it in pieces. If your mindset is 'I have to run thirteen miles', you'll psyche yourself out and never make it. Just concentrate on how to train *today*."

Maggie comes over with her chalk and begins to trace my feet. "So what do I do today? This week?"

"A hard run four days a week, a light run two days a week, and no run one day a week. You have to build in that rest day otherwise you'll burn out. And stay consistent. If Sunday is your day off, then no running on Sunday. Period."

"Thou shalt not run on Sunday. Got it."

"Eventually we'll build you up to where you can run ten miles a day, but we'll do it gradually."

I like *we*. I'm not too crazy about *ten*. "Right. Sure we will."

Seth places both of his hands on my shoulders. "Gradually, Holly. This isn't a sprint, it's a marathon, and you've got time. You know how we talked about artistic creative bursts? Well this is the opposite. You train because you've *decided* to run a half, you've already made the commitment. Not because you feel like it. Not because you feel inspired."

"Inspiration is overrated, got it."

"No, I'm not saying that. It's just… running is different. Everything else in my life sometimes feels undisciplined, out of control. But not running. Somehow having that one area under control frees me up to be creative and impulsive with everything else. Somehow, and it's a bit of a mystery, but somehow it affects the art, makes it better. I can give myself to the art if I've been disciplined with my running." He's lost in his own musings. I grin at him until he comes back to me, turns his gaze from the sky back to me. "Might sound like nonsense but that's how it works. For me, at least."

"Fascinating," I say.

Following Maggie's lead, Ava sits beneath Seth and traces his feet. She plants her palm on the top of his sneaker to make sure it stays put.

"What about weight training?" I ask. "Shouldn't I be lifting weights? Pumping iron?"

"Not yet, Rocky. That'll come. Maybe in the winter. Right now just concentrate on increasing your run time. If you do four miles today, shoot for four and a half tomorrow."

"Mom," Maggie commands. "Hold still."

Seth's lips twist into a smile. "Better hold still."

"There," Maggie says. "You're tied together and now you can't go anywhere."

I glance at my feet. She's drawn a chalk chain connecting the circle around my feet with Seth's.

"That sounds interesting," Seth says, still looking at me. "Hope we don't fall."

I feel like a toy, a little top spinning in his hand. I clear my throat. "Well, for the next couple of days I'm not sure if I can fit in any running at all."

He frowns. "Why not?"

"I'm in charge of the chocolate for my friend Laura's wedding."

"Likely excuse."

"No you don't understand. It's a lot of chocolate. They're not serving a meal so I'm running around tomorrow, picking up all these cakes and things and then Annalisa and I need to decorate the porch."

"The porch?"

"Yes, this is all taking place on the groom's cranberry marsh."

"Jake died," Maggie says, still at my feet.

Seth wrinkles his brow.

"Laura's first husband," I explain. "It sure was sad, wasn't it Magpie?"

Maggie says yes, it was, and then asks if she and Ava can have popsicles. After they clean up at the hose, I tell them.

"How did he die?" Seth asks once the girls are out of earshot.

"Brain aneurysm. He was thirty-nine. It was awful. No one got a chance to say goodbye. Not even Laura or TJ, their four-year-old son."

"That is awful."

"He came home from work one day with a horrible headache. Thought he was coming down with the flu or something and went to bed. Laura and I had plans to see *Wicked* at the Performing Arts Center so I suggested we drop TJ at his grandma's house. So while Jake was home alone dying, Laura and I were laughing at some stupid show." I watch the girls scamper into the house. "I think they left the hose on."

I turn and walk to the side of the house. I tighten the spigot and begin making wide green loops with the hose.

"Sounds like you have some guilt over this."

I shrug. "It was my idea. I bought the tickets. I suggested Laura call her mom."

"Holly, you know that's crazy, right? You couldn't have stopped him from dying."

"But if it wasn't for me, Laura would have been there *with* him." I suddenly stop. I will not start crying in front of him again. "How'd we get here? I don't know why I'm telling you this. I haven't admitted this to anyone, not even..." I fall silent.

"Your husband?"

"He doesn't like to talk about that kind of thing." I laugh a little. "Or anything." I secure the hose over the spigot and face him. "Anyway, Laura's getting married, I'm bringing chocolate, so I can't run these next two days."

He studies me. "Okay, you win. But don't make this a habit."

"Yes, coach."

"After this weekend, get yourself on a schedule. And if you need a kick in the butt to get going again, stop by. Or if you need a running buddy. Or stop by for any reason at all."

A breeze plays at my hair and I tuck a strand behind my ear.

"You do still owe me a muffin or two you know."

"Then stop by for a muffin."

"I might just do that someday. Ring your doorbell and demand my muffin."

"Sounds good to me." His eyes are steady on mine. "I should get going. Ava's going to her mom's this weekend. I'm flying solo tonight."

"I am too." My face grows hot. I look down at my hands, slightly muddy from the hose. "I should go." *No. I live here. He should go.* But I don't want him to.

In silence, we walk back to the driveway embellished with chalk castles and wedding cakes and tracings of our feet linked together by purple chains. He turns to me, looking like he wants to say something, but shakes his head and walks up the steps to my front door. He sticks his head in and calls for Ava.

I collect pieces of chalk and drop them into a bucket.

Before he leaves with Ava, he gives me a smile, a smile that seems to hold a question.

That afternoon, alone in my house, I slip into a hot bath. I loosen my ponytail and let the weight of my hair spill down my shoulders and float on the surface of the water. Then I gather it together and drape it over one shoulder and think of the first day I stepped into Seth's studio. Holding my breath, I close my eyes and bury myself. The silent, liquid darkness causes me to think of Jake. Where is he right now? What does he see? Does he know about Laura? Does he know that tomorrow his wife will marry? I count the seconds and I wonder how long I can hold my breath.

Seven, eight, nine...

The water embraces every inch of my body, my eyelids, the soles of my feet, my thighs. It's so warm, so gentle in its caress. I wish I could stay here. I wish I could make this last.

Fifteen, sixteen, seventeen...

My insides feel tight. I'm on the brink of panic. It's all up to me, of course. I can rise anytime I want to. I wait. Think. When I surface, gasping for air, I know what I want to do. I dry and dress quickly. Then I make a phone call and get into my van, vanquishing all doubt, all thoughts of John. This is, after all, my decision.

I wake up the next morning, laced with regret. What's done is done. There's no undoing it now. I spend the morning sitting at the computer, trying to work on the law offices of Daniel D. Nickels but accomplish little.

At one-thirty, I hear John's truck pull into the driveway. I jump up and glance in the mirror. Fuss with my hair. Smooth my blouse.

John steps in, takes one look at me, and stops dead in his tracks. "What have you done?"

His words cut deep. But then again, what did I expect him to say? He stands there, staring at me with confused and wounded eyes. I take his lunch cooler from him and head to the kitchen and start dumping food wrappers into the garbage.

"Why did you do it?" he asks.

"Why? Because it's my hair and I wanted to. I didn't think I needed your permission."

"I'd think you'd at least want my opinion. But then you already knew my opinion."

"It's a haircut, John. It gets so hot when I run. I needed a change."

"It's a change. That's for damn sure." He goes to the sink and washes his hands.

"So you hate it."

"I don't know. I haven't had enough time to know what I think. I hardly recognize you."

"You sure know your way to a girl's heart," I say as I brush past him. I shut myself in the bathroom and study the woman in the mirror. I hardly recognize her either. My hair's been long ever since Ben was born. I run my hands through my new bob, the ends now falling just south of my chin.

I feel a pang of remorse and wish, for a moment, that my stylist hadn't had a cancelation and wasn't able to squeeze me in last night. I was confident as I sat in her chair, explaining what I wanted. She, however, was hesitant. "Are you sure?" she had asked. "You have a gorgeous head of hair. This will be a drastic change for you."

I was sure, I said. Bring on change. And in the mirror I saw my chin tilt up in resolve, just like Maggie's does when she wants what she wants. And then my hair, my rich, glossy, beautiful hair began to fall in clumps at my feet, and when it was finished—after the cut and color and rinse and style—my hair was swept up and tossed out with the coffee filters and everyone else's hair as if all of those years of growing and grooming it never existed.

I toss my head around, letting my gold-highlighted bangs fall into my eyes before I push them back. It is a great cut. Exactly what I wanted. Even still my eyes fill with tears. All this fuss over dead cells. I remember when I learned this fact, back in grade school, during science class. How, I had asked my teacher, could hair be dead and still grow? What's underneath, the hidden part, she said, is alive and growing all the time.

I hear John outside the door, moving around in our bedroom, most likely waiting for the shower. What would he have said had I asked him? Would he have tried to stop me? Talked me out of it? Ran his fingers through the length of my mane and whispered, *Please don't cut this?* Would I have listened?

It's only hair. Unlike Maggie's poor dolls, it'll grow back. Maggie and I like to think we're rescuing those dolls, but are we? Or are we simply taking them captive to exert our control and impulsivity? Their smiling lips can offer no protest.

I lift my chin and sweep my hand through the soft layers.

Yes, I decide. I like it.

12

The day of the wedding dawns wet and grey. From the window, Maggie watches her chalk drawings melt away. Mercifully, by ten o'clock, when Annalisa pulls her van into my driveway so we can head to the marsh, the skies have cleared. I dodge puddles as I make my way to her van.

"Whoa," she says when I get in and shut the door. "When did you do that?"

"Yesterday."

She gapes at me. "I didn't know you were even thinking about it."

"Kind of a spur of the moment thing."

"I guess."

I run my fingers through it, self-conscious. "So you don't like it?"

"I love it. I'm just... shocked. You didn't mention anything to me."

"Was I supposed to?"

"Well, no. I just thought... I don't know, usually you talk to me about things like that. The timing is kind of..." She wrinkles her nose and shrugs.

"What? What do you mean, the timing?"

"Right before the wedding?"

"So?"

"I'm just surprised you didn't wait until after the wedding, you know, *after* Laura's big day."

"Hold on. You think I did this for *attention*? It's a haircut. I wasn't even thinking about Laura."

"Maybe you should have been," she says quietly.

I'm stunned silent.

She backs out of my driveway. We travel without speaking, stopping at various houses along the way to pick up food. As city morphs into country, I glimpse a dim reflection of myself in my window, of the haircut that, for some reason, seems to have knocked the world off its axis. When we turn onto the gravel driveway that leads to the house Annalisa sighs. "I don't want to fight. This is Laura's wedding day. You just caught me off guard. You loved your hair, everyone loved your hair."

"You think I'm trying to upstage Laura."

"No, I'm being silly. I'm just emotional I guess. I'm sorry. You look adorable, Holly. Really. It suits you. And you're right. It's a haircut and nothing more and I'm sorry."

I nod, my stomach growing queasy. Does Annalisa's initial accusation hold any truth? Why couldn't I have waited one more day, for Laura's sake? What kind of friend am I?

Even though I've been to Phil's twice before, the beauty of this place eclipses everything else when I step out of the van. The house is stunning, with its gable windows and never-ending, wraparound porch. Behind it, the gentle green hills rise in the distance, and the cranberry bogs lay a quarter mile down the gravel road. This marsh, this land, which has been passed down from one generation to the next, whispers stability and honesty and hard work. A calm sweeps over me. And then I spot Laura on the porch.

She runs to us, her flip-flops smacking the gravel. "Holly! Look at you, you hot mama! You're stunning."

I want to weep. "No, this place is stunning and you're stunning."

She chortles, glancing down at her frayed, cut off shorts. "Not yet, but I will be."

"The groom's not here, is he?" Annalisa wants to know.

"Of course not. He and TJ are with my mom. No way am I going to let him see me until I walk down the aisle."

The three of us unload the van—carrying cheesecakes and brownies and containers of fruit to the kitchen—and then survey the porch. After playing with various techniques, Annalisa suggests we wrap tulle and white lights around the pillars, embellish with wild blue asters, and hold it all in place with wire that we hide in folds of fabric. Then we turn our attention to the tables. Phil borrowed an assortment from his church while Annalisa and I ran around collecting any white and off-white tablecloths we could get our hands on. The textiles vary—linen, lace, cotton—but each table is topped by a Mason jar holding a floating candle. Finished, we climb down the porch steps and assess our handiwork.

The array of fabric creates a soft, whimsical palette. When the wind blows, the tulle around the pillars swirl like a ballerina and the gentle green hills in the background lend a storybook charm to the scene. Satisfied, Annalisa and I slice desserts in the kitchen while Laura goes upstairs to take a bubble bath. Just after Annalisa and I hollered up the stairs promising Laura we'll be back by six, Laura's two aunts arrive to take over bustling about the kitchen.

When I return home, Bernice greets me with a whine. I pour food into her empty dish and yell at Ben that he forgot to feed his dog. Just then I notice Ava underneath my dining room table, lying on her stomach next to Maggie.

I crouch down. "Hello, girls." Piles of paper surround them and their cheeks bear marker drawn rainbows. "Margaret Anne. Why is there marker on your face? We have a wedding to go to. Where's your dad?"

Maggie shrugs and returns to her coloring.

As I make my way down the hall, I pop my head in Ben's room and tell him to get in the shower. John's not in our bedroom. I head out the front door and find him in the garage. "Why is Ava here?" I ask after the table saw powers down and stops screaming.

He takes a pencil from behind his ear and makes a mark on the wood. "Maggie invited her."

They've met. Seth and John. "What time is she going home?"

"We didn't talk about it."

"I'll text him."

John glances at me. "Text him?"

"Yes. He's a client."

"That guy's a client?"

"He's an artist. A designer. I'm doing his website." My fingers are already flying across my phone. "You do remember about the wedding today, right?"

"What wedding."

I roll my eyes. "Just be ready to go at five thirty. I asked Seth to get her by five."

I head inside through the back door. As soon as I step into my kitchen I want to step out again. This room, this outdated, claustrophobic room with towers of dishes evokes the opposite emotion I felt at the marsh. I open the dishwasher. Dirty and crammed to capacity. For some reason pouring soap into a plastic cup and pushing *start* is beyond John. I want to run away. Hide in the play fort. But, as I told Seth, there's no time for running today. I set the dishwasher into motion, empty and fill the sink with hot water and suds, and unleash my anger on the pans.

When I've conquered the worst of it, I dry my hands and head to Ben's room. He's still gaming on his bed. "Benjamin! I told you to get in the shower. Get in the shower! What is wrong with you? Why don't you listen for once?"

A little voice inside of me says to stop. Stop, drop, and roll? Stop and count to ten? Stop and smell the roses?

"You don't have to yell. You always *yell*."

"Then *do* as you're *told*."

He rolls his eyes, drops his Kindle, and stomps past me.

I return to the dining room. The girls have abandoned their artwork and are now shooting Hungry Hungry Hippo marbles all over the place. "Maggie, pick up this mess. When Ben gets out of the shower, you get in. And scrub hard to get that rainbow off."

"No. I'm wearing it to the wedding."

"You are not wearing marker on your face to the wedding."

Maggie's eyes turn fierce. "Yes I *am*."

I grab her arm. Pull her to her feet and match her lethal glare. "No you're *not*." I might be scaring Ava, but it's too late now. Besides, she doesn't seem traumatized. If anyone is traumatized it's Bernice who's being assaulted by little, white marbles.

"Ava, please stop doing that. Get your things together. Your dad will be here soon."

I retreat to my room to get ready.

I'm shower clean and wrapped in a towel when John enters. He smirks and makes a grab for my towel. I pull it tighter. "Like we have time for that."

"You never have time for that."

I rummage through my underwear drawer, trying to find a good pair. "John, come on. Maybe later."

"It's never later."

I glare at him. "Well, I am sorry," I say, trying to step into underwear without dropping my towel. "I've been a little busy with this little thing called my job, and the kids, and the laundry, and getting everything and everybody ready for the wedding, and coming home to find every dish we own dirty. Maybe if I'd had a little help with any of that, then maybe, just *maybe*, I'd have time for *sex*."

"Let me know if that ever happens because that'll be the event of the century."

Facing away from him, I put on my bra. "Just go make sure Ben wears khakis and a shirt with buttons."

By the time the doorbell rings, I'm dried, dressed, and all made up. Seth's eyes grow large when I open the front door to him.

"Wow. I like the hair."

I'm blushing. I can feel it. "Thanks."

"Maybe you've shaved a few seconds off your time." All of a sudden, he smacks his forehead. "This is the day of the wedding, right? I forgot when I dropped off Ava."

"Oh, she wasn't any trouble at all."

"Shoot. Sorry."

"No problem, really. They decided to tattoo each other with markers but I'm sure it'll wash off."

"Crazy monkeys. They do like to get creative."

"Like dumping an entire bag of chocolate chips into pancake batter?"

He laughs. "Yeah, like that."

I hear sounds of movement behind me. I turn around and see John standing at the table, sorting through the paper. He raises his hand in greeting. Seth does the same.

"Do you know where the girls are?" I ask John, my tone light.

His eyebrows rise. "I'll go find them, dear."

A moment later Ava emerges, the rainbow still shining from her check.

"Nice," Seth says.

"Maggie did it," she says proudly.

"Looks like Maggie may have a career in the fine art of tattooing," Seth says.

I smile at the two of them. "One can only hope."

When the door is closed, I turn to my kids. "Hang up your wet towels, comb your hair, and find your good shoes. Not the best day to invite a friend over, Maggie. You knew that."

"What do you mean?" John says, a necktie draped over his shirt. "You said she was no trouble at all."

"I was being nice."

"You sure were. Being *nice*."

"What's that supposed to mean?"

"You tell me. Bring back Nice Holly. I'll take her to the wedding."

"If you are trying to ruin this day for me, congratulations. You're succeeding."

"It's not your day. It's Laura's."

For as long as I've known him, ties have troubled John. I watch him struggle with the striped grey and purple one Ben picked out for Father's Day. I wait for him to ask for my help, like he always does, but he doesn't. When he's finished, the knot is bubbled and lumpy and, I notice as we're walking out the door, twisted in the back, underneath his collar. I'm not going to fix it. I'm done trying to fix everything.

For the second time today, someone drives me to the marsh in silence. We park alongside the gravel driveway and walk toward the front lawn where the ceremony is to take place. What greets me takes my breath away: a multitude of mismatched, multi-colored chairs. "Welcome to the Mad Hatter's tea party," I say to no one in particular.

According to Laura, a family from Phil's church had offered to collect chairs for the ceremony. I've never seen such a collection. No two are alike. Even a lone rocker graces the last row. They do share one commonality: they all face west. This artistic offering had to be deliberate, calculated even, because people around here must own folding chairs. This is a nod. A crazy gift. And somehow it works, this kaleidoscope of furniture. Somehow it goes with the porch, Laura's dress, even the hodgepodge of desserts we've assembled.

"It's like a rainbow!" Maggie says. She scouts out a pale pink one with a rounded spindled back. Laura meant it for her, she insists, since it matches her dress. Thankfully, the marker tattoo has been scrubbed clean so I nod in agreement and watch her fan out her skirt before planting herself on her throne. John and Ben claim the chairs beside Maggie while I head to the house.

I find Annalisa in the kitchen, arranging gladiolas in a huge metal pail, and looking ethereal in a delicate lilac dress. "Look what the neighbors brought over."

I inhale the blossoms. "Beautiful."

"And so many. Find anything that will hold water and we'll scatter them around the porch."

I glance around, my eyes landing on an imposing looking ceramic rooster on the top of the eight-foot cupboards. Marco steps out from the pantry holding a metal Saltine box for Annalisa's inspection.

Annalisa wrinkles her nose. "Too much like a grocery story."

He disappears again.

I bend down and search the lazy susan. "How's the bride?"

"Nervous. I don't think she's having cold feet or anything but the reality of it has hit. She's ready. Just a little emotional."

Marco pops out again, holding a large green vase. Annalisa nods her approval. I find a glass pitcher for the remaining blossoms and the three of us disperse them all over the porch and ceremony area. Then Laura and I return to the house, leave our heels at the foot of the stairs, and climb up to find Laura.

She's perched on the edge of a bed, in the room I imagine will be hers and Phil's, facing a window that overlooks the cranberry beds. This is magic hour, the prelude to sunset; heaven itself pours through the glass and covers Laura like a blessing. She peers over her shoulder and notices us. The moment, the fact that she's sitting here in a wedding dress, feels nothing short of miraculous. Death to life. Grief to radiance. She's not the sort of woman you'd ever see on the cover of anything, but right now, I've never witnessed one more beautiful.

She stands and smoothes her dress. Then she picks up her simple bouquet of asters and lavender, tied at the stems with twine and tulle and says to us, "This is it. For better or for worse."

She's known worse. Here's to better.

We come alongside her and I smooth a crease in her veil as Annalisa begins to pray, simple and short and earnest. Then Laura smiles at us and at her reflection in the full-length mirror. TJ enters with her parents. Annalisa and I exit and take our seats with our families.

Laura is lovely as she glides down the grassy aisle, hand in hand with TJ. She is lovely when she stands before Phil and vows her devotion. And she is lovely when she leans in to kiss him while the sun buries itself into this land that is now her home. It's poetry, all of it. Poetry so beautiful and pure it makes me ache. John's right of course, this is Laura's day; I've known this all too well. This is not my story and as happy as I am for her, I feel an unyielding, aching emptiness for beside me sits a man I do not know anymore, a man I do not love. This awareness washes over me without ceremony, void of emotion. Hatred hasn't sprouted between us, only apathy, thickened over time. It's grown between us without our full realization, little by little, until the problem's too daunting to deal with.

If John took my hand right now, would it matter? Would it change anything? He won't, and doesn't, and what's more, I don't want him to. Our hands lie in our laps like dead fish. We clap along with everyone else when Laura and Phil make their way up the aisle as husband and wife but when the applause dies down, our hands don't seek out each other's. They only fall to our sides, or to the children, or to our belongings, but not to each other. Never to each other.

"The porch looks good," John says as we make our way over. And it does. It's picturesque, especially now, with the pillars twinkling and the candles flickering on the tables. Guests mingle about sipping wine and snacking on cheesecake bites.

John and I meander through the crowd, together but not together—like we both ended up here by chance. Eventually we drift apart, he to find Marco and I to find Annalisa.

Then, out of nowhere, the gentle strains of a violin sweep in. A woman appears, cradling the instrument against her shoulder like a long lost love. Before long, a cellist, another violinist, and a man with a viola join her. As if on cue, Marco and John set out four chairs in front of the porch and the quartet sits. They knew, I realize. John knew about this surprise.

And then Phil—stiff as a barn door Phil—extends his hand to his bride. The crowd parts to make room as he and Laura begin to move about the grassy, impromptu dance floor. I've underestimated Phil yet again.

"It worked," Annalisa says. "He surprised her!"

"You knew about this? The string quartet?"

"You didn't? John didn't tell you?"

"No."

"Oh. Maybe he wanted it to be a surprise for you, too."

"Right." I turn my attention back to the happy couple attempting to waltz. They're horrible, comically so, but by the breadth of their smiles, they don't seem to know or care. When the song ends, the quartet breaks into an up-tempo piece and the bride and groom motion for everyone to join them. Maggie and TJ are among the first to hit the dance floor, linking arms and swinging each other so turbulently they end up in the grass.

I scan the area for John and find him, jacket off and tie loosened, talking with Laura's brother. I tug on Annalisa's arm. "Come on. We can't be wallflowers."

She doesn't budge, doesn't even look at me.

"I won't step on you, promise."

She still doesn't respond. I follow her fixed gaze to whatever has captured her attention. In the crowd by the wine table, I spot Marco next to a tall, dark-haired woman. One long leg protrudes from her short dress, as if she's blocking his escape. Marco is smiling stiffly. He takes a step backward and bumps into the person behind him. The brunette laughs and grabs his lapel.

I glance at Annalisa. Her narrowed eyes shine green. "Here," she says, handing me her wine.

She squares her shoulders and runs her hands through her curls as she makes her way over. Smiling, she steps up to Marco and places a hand on his back, just north of his belt. Then, still smiling, she turns to the woman and says something. The brunette's expression changes, tightens, and she retracts the long leg.

And then my little friend Annalisa, still grinning, grabs Marco by the tie, pulls him to her, and kisses him. Right there, on the mouth, in front of everybody.

I laugh out loud.

By the time they break apart, the woman is gone.

Marco leads Annalisa to the dance area where they glide to a haunting rendition of *Time After Time*. Laura and Phil, lurching about, wave to them. I scan the porch. John's still there talking, or rather, listening to Laura's brother.

I walk to the wine table, throw away the plastic cups and grab my clutch purse. The song ends and another follows as I head into the darkness. The charming green hills from hours ago now loom before me like a sleeping beast. I walk on, away from the noise, the half moon lighting my way.

As the tune of the quartet fades, the crickets' song intensifies. Before long I reach the main dirt path that runs through the cranberry beds. It's such an organized crop, boasting these giant, recessed, rectangles. Like a giant grid. A half dozen beds stretch out on both sides of the road and I wonder where, exactly, Phil proposed.

I turn around and begin walking back. The party is only a faint, distant glow, a seemingly inconsequential event to which I'm not ready to return. I veer off the main road and wander down a smaller path, the moonlight spilling over a boulder up ahead. When I reach it, I spread out the skirt of my dress and take a seat, the night sounds my symphony.

My purse tweets. I pull out my phone. It's a text from Seth.

Sorry if I made your day crazier. Thanks for taking Ava. She loves being at your house.

Even in the coolness, my face grows warm. I begin to text him back but reconsider and push *call* instead.

"You're welcome," I say when he picks up. "For having Ava over today."

"Holly?" He sounds surprised. "I thought you were at a wedding."

"I am. I took a walk."

"Oh."

"I'm next to the cranberry fields. It's quiet. Well, maybe not quiet. The frogs and crickets are having some kind of sing-off. You should hear them."

He laughs. "I've heard frogs before."

"Not these frogs you haven't. These are like Juilliard frogs. Here, listen." I hold out the phone for a few seconds. "Did you hear them?"

"You're right. Those are truly gifted frogs."

We fall silent. I've never called him before without a specific reason. It's always been about the girls or his website or a question I have about training.

"So how was it?" he asks.

"The wedding? Lovely. Lonely."

"Lonely?"

I close my eyes. "Oh it's just these bullfrogs. I've always thought bullfrogs sounded lonely, even with the racket they make. The wedding was *lovely*. Laura was lovely. She and Phil are going to be very happy I think."

"That's good," he says. "So back on schedule tomorrow, I assume. I'll see you on the street bright and early?"

"This is a test, right? Sunday is my day off. And my trainer told me not to run on my day off or else. "

"Sounds like a jerk."

A breeze ruffles the hem of my dress and I smooth it down. "Oh, he's alright. Once you get to know him."

"He thinks pretty highly of you."

"Does he now?"

"He does. In fact, he'd like to get to know you better."

My pulse quickens. "He would, huh?"

"He would."

I hear something rustling behind me, at the edge of the woods. I jump off the boulder and glance around but the darkness conceals whatever is lurking.

"Holly?" Seth says.

"I'm sorry but I need to go—"

"Oh, sure. See you soon?"

"See you soon." I slip the phone back into my purse, my heart now beating at full speed. Why did I hang up? Why did I leave myself all alone with whatever or whoever is behind those bushes?

"John?"

How would I explain this, why I'm way out here, talking on my phone? The rustling grows louder. Suddenly, I desperately want it to be John.

"John? Is that you?"

Something darts out. I scream. Whatever it is screams back.

A cat, I realize. A stupid, rotten cat.

Adrenaline prickles my arms and legs and escapes through an eruption of laughter. Wait till I tell Seth about this. Hands trembling, I grab my purse and head back to the party.

Phil and Laura seem to be making their exit rounds when I rejoin the festivities. Laura spots me and pulls me into a hug. "There you are! I've been looking for you to say goodbye. Thank you for everything."

We break away. I know I won't be able to put into words what I want to say, what this day has meant. "You and Phil are going to be very happy," I try, my voice breaking.

She brushes off a few stray leaves from my skirt. "You alright?"

Before I can answer, the groom joins us. "Phil," I say. "That string quartet? Brilliant."

He smiles at his bride. "My gift to Laura."

Laura kisses him, turns to me and smiles one last time, and off they go. Off to their honeymoon, off to their new life together.

One by one, the quartet packs up and the guests leave. Laura and Phil's relatives blow out candles and unstring lights as Annalisa and I deal with the leftovers. "I almost forgot," I say to her. "What did you say? To that woman with Marco?"

Annalisa snaps a lid on a Tupperware container. "I said, 'Don't you just love weddings? Makes me think of my own wedding day.'"

"And sealed it with a big, juicy kiss."

She smiles and shrugs. "Sometimes you've got to fight for it."

I slide a plate of mint brownies into Laura's fridge. But when do you give up the fight? When do you call a truce? Call it quits? I'm still pondering this as John drives the kids and me home. Sometimes you have to fight for your marriage, like Annalisa did tonight, but it takes two people to fight for it, doesn't it? Two people committed to each other, rowing the same boat, pausing to dance now and again. Two people who believe the marriage is worth fighting *for*.

"Laura's brother is a tax accountant," John says from behind the steering wheel. "I told him I might give him a call next season."

"Oh. Good."

Did John even notice when I disappeared? Did he realize I was gone for more than a few minutes? Did he like any of the desserts I slaved over? Or my dress? These questions will remain mysteries because he doesn't say a thing.

The cornfields out my window seem to spread into eternity. Above them the solitary moon gazes down, detached from the rest of the world, the lonely half of what should be a whole.

13

By the time school starts, I have hit my weight loss goal. To celebrate, Seth makes fruit smoothies after our run one morning and we drink them through straws on his backyard deck.

We don't run together every day, but when we happen to bump into each other, usually early in the morning, it feels right to conquer the pavement side by side. Some days I run after walking the kids to school, even though Ben makes it clear he rather I not walk him at all.

"I'm not a baby," he tells me on the third day of school. "I don't need help crossing streets or anything."

"Of course you don't. You're in fifth grade. But maybe I like walking you and Mags to school sometimes."

He sighs. "Fine. But stay closer to Maggie."

I promise I will and once we reach the school doors, only offer him a hasty wave. Maggie, however, wants me to accompany her all the way to her classroom. I watch as she attempts to shove her backpack through the narrow mouth of her locker, ultimately giving the bag a rough kick. No wonder she goes through a couple backpacks a year. She hugs me tight and skips into her classroom.

As I'm about to leave, I spot Ava down the hall by the second grade rooms, giving her mother a hug.

Tori tweaks Ava's nose then straightens and starts down the hall, toward me. I fumble with Maggie's locker, unnecessarily re-hang her hooded sweatshirt, covertly watching Tori. For an inconsequential second our eyes meet. I should introduce myself; that would be the proper thing to do given her daughter's been to my house multiple times. But something stops me. I want to watch her first, figure out who she is before she knows anything about me.

She breezes past me and I notice two things: one, she smells great, like oranges and the beach and two, her complexion is blemished. Patches of acne lay hidden beneath heavy makeup. Not quite the model-perfect woman smiling from the frame in Ava's bedroom. No question about it, she's attractive, and she walks with long, confident strides. But observing her flaws bolsters me, gives me an unjustifiable sense of satisfaction.

Tori exits through the main doors. I shut Maggie's locker and follow. When she pauses to chat with another parent, I stretch my legs by the flagpole. When she crosses the street and ducks into a black Volvo, I start jogging. Due to the frequent crosswalks and sluggish school traffic, I'm able to keep up for a few blocks but when she turns onto the main drag, I know I've lost her.

Why, exactly, am I following her in the first place? What do I want to know?

I turn around. Today is a light run day so I circle back to my neighborhood and turn on Cherry St. As I pass Seth's house, he appears from his studio side door and waves. "Holly! I want to show you something."

I jog in place. "My trainer would tell me to keep going."

"Forget your trainer. I finished it. The loveseat."

"The one with the birds?"

"Want to see it?"

"Definitely."

I head up his driveway and follow him into the studio. Music plays from a radio on top of metal shelves. He hands me an opened water bottle and waits for me to take a swig, then leads me to a sheet-covered lump in the corner of the garage. With one swift move, he removes the cloth.

I step closer. The vintage fabric is expertly stretched along the rounded back of the loveseat, as if it were the original. "Seth, It's beautiful. He's going to love it."

"Thanks. I was hoping you'd get to see it before Jim picks it up. It's going to be hard to let this one go."

"I never thought of that. All of that work and now you have to give it away."

"Not exactly *give* it away. I mean, it is my bread and butter. But yeah, sometimes it's hard to let it go, even though this was never mine to keep."

I gently trace one of the birds. He watches me for a moment and then says, "Kind of wish I could give it to you, since you like it so much, but I can't even ask you to sit down."

I look down at my running shorts. "I wouldn't dream of it."

"Although..." He drapes the birds with the sheet, sits down, and pats the space next to him.

At first, I hesitate. But then I realize I'm being absurd and sit down next to him. I lean my head back and softly sing along to the Billy Joel song playing.

"You can sing," he says.

"I can carry a tune."

"I'm tone deaf."

"Really?"

"My mom told me so it has to be true."

I laugh.

"Holly."

"Hm?"

He's quiet for a while. "I'm don't know how to say this."

But I know where he's going. Somehow I knew the second I sat down.

"I like being with you," he says.

I smile. "I like being with you. If it weren't for you I never would have started running, or lost my mind and signed up for a half marathon."

"Or gotten your dog back."

"Yes, or gotten my dog back. This is all because of Bernice."

"Good old Bernice." He slips his arm around my shoulder. The gesture is so casual, so natural, I close my eyes. "There's more I want to say to you," he says. "A lot more."

I don't want this moment to end. I want to savor this lovely, hazy feeling. His scent. His nearness. His arm around me. His thigh pressed to mine.

"It's not fair and I don't want to pressure you." His fingers draw tiny circles on the top of my bare shoulder. "But you need to know how I feel."

If I open my eyes, this moment—this dizzy, spinning, sensation—might evaporate. I'm floating, free falling, and I don't want to thud to the ground. How long can I keep my eyes shut? How long can I hold my breath? "And how do you feel?" I ask him.

He chuckles. Then his mouth gently grazes my bare shoulder in something very close to a kiss as I sink deeper and deeper—

Until there's a knock at the door.

I open my eyes.

He jumps up.

I do too and rush to the worktable.

He waits a moment, runs his hands through his hair, then opens the side door, the same door we entered… minutes ago? Or longer? I begin cleaning up the worktable, collecting candy wrappers, empty soda cans, plastic cups coated with dried paint.

A man wearing a golf shirt and a big grin walks in and claps Seth on the shoulder. "All finished?"

"She's all yours." He leads the man over to the loveseat—*our* loveseat—and uncovers it, still bearing our imprints.

"Look at that," the man says.

"Look okay?"

"Looks great. Sharon is going to love it." He notices me and smiles.

"This is Holly," Seth says. "My web site guru. Holly, this is Jim."

He puts up a hand. "Nice to meet you."

I return the wave and toss out the garbage I'm holding.

Jim circles the loveseat before sitting down. "Sharon's been on me for years to get this thing recovered. See she inherited it from her grandmother and I've been promising her for years but never got around to it. Better late than never, right?" He seems to be asking me.

"Yes. She'll love it." My eyes flit to Seth. "It's beautiful."

Jim extracts a white envelope from his back pocket and hands it to Seth. "The remainder of what I owe you. Don't be shy. You can count it out."

"No need. I suppose we should get her loaded up." He pushes a button and the garage door opens.

I follow the two men out to the driveway and watch as they load my beautiful flock of birds into the back of Jim's truck. "I should get going," I say to Seth. "I'll get back to you about… those changes."

His eyes meet mine. "See you soon."

I jog off, my mind replaying our interlude on the loveseat, before Jim's interruption. As I relive the moment, the floating sensation returns. My feet barely touch the pavement. And these colors—these green trees and this sapphire sky and these white, whipped clouds—all of it seems to glow in impossible brilliance.

I cross Annalisa's street. Her house sits more than a block away but it casts a sudden shadow; the colors dull and my footsteps grow heavy. I run home.

All throughout the day, as I shower, sort laundry, plan dinner, work at my computer, Seth's words wash over me again and again. I feel his lips tantalize my shoulder, his fingers in my hair, caressing my neck. The doorbell rings. Interrupted again.

Through the window I spy Jackson's stroller. I'm swamped

with work, I'll tell her. I can't stop to talk. I need to keep plugging away because the kids get home in less than thirty minutes. She rings again.

As soon as I open the door, she thrusts a piece of paper at me. "Have you seen this?"

"Well hello to you too." This isn't an anomaly. Annalisa and I drop in on each other all the time but today her unannounced presence rubs me the wrong way.

"Have you read this letter yet?" She's already in my family room, Jackson on her hip.

"No. I'm really swamped today..."

"You need to read this."

I sigh, take the paper, and begin skimming. A few lines in, I sit down on the couch. "An attempted child abduction? Three blocks from school?"

"On Friday."

I examine the letter again. "Who was the child?"

"It doesn't say. I don't think they can say." She sets Jackson down. He goes straight for Bernice who's been lounging under the table for most of the day.

"The only thing the poor kid can remember," Annalisa continues, "is that the creep was wearing a black baseball cap and said he was *looking for his lost puppy*. Can you believe that? The pervert used that old line to try to lure the kid into his van. I'm sick, just sick. Thank God the kid ran away. Right here. It happened right here in our neighborhood. Right by our school."

My children's faces take front and center in my mind. I examine the letter again. *Increased police surveillance on school grounds. Crossing guards alerted. Parents please talk to your children.* "So they didn't get a license plate number?"

"Nope. Jackson and I are going to walk the boys home from school for a few days, aren't we buddy?"

I nod. "I'll come with you."

Judging by the buzz of moms and dads circling the flagpole,

Annalisa and I are not the only anxious parents. I notice Tori, her hands shoved into the pockets of her faded jeans, fixing her stare on the brick building as if to will her daughter to emerge, safe and sound.

When Ben and Maggie appear, I forget I'm supposed to play cool around Ben and hug them both extra tight. Annalisa and her troop head to the school library and my kids and I head home, Maggie's soft little palm pressed inside of mine. I want to keep it there forever, tucked away, under my control. I ask how school was and Ben says fine. But Maggie says, "Mrs. Larson says there was a not safe man around our school this week."

"A not safe man?" I play dumb. I want to hear her interpretation.

"He tried to get Lily into his truck."

Lily. I don't know a Lily. "What grade is Lily in?"

"Fourth. And you know what? He *lied*. He said he was looking for his dog but guess what? He wasn't. Mrs. Larson said he was trying to trick her into his van. Isn't that bad? That he *lied*?"

If only that were the worst of it. "It's not good to lie, is it?"

"No and Mrs. Larson says we need to be extra careful walking home from school."

"Yes, you do. And if anyone ever tries to get you into their car you scream and fight and kick and run away. You throw the biggest fit of your life, understand?"

Maggie's eyes light up at the prospect. "And then tell a grown-up-you-trust about it, right?"

"And then tell a grown-up-you-trust."

Ben, a few steps ahead of us, turns around. "It's okay, Mom. We'll be careful. You don't have to worry about us." He rests a protective hand on his sister's shoulder and my vision blurs.

"I know you'll be careful Ben. And I know you'll look out for your sister."

Does he sense the greater danger? At eleven years old, how much has he gleaned about the evil I'm urging them to scream and run from, evil a hundred times worse than a lie? If it were in my power I'd protect their innocence for as long as I could, but a bubble can only float for so long before it brushes reality and disappears forever.

After supper I show the letter to John. He takes his time reading it, as if there will be a test. Finally, he puts the letter down.

"Well?" I ask. "Do you think we should do anything? Say anything more?"

He props his elbows on the table and makes a chapel with his fingers.

"I talked with both of them," I continue. "Reminded them never to get in a car with a stranger."

John nods. "Good."

"Do you think you should talk to them?"

He shakes his head. "I don't want to scare them. You already talked to them."

"But maybe you should, too. Reinforce everything."

"You talked to them, their teacher talked to them, the school talked to them. I don't want them to be afraid to walk down the street."

"Yes, but you're their *father*."

"I don't want them to end up with a phobia or something. It's been handled." He rises from the table and I know we're done here.

I go to the kitchen. Fill the sink. Plunge my hands into scalding hot water.

Even with John in the next room and the TV on, and the kids jumping around in Ben's room, I am alone. So much for partnership. So much for carrying the burden together. Is it any wonder I have laid my head on another man's shoulder? John's shoulder is never available.

I scrub the bottom of a pot and let my thoughts drift back to this morning, to Seth and his softly spoken words. His invitation. I no longer feel alone.

14

My parents announced in between sips of coffee that they were getting a divorce. I was twelve and it was a Saturday morning in June and my younger brother and I were enjoying blueberry pancakes. My fork was in midair, syrup dripping from warm golden dough, when my father cleared his throat and said, "Your mother and I have decided it's best for all of us if we get a divorce." His tone was casual; he might as well have been mentioning we were having chicken for dinner.

I looked at my younger brother's terror-stricken face. I looked at my mother, her lips pressed together in what was supposed to pass for a smile. This had to be a trick. She'd amend Dad's pronouncement, say that they needed *time apart*, but a *divorce?*

Dad was gone all the time. He traveled endlessly for business and rarely stuck around on weekends. *Doing his own thing* is what Mom, with a noticeable bite, dubbed his absences. My parents didn't fight, not in the yelling and throwing things across the room kind of way, at least not in front of Robbie or me. Instead our house was characterized by periods of silence, as cold and long as the icicles that clung to our roof. I often resorted to telling knock-

knock jokes just to break up the tension, get us all moving again. I kept a book of them under my bed. When the silence turned unbearable, I'd find a good one and recite it to my dad. He'd smile at least. Tweak my nose. He once said all I needed was a microphone, which, at the time, I took as a compliment.

Some nights my parents would close themselves in their bedroom and snarl at each other in low tones. If I laid on my stomach and peer through the crack under their door I could glimpse their feet—Mom pacing in her socks, Dad firmly planted in his tasseled work shoes. More than once I overheard the word *Sheila*, the name of my father's not particularly attractive receptionist who spilled green Tic-Tacs into my palm whenever I came into Dad's office. My mother spat the name like a curse, and then I'd hear soft, muffled crying sounds.

On The Blueberry Pancake Morning however, my mother appeared unruffled, serene even. She and my father took turns selling us on the divorce. Divorce would make everything easier for everybody, they insisted. They'd both be happier. *We'd* be happier. Divorce, divorce, divorce. The more they spewed that word around the kitchen, the more they sounded like hissing snakes. Looking back, I imagine they read up on the subject, books like *How to Nicely Tell Your Child You're Getting a Divorce* or *Divorce Can Be Fun!*

Even at twelve, I saw right through Mom's brittle veneer. As she went from griddle to table, dolling out pancakes and the benefits of divorce, she failed to look me in the eye. She was being brave, I understood with adult-like clarity. She was convincing herself, not us.

I sat there, moving fork to mouth, trying to digest my breakfast and this new reality. I knew my role, the part my parents expected me to play: The Big Girl Who Could Handle It. Robert, head ducked, sat crying and I was not to add to this emotive display. I was older. So I swallowed my panic, my grief, my tears and snot, right along with the bites of pancake and blueberries. They both still loved us, my parents claimed; they just didn't love each other anymore. But that didn't mean we weren't a family.

It didn't?

I wanted to scream. Families were supposed to live in the same house. Families were supposed to tell the truth. Fathers weren't supposed to spend weekends with Tic-Tac pushing secretaries. How were we still a family?

"Finish up your blueberry pancakes," my father said when it was apparent the one-sided conversation was over and we were supposed to, somehow, move on through the day and the rest of our lives. My fork felt too heavy to lift.

"Come on now, Holly," Mom prodded after everyone else had cleared the room. "You love blueberry pancakes."

I stared down at my plate, at one of my favorite foods that now looked like a slab of flesh with multiple gunshot wounds.

Up until that morning, I was a girl who obeyed. My parents, my teachers, even my friends. Not anymore. I looked up at my mother who, in that moment, I loved, pitied, and despised and I pushed my plate away. "No. I don't. I hate them. I'm never eating them again." I stood up and locked myself in my room.

When I finally came out, suitcase packed, I told my mother I was staying with Aunt Bernice for a while. To her credit, she called her sister and made it happen.

Now, as I step out of the shower and reach for my phone to check if Seth called, I think about that morning in a whole new light. Flip the memory around and examine it from the other side. I place my mother on the glass slide and peer down to analyze her more thoroughly than I've allowed myself to before.

My mother was not simply my mother but a woman trapped in the rubble of a collapsed marriage. Who can fault her for her pretense? In her book, a mother who cries beneath the covers all day, who doesn't drive her kids to piano lessons or soccer practice, doesn't shower or put on lipstick, is useless. Hardly a mother at all. Deteriorating into that creature would be, in her eyes, the ultimate failure. Best to put on a brave face. Best to protect the kids. Best to continue to sing in the church choir and host Girl Scout meetings and, after the kids are grown, invent a new life in California. What I called pretense, she called self-preservation.

But my father.

Since that day, since realizing what Sheila was to him, I've given him little more than my resentment. But now, even though it makes my stomach churn, I recognize how convoluted and clandestine marriage can become. How unhealed injuries and dashed expectations can drive people to the arms of their receptionist, as cruel and cliché as that is. Am I on the brink of forgiveness? Possibly. Although in my child's heart I'm still angry, still abandoned, and it feels safer to view him as a one-dimensional caricature. But he was, is, merely a man. A discontent man. He and Sheila didn't last but what if, way back then, they were truly in love? Then what? What should have he done?

Stay. He should have stayed. With us and for us because that's what fathers do. We needed him. Mom needed him. That should have mattered more than his happiness.

Do I actually believe that?

My head begins to ache. I find the Tylenol and swallow two.

After blow-drying and styling my hair, I slip into a pair of yoga pants and a clean shirt. Then I flop down on my bed and call Seth. I feel shy, like I'm back in high school. "I saw you called," I say. "I didn't see you on my run this morning."

I hear music in the background and I imagine him in his studio. "Did you see that letter from the school?"

"Yeah. Scary isn't it?"

"Sickening. I had a long talk with Ava."

"I did too, with my kids."

He pauses and then says, "So I hope I didn't scare you away yesterday. I just needed to let you know how I'm feeling."

"You didn't scare me away. I called you back, right?"

He sighs. Actually it's more like a groan. "What are we going to do Holly Lewis and the News?"

"I don't know."

"When can I see you again?"

My heart is ricocheting all over the place and even though no one else is home I glance around the room, as if at any moment someone might pop out of the closet. "We'll have to get the girls together."

"That's not what I mean."

"Seth, I..."

"I know," he cuts in. "I'm not being fair. I'm not trying to complicate your life."

"I need some time. To think. To figure this out. I need to talk to my mom," I tell him and realize it's the truth.

"Your mom? Okay. Do what you need to do. I'll try to leave you alone for a while so you can figure out what you want."

I know what I want; this isn't a question of *want*. This is a question of *should*. And *at what cost*. Because right there, above my dresser in a pale yellow frame, beam the two sweetest faces in the world, the two little people I love more than anything. How could I ever deal them a blueberry pancake morning? How could I turn Ben into my brother and Maggie into myself and myself into—Lord have mercy—my father? What's the lesser of two evils? What's the better choice? To give my children the semblance of an intact family, or to raise them under the gloom of an unhappy marriage, an unhappy mother?

In some ways, after my parents split, my mom seemed happier. Humming around the house, popping flowers into vases and taking bubble baths—she never did these things before the divorce.

"Don't think this isn't hard for me," I say.

He's silent for a while. "We'd be good together Holly, you and me."

I let the tears slide down my cheeks. I still feel him beside me, see his eyes searching mine in question. But I also see a twelve-year-old girl trying not to cry on her plate of blueberry pancakes.

A day later, I tell John that Maggie and I are going to my mom's for a few days. We're in the garage and he looks at me over the dipstick he's extracted from his truck. "Since when?"

"We're using our frequent flyer miles. The ones you didn't want to use."

"What about Ben?"

"He'll be fine. It's a girls' trip and the two of you can do boy things. Annalisa said she'd take him when you need to be gone for work."

"Thanks for checking with me."

"I didn't think you'd care. We have to use those miles before they expire and I knew you didn't want to go anywhere." I turn to leave

"Why?" I hear him ask when I reach the back door.

I don't turn around. "I need to get away. To think. To just… get away."

I wait, half wanting him to press me further, to chase me.

"Great," he says flatly. "Have fun."

I turn the doorknob and glance behind my shoulder in time to see him slam the hood of the Chevy so hard the truck shakes.

Maggie throws up just as the plane touches ground. Fortunately, she's quick enough to have grabbed the barf bag from the seat pocket and only gets a little spittle on her shirt. In the airport, I stop at the first joint we pass and get her a 7-Up. She sits and sips as I rub her back. By the time we meet my mother, she's bounced back to normal and relays the puking details as if it's the plot for a blockbuster movie.

My mother lives in one of those retirement communities that, on particularly frenzied days, occupy my fantasies. She has little to no responsibility; she doesn't keep up the lawn and needless to say, no one in California owns a snow shovel. If the microwave blows she simply makes a phone call and maintenance supplies her with a new one. No doubt she pays a pretty penny for the freedom to lounge on her second floor balcony flipping through magazines all day, but after working as a nurse for over thirty years, she's earned a few years of luxury I suppose.

"So, why the visit?" my mother asks when the two of us retire to her balcony that evening. After spending the afternoon watching the seals at La Jolla Cove and eating fish tacos close to the beach, Maggie's sacked out on the couch for the night.

"Can't a girl visit her mother without facing the grand inquisition?"

"It was one question, Holly. I'm delighted you and Maggie are here. I just thought that maybe there was a reason for it."

I'm here for four days; I don't have time to be coy. "John and I aren't doing the best. I just needed some time away."

The expression on her face remains neutral. "When I was there for your birthday, you hardly spoke two words to each other. I was wondering if something was wrong."

"Yeah, well things haven't gotten better since then." I take a sip of my tea. "I'm wondering if I should leave him." I stare straight ahead, waiting for the dose of maternal wisdom I guess I've come for.

"So, who is he sleeping with?"

I turn to her. "*Mom*! No one."

"Are you sure?"

"You watch too much HBO. Yes. I mean, I *was* sure. Until now."

She looks at me quizzically. "Then why in the world would you leave him?"

"Mom, there are others reasons for getting a divorce besides your husband sleeping with his secretary. We're just not happy."

She begins to laugh. She actually *laughs* at me.

"We fight all the time," I go on, irritated that I have to justify myself. "We're not *connected*. He doesn't understand me at all. He doesn't even *try* to understand me."

"Oh for pity's sake. Is that all?"

"Thanks, Mom. Thanks so much for your love and understanding." I get up and reach for the handle on the sliding glass door.

"Sit down, Holly. You came to me. Now *sit down*."

I sit down.

"Being unhappy from time to time is just a part of marriage," she says. "You're not going to feel connected *all* of the time. You're not going to be on the same page *all* of the time."

"But shouldn't we at least be in the same book? Shouldn't we feel connected *some* of the time? I can't remember when we last had a real conversation without it turning into a fight."

She studies me for a moment. "Does he work hard at his job?"

"Like a dog."

"Does he come home to you at night?"

"Most nights. Some nights he goes out with the guys, but yes, he always comes home eventually."

"Is he abusive toward you?"

"No."

"Is he abusing the children?"

"*No.* Geez, Mom. You act like you don't even know John!"

"I know John. You're the one who's thinking about leaving him."

"Oh, so it must be my fault, is that it? I'm the problem because John is so perfect."

"I never said that. Don't put words in my mouth. I know he's not perfect. But so far you've told me he's not sleeping with anyone, he's not abusive, he works hard, and he comes home to you at night." She ticks off this list on her fingers and looks at me as if she's made some irrefutable point.

"There's more to marriage than that."

"Maybe, but those are pretty major deal breakers if you ask me, and John isn't breaking any of them."

"What about love? Can you add that to your list? He doesn't love me anymore, and I don't love him so if he's not happy and I'm not happy then why the hell should we stay married?"

Her eyebrows lift and she tips her head toward the sliding glass door, toward Maggie asleep on the couch.

I shake my head. "You're one to talk," I say and immediately regret it.

"Holly, my situation was completely different and you know it. I didn't want a divorce, but I had no choice. What was I supposed to do? Let him sleep with her on weekends and come home to me Monday thru Friday? He refused to give her up. He *forced* me into a divorce. I'm sorry dear, but I don't think you get it. I don't think you understand the difference between a wife who feels stuck and perhaps a little bored and yes, maybe even unhappy, and a wife who has no choice because her husband has *left her for another woman.*"

I study my hands, my wedding ring—a white gold band topped by a solitaire diamond secured by six prongs instead of four. Six, John insisted, in case one or two of the prongs wore down, the diamond would still be protected.

"Your father and I hardly provided you with the model marriage," my mother continues, "so maybe I'm the last one who should dole out advice, but listen to me. John's not perfect. Not even close. But he's a good man. A steady man. So your marriage has lost its spark. Get it back. You've just turned forty. Everyone goes a little haywire when they turn forty. Maybe your life hasn't turned out exactly as you hoped it would. Maybe most days are more frustrating than satisfying. Maybe marriage and parenting is a hell of a lot more work than you ever imagined. But honey, find the moments that are good. Not perfect, *good.* Because there is no perfect. No perfect marriage and no perfect man, so don't waste your time running after something that doesn't exist."

Seth exists, I want to say. He's very real and he makes me very happy and what's more, I make him happy. If I speak his name, if I explain to my mother what I've found with him, would she change her position? "Can I ask you a question?" I say after a while. "And be honest."

"I'm listening."

"After you and Dad split up, were you happier?"

She leans back in her chair and sighs. "Yes. Not at first, but yes. After I got over the heartbreak, yes. I was."

I lean forward, desperately wanting her to understand. "That's what I'm chasing. That's what I want. Happiness."

She touches my arm. "I want you to be happy. But chase it with John."

"I've tried. I'm tired."

"And you think leaving John will make you happy?"

I study the pool below and speculate how often it's used by this community of seniors. According to Maggie, we're diving in first thing tomorrow morning. We're jumping in and touching the bottom and then soaking up the sun.

I keep my eyes on that pool, as still as glass. "Yes."

Late that night, as I'm under the covers of my mother's daybed in her guest room, Seth texts me.

How's California? How are you?

Sunny. Beautiful. Confusing.

Sounds like you.

Aw shucks.

I glance at my closed door, as if my mother may open it at any second and catch me with a smutty romance novel.

Come back, he writes. *I miss you.*

I miss you too. Trying to figure this thing out.

Don't use your head so much. Use your heart.

At this, I smile. We say goodnight and I get up to plug in my phone and survey the collection of photographs lining the top of the dresser. One is of my Aunt Bernice, her red hair pulled back with a yellow scarf. She's standing with my mother on the beach, laughing, the waves behind them crashing against the rocks. I can almost feel the spray of water, hear Aunt B's chime-like laugh. I miss her all over again, as if she died ten days ago and not ten years.

I turn off the light and snuggle deep into my mother's comforter. Sleep comes quickly. I dream about jumping into a pool as big as a city block. It's crowded and horrible at first, with swarms of people bumping into me left and right, but when I dive underneath the water I swim and swim and realize that the bottom of the pool doesn't exist, and in my dream it dawns on me that I can swim underwater forever and never come up for air.

I'm awakened by the scent of cinnamon. I hobble down the hall and find my mother in the kitchen pulling muffins from the oven. The carrot peelings in the sink and the box of raisins on the counter disappoint me—before her health craze she used to make killer chocolate chip banana muffins—but when she hands me a plate and I take a nibble, I decide it's not half bad.

We're discussing our plans for the day when Maggie stumbles in, her hair a matted mess. She sides up to me and I kiss her sweaty head. She scoots herself onto my lap, reaches for a strip of bacon, and holds it vertically. "What is this?"

"Bacon," I tell her.

"That's not bacon."

"It's turkey bacon," my mother explains.

"Grandma," she says with a teacher tone, "bacon doesn't come from turkeys. It comes from pigs."

"Yes, but sometimes bacon comes from turkeys."

Maggie takes a bite and makes a face. "It shouldn't."

I laugh and squeeze her.

My mother smiles. "This kind is better for Grandma. It has less saturated fat."

My mother gets up to pour Maggie some juice and Maggie gives the turkey bacon a second chance. She makes the same face and lets it drop on my plate. It's so stiff it makes a clacking sound against the porcelain. "This is fake. I like the real kind."

I whisper into her ear, "Me too."

She giggles.

"Are you two making fun of my turkey bacon?" my mother says from where she's standing at the counter.

"Sorry, Mom. But we think your turkey bacon is for the birds."

Maggie laughs and laughs.

My mother sets a cup of juice and a carrot muffin in front of Maggie. With a look, I try to communicate to be polite; no gagging sounds. But to my surprise, Maggie devours the whole thing with a splotch of honey and asks for a second.

Minutes later, as I'm clearing the table, my phone buzzes. Maggie grabs it and checks the screen before I get the chance. "It's Daddy!"

She answers and launches into a scathing editorial about Grandma's fake bacon. My mother snaps the lid on her fake butter. "I'm going to go put my suit on," I say and she only nods.

We spend most of the day at the pool. In the evening, my mother takes us to a restaurant with an aquarium and Maggie names all the fish. The small white one is Ava. The following day the three of us wander through the San Diego Zoo and return to the condo exhausted. We order pizza and make root beer floats. Since she's missing a couple days of school, I force Maggie to write a paragraph about her trip to San Diego. Nestled on one side of her sofa, my mother watches Wheel of Fortune while I sprawl out in the recliner. My phone buzzes. It's a text from Seth. He wants to know if I've been running.

Yes, I type back, *by the ocean.*

Lucky. Wish I were there.

Me too. I can't help smiling.

I glance up to my mother watching me. Stashing the phone in my pocket, I turn my attention to the TV and shout out the wrong answer to the puzzle.

On our last morning, while Maggie's in the shower and I'm packing up, my mother comes into the guestroom with a stack of clean sheets. She places them on top of the dresser, straightens the covers a little, and sits down on the bed. I fold a pair of Maggie's jeans and give her a smile. She fiddles with the clasp on her watch. I fit the jeans into the suitcase and bend to retrieve a balled up pair of socks. "I miss Aunt B," I say, glancing at the photograph again.

"Me too," Mom says.

I toss the socks into our dirty laundry bag and refold a shirt.

She takes a deep breath. "Sometimes happiness is a choice. Take a good look at what you have. See if you can find your happiness in that. My advice? Don't jump ship too quickly."

The shower shuts off. I stare at the photograph of Aunt Bernice. What my mother doesn't know, what I haven't told her, is that I have felt greater stirrings, greater happiness, in these last few months of knowing Seth than I have with John in the last few years. I've tasted *What Could Be* and I want more. Yes, it comes with risks, but I want the better, the real, saturated fat and all.

Sometimes you have to count your losses and jump ship. Sometimes the ship is riddled with battle holes and you have no other choice. Sure it's going to be messy and people will get hurt but, in the end, won't it be worth it?

She doesn't know these things and there isn't time to explain. What's more, she hasn't lived in my house or walked in my shoes. She's right: John isn't the worst of all husbands. He's not cheating on me or beating me—as if these deficiencies define a good marriage—but I'm finding fewer and fewer reasons to continue the charade. I love my kids. But kids are resilient. And I'm only forty; I have half a lifetime left.

So I nod at my mother's advice. I smile because whatever I do, whatever I decide, I must first return to John, return home, to my sinking ship, which happens to be empty when Maggie and I drop our luggage inside the door.

Maggie rolls her suitcase down the hall eager, no doubt, to introduce her new Californian trinkets to her room. I stand in the dining room, the center of my house, and survey the ship. Where I'm standing, I can see a pile of clothes littering the bathroom floor and Legos and soda cans and a beer bottle in the living room. Papers are spread across the dining room table and dishes cover the kitchen counter.

I don't want to clean it up. I want to break every single dish into a million pieces. I want to throw away the Legos and burn the clothes in the bathroom. Light a match, grab Maggie, and watch the whole thing go up in flames. Start over.

John doesn't want a wife; he wants a housekeeper.

Cursing softly, I start scraping plates. Fill the sink. Scour dishes in scalding hot water. I scrub so hard I break open an old cut, but I keep scraping and scrubbing and when I'm done the kitchen is pristine and my hands are raw.

When John comes home, I don't even look at him.

"I was going to get to those," he says, eyeing the drying rack.

I set my jaw and don't say a word.

After feeding my family a frozen pizza and a bag of past-expiration-date baby carrots—because no one thought to go to the store—and after snuggling with Ben on the couch and watching his face light up when I give him the shark tooth necklace I bought him, I grab my favorite quilt and head down to the basement to sleep on the futon.

And the next morning, after the kids are off and John has left for work—both of us as silent as walls—I put on a sundress and a little makeup and head to Seth's.

The minute his front door closes behind me, he enfolds me in his arms. "Next time you go somewhere, take me along."

He wants to kiss me, I can tell, but he releases me and takes a step backward. "Sorry. I said I was going to give you space. How was California?"

"Fine." I drop my gaze and stare at my chapped hands.

He takes my hands in his and inspects my fingers. Then he proceeds to kiss them, one by one, and this is the thread that undoes me. I begin to cry.

"I don't want to hurt the kids," I say. "I want to do this right."

Right? Is there a right way to have an affair?

"I know," he says, and kisses the inside of my palm. "Me too. So what do we do?"

I feel so weak I may sink to the floor. "I don't know."

He stops and looks at me. "What do you *want* to do, Holly?"

I blink back my tears. "I want to be with you."

His eyes ignite.

"But we need to figure this thing out," I quickly add.

He plays with a strand of my hair. "I'm gone this weekend. I promised to take Ava to this American Girl thing in Madison. Come over on Monday," he says and plants a soft kiss on the inside of my wrist, "and we'll figure this *thing* out." He's teasing me, I know.

"Okay." I let him kiss my other wrist. "Monday."

Then he pulls me to himself and kisses me, finally, on the mouth. A fire of pleasure rushes through me, trailed by something thick and ruinous, like black tar coating a clean white canvas. I pull away. Manage to find the doorknob. "I gotta go," I say and even though my body is begging me to stay, I step into the world outside that, to my surprise, looks the same as when I left it minutes ago. Knees trembling, I start for home.

I'm halfway down the block when I hear someone call my name. Even without turning around, I know who it is.

"Holly!" she calls again and I have no choice.

I pivot on my heel and wait for Annalisa to catch up to me.

15

She's pushing Jackson in the stroller and breaks into a jog to close the distance between us. "When did you get back?" she wants to know.

"Yesterday. Thanks for taking Ben."

"No problem. Did you have fun? Good girl time?"

"Yeah. Maggie loved the seals."

She glances in the direction of Seth's house. "You had a work appointment today?"

I can't say I was jogging; my sundress and flip-flops prohibit it. "Not so much of a work appointment."

"Oh. What then?"

I continue to walk and she falls into step with me. "Just dropping by to say hi to a friend."

She's quiet for a moment. "It's that guy, right? From the pool? I know he lives around here."

"Seth? Yes."

"Holly, is everything... alright?"

I shrug. Where would I even find the words?

"Come over," she says. "Let's talk."

"I have a ton to do. I'm way behind on everything."

"You have time for Seth but you can't carve out an hour for your best friend?"

"Wow. Can I have some jam to go with that guilt?" I smile. She merely looks at me with somber grey eyes.

"Thirty minutes," she says. "You have time."

Deep down I knew this day would come, *had* to come. I knew I'd spill to Annalisa even before telling John.

We make our way to her house, a foreign quietness swelling between us. In our twenty-plus years of friendship, we've had our disagreements. We've clashed in our parenting styles, bruised each other's feelings, and unraveled sticky misunderstandings. In some seasons we've called or seen each other daily, other times life's swift current prevents us from connecting for weeks. But when we finally do catch up, we jump in and pick up right where we left off with heightened eagerness.

But this. This is new ground for us, this eerie silence. Mercifully, Jackson fills the void with gibberish. Once we get to her house she promises to meet me on the back deck, after she's put Jackson down for a nap.

"You painted the trim on the play fort," I comment when she sets two glasses of lemonade on the patio table. "I like it."

"The boys rallied for that electric blue. Finally we thought, what the heck?"

We sit sipping our drinks. I'm about to fill the void by relating how Maggie and I accidently marched into the men's bathroom at a restaurant in California when Annalisa squints her eyes and says, "Are you and John doing alright?"

There's no sense beating around the bush. "No. We are not."

"What's going on?"

"Where do I start?" I stare at the play fort, vaguely wondering if the inside has been painted as well, or if it looks the same as it did last spring. "We're not happy. We don't talk, and if we do, we fight."

"Marco and I would be glad to take the kids for a weekend, let you guys get away. There's this marriage conference my church is hosting in a few weeks, maybe you and John—"

"It's a little late for that."

"It's never too late," she says, her face lit with hope. "What about a counselor? Laura really seemed to like hers."

I laugh. "John? Counseling? That'll be the day. And you may remember that I wanted to go to some marriage thing at your church a couple of years ago but John said no. Oh and a couple of months ago, I wanted to take a trip with him, just the two of us, but he didn't want to do that either. So I'm done trying to work on our marriage all by myself. I'm just done."

"Okay. I get that you're going through a rough patch, but when I see you coming out of some attractive, single guy's house... you have to know why I might be concerned, what I might be thinking."

I meet her gaze. "What are you thinking?"

"I don't know. That there could be... maybe... something..."

I don't give her an ounce of help. I just watch her squirm. Wait and see if she can reach her own conclusion for once in her life.

"I mean, I'm sure there's nothing going on between you," she rambles, "but it doesn't look good. To see you coming out of his house. In that little dress? I mean, I guess you could be there for work or something but even so... it doesn't look good."

I take a sip of tea.

She worries her lip and watches me, waits for me to refute her, to put her mind at ease. Finally she lowers her voice. "*Is* there something going on between you and Seth?"

I look away. How I wish I could be with him again, standing in his entryway with my knees quaking and my heart pounding, instead of here. I take a breath. "Yes."

Her cheeks pale.

"There is definitely something going on. I've fallen in love with him. And I'm pretty sure he's fallen in love with me." I give her a minute to absorb this.

"You can't really mean that," she finally says.

"I know this comes as a shock, but I do."

She's a statue, only the pupils of her eyes dart around. Now that I've released the words, undeniable as a rainfall, I second-guess myself. Maybe I should have waited to tell her until…. until when?

She blinks a few times, gathers her composure. "Okay. Well. Every marriage has its up and downs. I know that it may not seem possible but you and John can work this out. We'll help you any way we can. Don't give up."

Her optimism infuriates me. "You're not listening. I don't *want* to work it out. I think I love Seth and I'm pretty sure he loves me."

Her eyes narrow. "Did he *say* that? Did he actually have the audacity to say *I love you* to a married woman?"

"Not in so many words but he's… made his intentions clear."

"His *intentions*?" She stands, paces to the end of the deck, and grips the railing. After a minute she storms back to tower over me, all five foot two of her. "His *intentions*? And what, exactly, are his *intentions*? Other then than to get you under the covers."

I spring to my feet. "You don't know anything. You don't know what kind of connection we share. You don't know him."

"I know he's not your husband."

"No. He's not. He's nothing like John."

"Holly, *listen* to yourself."

"What do you know about anything? Just because you have your perfect little marriage—"

She gasps. "Are you serious? Marco and I have gone through our share of problems and you know that—"

"Marco is crazy about you. You don't know what it's like to be married to a roommate, a stranger, to be trapped in a marriage without friendship or love."

"You can get it back," she says, her voice reaching its upper register. "You can fight for your marriage."

"I'm sick of fighting. I'm done fighting." And as if to prove it I sit down, cross my arms over my chest.

Finally she sits too. "I'm going to pray for you and John, pray like crazy—"

I belt out a laugh. "You do that, Annalisa. You pray. That'll fix everything. Pray and all of our troubles will fly away. It's too late. Our marriage is dead."

"Then I'll pray that it will come back to life."

This woman is so didactic I think I may scream. If it's bleeding, bandage it. If it's crying, hug it. It it's hopeless, pray for it. If it's dead, resurrect it. "We're past the point of resuscitation."

"Does John know? About Seth?"

"No."

"How...?" she closes her eyes for a moment and shakes her head. "How far have things gone?"

I can still feel Seth's lips travel along my fingers, my hands, my wrists, my mouth. I turn away.

"Oh, Holly."

"No, not that far. Give me a little credit. But yes, I want to be with him."

She shakes her head, as if she can dodge the truth of my words. "I can't believe this. I can't believe what I'm hearing. You sound as if you're thinking about leaving your *husband*."

"I'm doing more than thinking. That's why I went to California, to decide. I've tried making things work with John. Tried and failed. One person can't make a marriage work. We're just so unhappy. It's like we don't even know each other. And with Seth, I'm happy."

All at once, like a three-year-old, she bursts into tears. "Holly, *please* don't do this. This can't be the answer. There has to be another way. Divorcing John isn't the answer."

"I'm sorry," I say, truly meaning it. "I'm sorry you feel like I've failed you, I am, but I can't keep living like this."

"What about your kids? You of all people should know what this would do to your kids."

"Don't you dare. Don't talk to me about my kids, as if I don't think about them every minute of the day. As if I don't want what's best for them. I'm not saying it'll be easy, but it's not fair to constantly subject them to our fighting, is it? They deserve a happy mother, don't they?"

"I just want to help you."

"Then help me be happy."

She shakes her head and stares at the play fort. "It won't make you happy. Not in the long run. You may think it will, but Holly—"

"If I'm going to do this," I cut in, "if I'm going to completely change my life, I'll need your friendship more than ever."

She sniffs and wipes her eyes. Her expression shifts into one of resolution. She looks at me with steady grey eyes. "No."

"No?"

"No. I can't help you with this."

"So you don't want me to be happy. You want me to stay miserable."

"Of course I want you to be happy, Holly. You're my friend. But John's my friend too and your children are my children's friends, and as your friend, I can't be part of this. As your friend, I can't help you throw your life away. I can't support what you're thinking about doing in any way whatsoever. *No.*"

She's never been so decisive in all her life. For a second I'm floored, even impressed. But then the full impact of her words hit. After over two decades of friendship she would cut me off. Slam the door. Just like that. I can't believe it. I can't breathe. Somehow I manage to draw from the air around me, fill my lungs like I do before a run, and fix my eyes on this woman who's supposed to be my friend. "Thanks a lot. I knew I could count on you."

"You *can* count on me, to help you work things out with John."

"You may think I'm throwing my life away, but I'm not. And for the record, I'm not the one walking away from our friendship. *You* are."

She leans forward. "If you don't break things off with Seth, how *could* we still be friends?"

"Are you really that narrow minded? I didn't realize our friendship came with conditions."

"Holly, think about it. You leaving John would affect everything. Me. Us. Our families. Our kids. *Everything*. How could our friendship possibly stay the same?"

"So you're giving me an ultimatum. Stay with John and be miserable, or lose your friendship."

"No, it's not an ultimatum. It's reality. It's not that I wouldn't *want* to be friends, I just don't know how we *could* be friends. Not how we are now. We'd be fake, phony. I stood beside you at your wedding and you stood beside me at mine and I know in the end it's your choice and I can't make you do anything, but *I'm not happy* is hardly grounds for divorce. Everyone who's ever gotten married would be divorced because at some point we've all been unhappy."

"I'm the one who's stuck in a lifeless marriage, not you."

"So let your friends help you. After all we've been through, all of us, you and me, John and Marco, Laura and Jake and now Phil—let us help you and John. Do you really think we'd all simply watch you walk out on John and welcome Seth around the Monopoly table as one of the gang?"

I slide my finger through the condensation on my glass. "We did with Phil."

Her jaw drops. "Tell me you're kidding. Please tell me you aren't comparing your situation to Laura's. Laura's husband *died*."

"Well my marriage *died*."

She closes her eyes and inhales through her nose. "Dead things aren't always dead."

"That is the stupidest thing you've ever said."

She says it again, louder. *"Dead things aren't always dead."*

"No, Annalisa. You're wrong. Dead means dead." I stand, ready to be done with this madness.

She jumps to her feet and grabs my hand, her eyes filling with tears. "Wait! You have to know how much I love you. No matter what happens, no matter what you do. Even if our friendship changes."

Tears threaten but I swallow hard. "I wish you could hear yourself. You're making no sense at all."

I yank my hand free and rush down the deck steps and hurry home, my eyes burning with tears I refuse to let fall. She isn't worth it, this woman, this fraud who refuses to accept the real world, refuses to allow people to make their own choices and live their own lives. Why does she get to decide the rules?

At home, I empty Maggie's and my suitcases and all the hampers and head down to the basement. I start the washer and pour in detergent. After twisting the cap back on the soap, I pause and examine my hands. Just this morning Seth gently kissed these hands. Kissed them and loved them minutes before Annalisa desperately grasped for them.

The washer starts churning. I turn to head upstairs but suddenly realize I've forgotten to add clothes. I dump in the pile of jeans and then take the stairs two at a time. In the kitchen, I start a grocery list—frozen pizza, boxed dinners, pasta—easy things to get us to Monday, and then get in my van and drive to the store.

Monday. Three days from now. I'll see him on Monday.

In spite of my list, I wander up and down aisles, contemplating products I've never purchased before. I'm loitering among the breakfast cereals when I hear a familiar voice. "Get the sugary kind. Your kids will thank me."

I leave my cart to hug Laura. "You look amazing!" I tell her, and she does. Her hair shines lustrously and now she's sun-tanned to boot. "How was the honeymoon?"

"Fantastic. The resort was amazing. I'll show you pictures tomorrow."

"Tomorrow?"

"Everyone's coming to the marsh, remember? You replied to my email, you goofball. You said you'd bring artichoke dip."

That's right. Some email floated back and forth between our three families days ago. "Oh man, is that tomorrow? I'll have to double check with John."

"Philip talked to him yesterday. John said it worked fine."

I can't think fast enough. "Okay. Great."

"You can tell me all about your trip to California. John

mentioned you and Maggie went to visit your mom. Come anytime after four and have the kids bring nets."

"Nets?"

"To catch frogs. We have lots of frogs."

"Right."

"The whole gang will be there," she enthuses before she wheels her cart away. I stare at the cereal boxes, trying to remember the ingredients needed for artichoke dip.

My van has been making a clicking sound. John wants to take a look at it so the following afternoon we take his truck to the marsh instead. Talking a mile a minute, Laura leads me to her kitchen where Annalisa is slicing cucumbers. She looks up when I enter and offers a shadow of a smile, and then slides the green circles into a salad bowl.

When Laura gets on a roll, the girl can talk. For the next twenty minutes she dishes out the PG details of the honeymoon and shows us picture after picture of white beaches and sapphire water and she and Phil looking absurdly happy. As Laura rambles, Annalisa and I interject comments and exclamations without technically speaking to one another. Later, when the three of us transfer the food to the porch, Annalisa and I pass each other carefully and cordially, like mere acquaintances.

Laura yells for the kids to gather on the porch. Phil peels off his John Deere baseball cap and offers a blessing. I keep my eyes open. As Phil thanks the Lord for good friends, I scan faces. Everyone, even Maggie, has his or her eyes closed. Everyone but Jackson. He grins at me and begins to chortle over our shared secret. On the heels of amen, Annalisa sets him down and he runs straight into my arms. I scoop him up and bury my nose in his curls. Annalisa's gaze flits in our direction and I set him down.

We heap our plates and automatically segregate ourselves. From time to time I glance at the men on the other side of the porch. What does Marco know? What has Annalisa told him? What are he and John talking about so intensely? I attempt to block out Laura and Annalisa's chattering and tune in to the men's voices. They look so serious, so grave. I eye Annalisa. She glances at me. She told him. She told Marco and now he's warning John.

Slowly, I rise to my feet, even though I have no idea what I'm going to do. Then I hear John say, "For that kind of clog I'd use a drain snake. I'll loan you mine."

I sit back down and stare at my potato salad.

Lucas spills his drink at the kids' table. Annalisa gets up, gets him started on cleaning up, and then glides back toward us, her oversized tunic, billowing in the breeze. She settles herself in the rocking chair and pokes her food around. For as long as I've known her she's rearranged her food so none of it touches. *Grow up*, I want to shout. If the watermelon cubes touch the cheese balls life would carry on. As if privy to my thoughts, she glances at me, her eyes a glittering jade against the eggplant hue of her blouse.

Phil passes us and Laura playfully tugs on the edge of his shirt. Then she turns to me and says, "You're looking particularly fit these days, Holly."

"Why thank you. I hope so with the half marathon coming up."

"That's right. You've gone crazy but I'm impressed. So you run every day?"

"Holly's always running," Annalisa remarks, nudging a pickle to the side of her plate.

"It's called *training*." I turn back to Laura. "Six days a week."

Laura nods, her eyes bouncing from me to Annalisa. TJ bounds over to show off an enormous bullfrog he's captured. Laura admires it then tells him to wash, eat, and *then* he can catch frogs. "He loves it out here," she says. "I was worried he'd miss our old neighborhood but with the creek and all the frogs he can catch, he loves it. He's so outdoorsy, just like his dad. And Philip."

"How's he doing with all the other changes?" Annalisa wants to know.

"It's an adjustment, for both him and Philip. The other day was rough. Philip tried to step in with something and TJ got angry and shouted 'you're not my dad', but they're learning the ropes."

"It hasn't been that long," I remind her.

"Right. So all in all, we're doing well." She smiles at Phil across the porch who grins back like a happy fool.

Annalisa and I exchange a knowing look. But then we remember and examine our food.

After the children run off to catch frogs, Annalisa serves pie. Laura brings out the Monopoly board and ceremoniously opens it on the porch table. "The time has come to initiate Philip."

"Here here," Marco says, raising a can of Mountain Dew.

Laura stands before Phil, the silver pawns displayed in her open hands. "You get first choice, my love."

Phil selects the wheelbarrow which prompts the rest of us to applaud. Laura nabs her iron, Marco swipes the car, Annalisa selects the hat, and John takes the dog. Today I don't want to be the boot. Today I am the cannon.

The game begins. We explain our house rules to Phil as we travel around the board. He catches on quickly, trading a bottle of cranberry wine for Marco's Reading Railroad on his third turn. Annalisa, as always, appears innocent but I know her better. She's hot after my Pennsylvania Avenue. Then she'll have a monopoly. Then she'll build houses that she'll turn into hotels and destroy us all.

She straightens in her chair. "Okay Holly. St Charles Place, my Get out of Jail Free card, and three hundred dollars for Pennsylvania."

I guffaw. "Get real."

"You'd have two purples."

"Big deal. You'd have a monopoly."

She tilts her head. "St. Charles Place. Get of Jail card. Three hundred dollars, *and* you can take home the rest of the pie. Honeycrisp."

Marco shakes his head. "Not the pie, babe."

"Take the pie," John says.

Annalisa's piecrust is a dessert unto itself, never mind the filling. But cannons don't surrender to the likes of little hats; cannons aim to win. "I'm watching my carb intake. Pass."

"Hang on," Annalisa says. "All of this, *and* the pie, *and* I'll be your running buddy for a week."

"Ha! Like you could keep up." I grab the dice and hand them to Laura.

"Try me. I may be the running partner you need."

"Right. Because you always know best about everything."

She shrugs. "Just trying to help."

"Well don't try to help."

"That's what friends do."

"Really? Is that what you call it?"

Whack! Laura's slapped the table so hard with her hand all the pawns jump. "What is with you two?"

Annalisa looks off toward the fields. I straighten my stack of bills. Phil scrapes back his chair. "Coffee anyone?"

Marco and John mumble coffee sounds good and follow Phil inside. Annalisa gets up and trots down the porch steps. Laura watches her go and turns to me. "Let's have it."

"What? We always get competitive."

"Not like this you don't. Something's up. You two are being weird."

"We're fine. We had a disagreement over something but we'll work it out."

"So go," Laura says, thumbing toward Annalisa. "Work it out."

I watch Annalisa's figure grow smaller and before long she rounds the bend and disappears completely. An unexpected bubble of panic rises inside of me. What would life be like without her? I can hardly imagine. But she, not me, is walking away. She is choosing to sever, cut me off. "I think we better let her cool off," I say. "You know how emotional she can get."

Laura looks dubious.

I turn toward the house. "I think I'll have a cup."

The coffee isn't done dripping. I glance at the kitchen counters, overwhelmed with dishes and food scraps. I sweep potato peelings into my hand and throw them in the garbage then fill the huge sink. In no time I'm scrubbing away at the scorched bottom of a big, black kettle.

Masculine laughter rings out from the next room. Above me that awful rooster scowls down. How long, I wonder, has Mr. High and Mighty reigned? How does Laura put up with him?

I pause in my task to shoot him a look. "Cock-a-doodle-do." Then my hands dip back into the water that's turning brown and gritty from burnt potatoes.

16

On Monday morning, I pack John's lunch and make the kids toaster waffles. I echo John's monotone goodbye as he shuffles out the door. I kiss the kids' foreheads, see them off to school, clean up the kitchen, and then run a bath. The tub is nearly full when my phone trills. *Hoover Elementary* flashes across my screen.

"I forgot my gym shoes," my son informs me.

"Benjamin. When do you need them?"

"Soon. For gym."

I glance at the clock. It's not quite nine. School hasn't even started yet. I swathe myself in a towel and start for the hall. "Where did you leave them?"

"I don't know."

I search the predictable places—by the back door, under the table, in the middle of the family room— and even check his closet on the small chance he had a burst of responsibility. "I don't see them. What are you wearing now?"

"Flip-flops."

"And you can't wear those to gym?"

"*Mom!*"

"When did you last have them?"

"I don't know. Oh, wait. At TJ's."

"At TJ's?"

"Yeah, we went wading at the creek so I took them off and put them in the van."

I think for a moment. "We didn't take the van. We took Dad's truck, remember?"

"Oh yeah. They're in Dad's truck."

"Dad's at work. Honey, he's not going to be able to bring you your shoes."

"But I *need* them."

"You'll just have to tell your teacher you don't have them."

"But I'll lose a point."

"Okay, well, you'll lose a point. You can call Dad if you want, but I doubt he's going to bring them. You're just going to have to make do."

He sighs. "Fine."

I end the call and slip into the tub. I scrub my scalp and deep condition my hair, immerse myself to rinse, then wedge a rolled up towel behind my neck. The day before me feels endless in its possibilities, like a clean, white sheet of paper. My heart begins to palpitate. We are simply getting together to talk, I remind myself as I shave my legs. To *figure this out*. It's been only three days since I last saw Seth but it feels much longer.

When I step out of the bath, I catch my reflection in the mirror, the sight of my body no longer causing me to cringe. Miracles aside, my stomach will never be taut but it's lost its dough-like quality and the sun has bronzed my toned arms. But these thighs. I sigh and head to my room.

I step into a soft cotton skirt that falls above my knees, pull on a tank top, and slide my arms into a long, thin cardigan. I latch my dangly charm bracelet around my wrist. The light from the lamp on my dresser hits the cascading crystals and causes dots of radiance to flicker across my dresser. But the delicate piece feels heavy, oppressive. It was a birthday gift from John, something I pointed out to him in the store weeks beforehand. When I opened it, I played it up. How in the world did he know? A little birdie told me, he had said.

I unfasten the bracelet and bury it in my jewelry box. I step out of my house, lock the door behind me, and make my way to Seth's.

Sunlight filters through the tops of the trees, throwing shifting shadows against the sidewalk beneath my feet. I pass under the umbrella of an over zealous maple, already blazing like fire among green leafed oaks and elms. When I reach Seth's house my heart quickens. I run a hand through my hair and knock.

His car is not in the driveway and the windows of his studio are dark. I knock again. I wait a minute and then try the doorbell. Another minute crawls by.

The mail truck pulls up and the mailman deposits slim white envelopes into the box and waves at me. Reluctantly, I wave back, unable to distinguish if he's my mailman. Does he recognize me?

Once more I press the door bell. The house remains quiet, unwelcoming, so I hurry down the steps and head home.

Thirty minutes later Annalisa is on my doorstep.

Annalisa. Of course. The pieces click into place. "What did you say to him?" I demand when I open the door.

She only stares. "Say to who?"

"Seth. You talked to him, didn't you? What did you say to him?"

"What?"

"You stuck your nose in my business, didn't you? Or you had Marco butt in." But even while I'm speaking I realize my mistake; I know her expressions too well.

"Holly," she says her eyes wide and wounded, "the only time I've ever talked to Seth was that day by that pool."

"Oh. Okay. Sorry."

"Can I come in?"

"I'm working. I'm way behind on the site for that new gymnastics place downtown."

She presses her lips together and shakes her head. "I hate this. I miss you."

For a second, I want to throw my arms around her, whisk her through the door, make her a fresh pot of coffee. Forget everything, forget Seth, and go back to before. But I was just there, standing at his doorstep, and when he calls, I'll run back to him. I shield my heart with my crossed arms. "I need to do what I need to do."

"So you haven't changed your mind."

Her words aren't a question, so I don't offer an answer.

"Okay then," she says in a watery voice, "I'll keep praying."

An incredulous laugh escapes me. "You do that."

"Holly, please—"

"I don't know what else to tell you. I'm sorry, Annalisa. I'm sorry for not living up to your expectations. I need to go." I close the door and turn to walk through the family room, the dining room, and all the way into the kitchen so I can't see how long she stands there.

In all our years, I've never shut her out, not like this. And, to be fair, she has never closed the door on me.

We'll work through this, I vow. We have to. In time, she'll come around. Of course she's going to make a fuss, resist me, even threaten me with withdrawing her friendship. I've upset the order of her well-oiled world. Why wouldn't her initial reaction be one of judgment and fear? But just as I presented myself on Seth's doorstep, Annalisa showed up at mine. That says something. We've been too connected for too long for her to turn her back on me forever.

I check my phone. Still nothing from Seth. I re-read his text from last night. *Can't wait to see you tomorrow.*

It's tomorrow. Where is he?

I've already texted him on the walk back from his house. Hopefully I came across as nonchalant and curious instead of uptight and crushed that he'd forgotten about me. It's now ten-thirty; enough time has passed to warrant a call. A no big deal, just wondering what he's up to, non-needy, call. "You artists types sure like to keep a girl waiting," I say when he answers.

"Holly?"

Anger rises. What other girl waits for him today? "Yes, it's me."

He doesn't respond.

"I dropped by," I go on, "but maybe I had the time wrong? You weren't there..."

His breathing is strange, like he's been running. But he never answers his phone when he's running unless it's from his neighbor who watches Ava. He likes going off the grid if only for an hour, he says. Something is off.

We are. *We* are off. The realization sinks in slowly, painfully, like swallowing ice. He's changed his mind. He sees me for who I am, an over-the-hill mom with thighs that refuse to slim down no matter how hard she runs.

I strive for lightheartedness. "Everything okay?"

"No," he finally says. "Someone's been after Ava."

I hang up the phone, sink to my sunny spot in the kitchen. Right now, with the sun trapped behind the clouds, the corner only holds shadows. Bernice trots over and lays her head on my leg. I weave my fingers through her fur and hold on tight. Seth's words lay at my feet like pieces of jagged glass and I must fit them together, make sense of them. He didn't speak sequentially, or even coherently at times, but I line up what I know: Ava was late for school, something about toothpaste. Even though Seth has told her a millions times not to, she took the alley as a shortcut. When she crossed over Pine Street, a man was there. The man grabbed her. The man tried to force her into his van. Another man appeared. The first man let go of Ava and Ava ran to school. An aide found her in at the bottom of the yellow tunnel slide. Ava wouldn't budge until Tori arrived. Tori and Seth and Ava and the school police liaison went down to the police department. That's where Seth was when he answered my call. At the police station. Because someone tried to *force his daughter into a van*. She has bruises on her arm. She hasn't fully stopped crying.

What can I do? I said to Seth. *How can I help?*

I don't know, he said. *I don't know. I don't know.*

I sit in my spot that should be filled with light and cling to my dog like a security blanket.

I do not envy Principal Dobbler, especially today. He's doing his best to pacify the parents of Hoover Elementary but we are a roomful of agitated wasps, ready to strike. "Thankfully," he says standing in front of the Arts and Literature section in the school library that afternoon, "the perpetrator has been caught and will be brought to justice. Please make sure your children are aware of this as you continue to talk to them about personal safety. We at Hoover Elementary want to work with parents to ensure your child not only *feels* safe, but *is* safe."

A mom I know by sight but not name pipes up. "What about the crossing guards and safety cadets? Why didn't they notice anything? What are they *there* for?"

Mr. Dobbler nods. "The incident happened after the second bell rang. Unfortunately the guards and cadets go off duty five minutes after nine."

As if this is idiocy, the mom crosses her arms and shakes her head.

He's right, I want to say. Ava was late for school. Because of toothpaste.

Mr. Dobbler laces his fingers together and holds them in front of his potbelly. "We want to assure you that we are committed to maintaining the safest school possible. Your child's safety is our utmost concern."

"Well, it certainly didn't seem like it today," persists ticked-off Mom.

"Lay off," I hear someone call out and realize it's me. I look at ticked-off Mom and soften my tone. "I understand you're angry but be angry with the pervert behind bars, not Mr. Dobbler. Not the school."

A few people murmur agreement. Mr. Dobbler gives me a brief, appreciative look. Ticked-off Mom turns to look out the window. I'm too far away to know for certain but I think she's fighting tears. Part of me wants to put my arm around her, tell her I know how she's feeling. I feel it, too. We all do. This world, this sick, dark world, is where we have to raise our kids and sometimes we feel so powerless we can hardly breathe. I smile at her but she never knows because she doesn't look my way again.

Annalisa does. I feel, then notice, her smile on me. Quickly, she turns to Jackson in the stroller in front of her and ruffles his hair.

Mr. Dobbler fields questions and when the final bell rings we disband, he, no doubt, to wipe the sweat from his forehead, we to find and hug our children.

"That bad man is going to jail, right?" Maggie says as the three of us walk home.

"That's right."

"Good. Now we don't have to worry about him anymore."

I close my eyes for a second. "You still need to be safe. Most people are nice people, but some people are not nice at all." I stop walking and grasp her shoulder so she'll stop and look at me. "Maggie, you *always* have to be safe. Always. Even when you're a big teenager. Even when you're a grown up lady. Not everyone is good. Not everyone is safe. There are some people you just need to run away from."

Her dark eyes are serious. "Don't worry Mom. I'm a fast runner. And you know how loud I can scream."

"The whole world knows how loud you scream," Ben says.

A strange, tight laugh leaks out of me and my eyes begin to burn. These two little people, these two gems. What if it had been either of them? In my mind I see Ava, swinging up into Seth's arms, her feet dangling from the ground. Then I see her beside a van, some stranger grabbing her, pulling her...

I swallow, concentrate on the oak in front of us, the tips of its leaves looking as if they've been dipped in orange paint. Ben asks if we can have pizza for supper.

I clear my throat. "Of course, sweetheart. Of course we can have pizza for supper."

Later that night we order plain cheese for Maggie and pepperoni and pineapple for Ben. I taste little of what I force into my mouth but watch, mesmerized, my children gobble and chatter. Every syllable is a melody, every grin a gift. After they clear their plates and run off to play video games, I remain at the table turning over *what ifs*. Now what? What do I do? Do I reach out to Seth? Give him a few days? I want to be there for him, and Ava. Even for Tori in a maternal solidarity kind of way.

I'm still sitting at the table when I hear John enter through the kitchen door. His cooler thuds to the counter. He grab a drink from the refrigerator.

"Any left?" he asks when he sits down across from me.

I nudge the boxes toward him.

He grabs a slice. "Any Parmesan?"

I look at him for a second before I scrape back my chair, trudge to the kitchen, search the fridge, seize the Parmesan cheese, and slam the cylinder on the table. "Anything else?"

"A napkin."

My insides are quaking. "You have no idea what kind of day I'd had."

"You have no idea what kind of day *I've* had," he says as he dusts his pizza.

"Maybe instead of coming home and demanding the world—"

"A napkin is the world?"

"—you could start by saying hello to your children, to me—"

"Hello."

"—because if you only knew what's been going on—"

"If *you* only knew."

"—what we've been through today—"

"Spent half my day down at the police station."

"—you might not be so concerned about the damn Parmesan

cheese." I stop. Study him. "What did you say?"

He bites off the tip of his slice. He's chewing but it seems difficult, like he's forcing himself to eat rotten food. Finally he swallows and drops the slice on his plate. He props his hands in front of him and stares past me.

I grip the back of my chair. "You were at the police station?"

He nods, still not meeting my gaze.

"What were you doing at the police station?"

He digs his thumbs into his eye sockets. "Giving a statement."

"John?"

"I saw something. When I brought Ben his shoes."

From where they're playing video games in the next room, my children's laughter rings out. One of them is collecting coins; the TV is making that blinging carnival sound. One of them has struck gold.

I sit down. Not across from John but beside him. "What? What did you see?"

He doesn't speak for a minute. He grabs the green parmesan cheese tower and mindlessly picks at the label with his thumbnail. "There was this van, in the alley. And this girl. This guy had her by the arms." He gives the cheese a little nudge, props his elbows on the table, his face half hidden by his fists again.

"And you rescued her." I say softly. "You rescued Ava."

He lifts his head and looks at me. His blue eyes look so tired, so earnest. He nods, so slightly if I hadn't been staring at him I would have missed it.

17

That night, John goes to bed early. Before he does, he listens to Maggie's twenty minutes of reading and plays a round of UNO with Ben. Then he showers and climbs under the covers. I sit on the edge of our bed, desperate for details, but he rolls to his side and faces the window. "I can't talk about it anymore tonight," he says.

And then, before I leave the room, my hands, all on their own, do the most peculiar thing; they pull the covers around his shoulders and tuck him in.

In the bathroom, the kids are making a mess as they brush their teeth—toothpaste on the counter, water on the floor—but they're laughing so infectiously at some shared joke I don't say a word. After they rinse and spit, I wipe the sticky blue splotches and puddles with a towel that needs to be laundered anyway. I put away Maggie's hair brush and recap the toothpaste.

Toothpaste. If it hadn't been for toothpaste, Ava wouldn't have been late.

If she hadn't been late, she wouldn't have taken the alley.

If she hadn't taken the alley, the man wouldn't have grabbed her.

It's like a sick version of one of those never ending children's books. My mind stubbornly strings one detail to the next.

If Ben hadn't forgotten his shoes, he wouldn't have called John.

If John hadn't brought the shoes, he wouldn't have driven past the alley.

If he hadn't driven past the alley...

I shudder. Toothpaste. Gym shoes. Inconsequential details altering the course of a day. Of a life, really. Including mine. Because even though it shouldn't matter in the light of the day's events, if there hadn't been a toothpaste issue, where would Seth and I be? I don't even know. Our plans, our Monday morning rendezvous, now seems like an alternate reality.

I knock, enter Ben's room, and kiss his forehead. Then I step into Maggie's room. She reaches for me so I climb into her bed. We whisper for a few minutes, my head propped on my elbow, and then I watch her drift off. Her lips part slightly as she gently, sweetly, exhales. When does that change? At what age does our breath go from sweet to rancid? What begins to rot inside of us to cause that to happen? How can someone be so sick to prey upon a little girl? What is wrong with the world?

In her sleep, Maggie smacks me in the face. I peel off her arm and stumble to the family room where all the lights have been left on. One by one I turn them off then curl up on the couch with my phone. No new messages or texts. Not from Seth, or Annalisa, or anybody.

Ordinarily Annalisa and I would talk this day out. Annalisa would interject phrases like *Lord have mercy* and right now I'd welcome her platitudes. I ache to talk to her, to sit at her kitchen table, to muddle through this mess together. Does she know the whole story? Is she aware that John and Seth are among the players? But for as much as I yearn to talk to Annalisa, I long to talk with Seth even more.

I get up and pace, like that restless, lone tiger Maggie and I saw at the San Diego Zoo. Ultimately, I pace my way to the kids' backpacks. I start sorting and purging Maggie's. I find a crumpled word scramble, a book order form, and a candy bar wrapper. I move on to Ben's and extract a pair of dirty socks, a math sheet that needs to be completed, a pencil drawing of a T-Rex eating a semi-truck, a field trip permission slip needing a signature, a handful of wadded up candy wrappers, and a tattered library book. At the very bottom, as if it's been hiding there since the first day of school, I find a sheet of notebook paper with the fringes cut off. *Sounds like fun!* is written across the top margin in red ink. I sit down to read.

My Summer Vacation by Ben Lewis
I got a new video game. I made it to level six. My dad took me camping. My friends and there dads came to. It was fun. They don't have real bathrooms there. They are gross. We told stories at night. Another fun thing is when we all were on my parents bed. We ate popcorn. My dog was there too. We told jokes. It was fun. We were all there. Me and my mom, my dad and my sister and my dog Bernice.

I reread the last few lines. It takes a moment to riffle through the events of the summer but eventually the memory surfaces. I had a head cold that day and went to bed early. Maggie burst in with her Fisher Price Doctor's Kit, stuck a plastic otoscope in my ear and diagnosed me with gingivitis. The treatment, she prescribed, was for her to rub my forehead. She was the doctor, so I enjoyed the massage for a few minutes and flipped on my stomach so she could rub my back for good measure. At some point Ben joined us, and eventually John. Perhaps sensing the rarity of the occasion, Bernice hopped on the bed and was allowed to stay. Someone brought in a bag of microwave popcorn and John and the kids practiced taking free shots into each other's mouths while I dozed.

In June we took the kids to the Shedd Aquarium in Chicago and let them ride the Ferris wheel at Navy Pier. When the heat wave hit, the kids and I fled to a water park in the Dells. We paid our dues to Chuck E. Cheese not once, but twice over the summer, and I can't count how many times we frequented the city pool. These excursions didn't make the cut. An evening spent on our bed, all of us, including our gassy dog, did. It became one of Ben's summer highlights.

I smooth out the wrinkled corners of the paper and hang it on the fridge.

I head to the bathroom, stick my toothbrush in my mouth, and check the kids. I peek in on John, too. After I spit and rinse, I pad back to the family room.

With the fleece blanket wrapped around my shoulders, I crouch down to where Bernice sleeps on her giant pillow. "Just you and me girl."

She looks at me curiously, heaves a sighs, and flops down again. I reach for one of her big, calloused paws, lay my head next to hers, and close my eyes.

When I open them, it's dawn. I push myself from the floor and groan. My neck won't turn. I stagger toward the kitchen and find John dumping grounds into the filter. "You slept there all night?" he asks.

"Yes. I shouldn't have," I say, needling my neck with my fingers, "You're going to work?"

He doesn't look up. "Yeah. Why wouldn't I?"

"I just thought…" What? If you thwart a kidnapping you get the day off? "Do you want eggs?" I ask him.

"I'm fine."

"Did you sleep okay?" I ask.

He nods.

I stand in the warm spot by the window. "Do you want to talk about it?"

He shrugs. "It's no big deal."

"John, it is a big deal. Especially to…" I'm about to say Seth but make a last minute amendment. "To Ava and her parents."

He rummages through the dishes in the drying rack and digs out his travel mug. "I don't want to keep talking about it."

"You haven't talked about it. Not with me." When he says nothing more I go to the fridge, find the salami and mustard, and set them on the counter. He's already untwisting the tie from the bread. I watch him assemble his sandwich—the same sandwich he's eaten for almost twenty years: wheat bread, salami, mustard. I grab an apple and a can of Coke and place them in his cooler.

He adds the sandwich and snaps the lid shut. "You seem to be pretty good friends with Seth. Ask him for the details, I guess."

Heat pours into my face. John grabs his lunch and coffee thermos and walks out the door.

I pour myself a cup of coffee. When John's father died three years ago, he didn't want to talk about it. When Maggie, at eighteen months, started pitching monumental fits that left me wondering how I was going to parent her into the afternoon—let alone the rest of her life—he didn't want to talk about it. When I miscarried our very first baby and I couldn't see through the fog of grief, he didn't want to talk about it. John never wants to talk about it.

But somehow, the local newspaper gets John to talk, or at least convinces him to meet with Seth, Tori, and the Chief of Police for a picture. "Nine-thirty tomorrow morning," he says that evening over a bucket of chicken. "We're supposed to meet in front of the courthouse."

We. Does he mean we, the two of us, or all of them? I plop a dollop of mashed potatoes on Maggie's plate, my heart racing. "Do you want... should I come along?"

He shrugs. "Up to you."

Maggie bounces in her chair. "Can I go, Daddy? Can I go? *Please* Daddy?"

"No Magpie," he tells her. "You have school."

Maggie spends the rest of the night flinging herself around the house, insisting the newspaper would want a picture of her too, since she's Ava's best friend. Right before bed she switches tactics. She tells us we're mean parents who never let her do anything because we hate her. She falls asleep fuming and wakes up fuming and when we drop her and Ben off at school her eyes are still smoldering coals. "You just *hate* me," she hisses. I reason this is a step above *I hate you*.

I smile at her. "I love you. Have a good day."

She stomps into school and we drive to the courthouse. I flip down my visor mirror and hiccup.

"You're nervous." John says.

"I'm not nervous."

"You have hiccups."

I fidget with my bangs. "Must be all the excitement from being married to a superhero."

He smirks. "I'll give you an autograph later."

John parallel parks in front of the courthouse and I spot them on the lawn: the Chief of Police, the photographer for the paper, Seth, and Tori. All hell breaks loose in my stomach. I hiccup/burp loudly and John looks at me and raises his eyebrows. Breathe through your nose, he instructs.

The walk across the lawn feels like a disconcerting dream, a conglomeration of strange characters all coming together. Even from a distance, Seth appears uncharacteristically anxious. He's shuffling through the grass and raking his hands through his hair. He glances my way. I want to hug him, calm him down. Sit with him and tell him everything will be all right. John's arm brushes mine and I remember, with a flush of shame, the last time Seth and I were face-to-face, when he kissed me in the entryway of his house. A rivulet of perspiration slides down my side. I swallow over a hiccup. Why, why, why am I here?

I'll say I need to go inside. Find a drinking fountain, or a restroom…

All of a sudden, Tori's charging us. She barrels into John, throws her arms around his neck, and sobs. I make out *thank you* and *you have no idea* although most of her utterances get lost in John's chest. John awkwardly pats her back. When she finally releases him, his polo shirt is splotched with tears.

Seth steps forward, extends his hand to John. They shake hands and then Seth initiates that peculiar man move, that half-hug, half-pat on the shoulder gesture. "There aren't words to express our gratitude," Seth says and his voice—usually smooth with confidence, even cockiness—sounds odd. Tight. He looks down at his shoes and sniffs. "Thank you."

John's uneasiness seems to have morphed into flat out embarrassment. He shrugs. "It was nothing."

Tori peers at him, almost sternly. "What you did was heroic. How you chased that scumbag across town for miles? How you went after him like that? If it weren't for you, who knows what have happened. And he might still be out there. You are a *hero*."

Chased him across town for miles? I look at Tori, hoping she'll spill more. Or will I have to read the story in the paper like any other citizen?

The photographer, who doesn't look old enough to legally drink, approaches Tori and asks if her daughter's going to be in the photograph as well.

Fury darkens Tori's face. "Are you kidding? Do you really think I'm going to let you plaster her little face all over town? After what she's been through?"

The guy takes a step backward. "Sorry. I didn't know."

"I'm sorry." She turns back to John. "I'm just a little sensitive about Ava right now."

"Sure. Makes sense." John says.

She nods, tears springing afresh. She grips his arm and John gives her hand a little pat.

I'm a mother. I get it. The sheer gratitude and fear that must overlay every second of her day, occupy every corner of her mind is understandable. But this drama, this over the top stage show, she sure does lay it on thick. As if she can read my mind, she grips my arm. "Sorry for all of my blubbering," she says. "I'm not meaning to fall all over your husband, but you're lucky to have someone like him. We're all lucky to have him in this town." She looks at John. "He's a guardian angel, straight from heaven."

I will smile and I will nod and I will keep my eyes from rolling into my head.

After Tori fixes herself up with whatever miracle products she totes around in that giant purse of hers, she looks ready for her close-up. Her smile is wide and white, her highlighted bangs fall perfectly across her forehead as she stands between my husband and my... Seth. That is how I've come to think of him, I realize. *My Seth.*

As the photographer clicks away, I study these two men, divided by the woman who, I imagine, at one time adored Seth and at this moment, adores John. Sunlight illuminates John's cropped blonde hair, reminding me of a boy at the beach. He's taller than Seth by a good inch, maybe two, and even though his midsection paunches slightly, his arms are strong. He has the self-conscious look of a second grader on picture day—blue shirt tucked into brown pants, stiff, unnatural smile.

And then Seth. Seth who emanates natural cool. Seth who can pull off wearing a black T-shirt and a tweed blazer and a pair of blue jeans. Seth and his wry smile, his laidback confidence. But not today. Today he looks bleary-eyed and tense. He glances my way. I smile. He averts his eyes again.

After the photographer packs up, the three of them stand around talking. "She slept a little better last night," I hear Tori say as I approach their huddle, "but she still won't let me leave the room."

Seth steps to the side to let me join them. I pick up a hint of his aftershave.

"I don't know how long it'll take her to go back to school," Tori goes on.

"You don't want to rush her," John says.

"No, of course not. The most important thing is that she feels safe."

"Anytime she's ready to come over for a play date with Maggie, she's welcome to," I offer.

Tori smiles. "Thanks. Maybe in a couple of days I'll ask her if she's up for it. Or maybe Maggie could come over instead?"

"Absolutely. Whatever Ava wants."

"I'm so glad she knows your family," Tori says. "When I explained to her that it was Maggie's daddy who helped catch the bad guy that seemed to help. But she's so young, and she's so shy, you probably won't get a thank you out of her."

John looks puzzled. "She shouldn't thank me. Something like that shouldn't ever happen."

Tori nods, turning to water again. "Well, on her behalf, I'll be saying it until the day I die. Thank you."

"How long did you chase him across town?" I ask John as we drive home.

"Until the police came."

I silently beg for more. He offers me nothing. What exactly happened that morning? I don't find out until a day later, when the story comes out in the paper.

The photograph itself takes up half of the page. Tori looks stunning, Seth looks exhausted, John looks stiff. *Local Hero Thwarts Attempted Child Abduction,* reads the headline. I glean the article for details. An Officer Stanford relays how the police received an emergency call at 9:10 in the morning from a John Lewis claiming to be "chasing a kidnapper". According to the article, after the perpetrator bolted, John jumped in his truck and went after the accused, calling 911 during the nine-mile chase. John Lewis, the paper informs me, will be the recipient of a Chief's Award and will receive a plaque for his bravery. "Our whole community can be grateful for conscientious citizens like John Lewis," concludes Officer Stanford. "It's courageous and caring residents like him that make our community great." The news reporter ends with a reality I know all too well: "All attempts to interview Mr. Lewis have been declined."

Laura is the first to contact me. "You must be bursting with pride," she says over the phone.

"Of course."

"Your guy has guts. Thank God he was there."

Yes, I tell Laura. Thank God. After a few more exchanges

about the sad state of the world and the gallantry of my husband, I steer the conversation toward the impending cranberry harvest. "We're flooding the beds on Saturday," she says. "Come on out and watch. Bring John and the kids. And I'll call Annalisa. I'll make chili. I miss you guys!"

"I need to check my calendar," I say.

"For a *Saturday*? No you don't. Harvest comes once a year. Just get your skinny butt out here and bring me a latte while you're at it."

The following afternoon, on my way to meet the kids after school, I walk past Seth's house. Regardless of anything else, I am his friend and it's only right for me to stop by. I rap on the door. He opens it and slides into flip-flops before we start walking toward school together. If Annalisa should see us, I decide, she can fume and flail all she wants.

"How is she doing?" I ask.

"Better. Although she still refuses to sleep alone. What really gets me is that she doesn't understand the true danger. To her, a bad man grabbed her. She doesn't know...she doesn't understand what could have..." His voice breaks and I briefly touch his arm.

"That's good," I suggest. "Don't you think? She's innocent. She shouldn't understand everything yet."

"Yes, but I've been on the verge of throwing up ever since it happened. I shouldn't have let her walk to school when it was so late."

"Seth. It's not your fault. I'm so sorry this happened. I can only imagine how scary this has been. I just want you to know... how much I want to be there for you. For both you and Ava."

If he's trying to smile he's failing horribly.

"I miss you," I say quietly.

"I miss you too."

Hoover Elementary sits a block away. He stops walking and

turns to me. I sense he wants to say more, but a car pulls up to the curb and idles while three kids tumble out. We walk on. As we near the school, someone calls to him. "We'll talk more later," he promises and runs off, just as the bell rings.

Minutes later, Ben and Antonio flank me, begging to play videogames at my house. I agree to it, as long as Antonio checks in with Annalisa. The boys rush off leaving me to listen to Maggie prattle on about the new girl from California who, to her astonishment, hasn't met Grandma.

"California is a big state," I remind her.

But she's moved on to the bake sale for which I'm to supply four-dozen Rice Krispie treats.

The doorbell rings around supper time. It's Annalisa, collecting her child, but I don't want to let her in. With no other choice, I open the door and fake a smile.

"I can't believe it was John," she says, shaking her head. "What a crazy week you must've had."

"You could say that."

"Will John have to go to court and testify once it goes to trial?"

"I'm guessing so. Although it sounds like that won't be for another few months. Fortunately they set a super high cash bond on the creep."

She nods. "I saw Ava was at school today."

"It's a step, although Seth says she only sleeps if she's with him or Tori."

Something flickers in her eyes.

I sigh. "He's my friend, Annalisa. Friends talk to each other. Friends should be there for one another when everything falls apart."

"What about John? How is he doing?"

"I don't know. He won't talk to me. Most of what I know I found out from the paper, like everyone else."

"Give him time. He'll talk when he's ready. In the meantime, just let him know you're there for him. That is... if you *are* there for him."

I look at her and say nothing.

"Holly, open your eyes. This horrible thing happened—*almost* happened—and John stopped it. How can that not change anything for you?"

"John was the hero, I get it. But that doesn't change our marriage."

"It could. It could be a start. If you let it."

I cross my arms over my sweatshirt. "Antonio!" I holler. "Your mom's here and she needs to get going!"

The boys appear pelting each other with Nerf guns. Between shots, Antonio asks if Ben can come over tomorrow.

"I don't know," I say, glancing at the back of Annalisa who's heading down my steps. "I don't think tomorrow will work."

"Why not?" Ben wants to know.

"It just doesn't."

His protests increase. Annalisa calls for Antonio. Ben follows them outside only to return seconds later with a slam of the door. "You're so *unfair*."

I watch my angry, preadolescent son stomp off to his bedroom. Then I glance out the window to see, yet again, Annalisa walking away from me.

18

Over the next couple of days, my resolve and my desire to be with Seth thicken. It courses through my veins, fortifying my will to wait for him. Wait until he's ready to talk. To come back to me.

Of course he's consumed with Ava right now. In time, things will calm down. Life will veer back into normal and panic will fade to fear, and fear to caution, and we'll set up another day to *figure things out.*

After two days of no contact, I text him over my second cup of morning coffee.

Would love to see you. Can we get together sometime?

By ten o'clock, I still haven't heard back. I do, however, hear back from the owner of the gymnastics place who complains that the color scheme I've chosen is too feminine and won't appeal to boys. I tell her I understand and promise to rework everything, even though the plum hue I incorporated into the site *is,* in my estimation, a gender-neutral color. I hang up the phone and pull at my hair for a minute. After trying a dozen different color combinations, I settle on boring old navy and grey and finally, my phone chimes.

Sorry, Seth has texted. *Crazy day. Wish it worked to see you. I miss you.*

I obsess over these words. He wishes it worked to see me *today*, or at all? He misses me. That much is clear, so of course he wants to see me. It's just too soon. I refuse to come across as desperate so I let ten minutes slide by before texting back: *Miss you too. Thinking of you all the time.*

I call for Bernice. From her pillow, she lifts her head and flops back down. It's probably just as well; today I'm going for broke.

I step into the September afternoon and run as if I'm being chased. Or maybe I'm the one doing the chasing. Either way the push feels good, each stomp a defiant retaliation to the whirlwind of aggravations: Annalisa's rebuke and John's refusal to talk and Seth's preoccupation and even my mother's calm admonition from weeks ago. I accomplish six miles and much of it feels like a tantrum. By the time I'm panting up my driveway, my shirt is stuck to my back but I feel, somehow, like I've won. Won what, I don't know, but it still feels good.

In the evening John and I park ourselves on either end of the couch and gape at the TV. Periodically I glance at my phone but the only thing displayed on my screen is a picture Maggie assigned as my wallpaper, a candid of the four of us from last summer at the beach. Ben's wearing his serious expression, Maggie has her tongue out, John's shoulders shine from sunburn and I look pleased in my chocolate brown one piece, a striped towel tucked around my waist. I remember a newfound sense of confidence that day, as this picture was taken days after I'd hit my weight loss goal. I study the photo for a moment, at this seemingly happy family of four, and then I scroll through my photos and find one of Maggie and Bernice napping side by side. I make that my new wallpaper.

The following morning Tori calls and asks if my offer still stands. My mind goes blank.

"For Ava to come over? She asked if she could go to Maggie's house and it's the first time she's volunteered to go anywhere. But if it doesn't work…"

"No," I interject. "We'd love to have her. The kids and I are home all day. Anytime."

When I tell Maggie, she screams and runs to the bathroom to fetch the tote bag of nail polish. She arranges the bottles and emery boards on the dining room table and announces, "We're playing salon."

I'm about to tell her no, too messy, but the pockmarked surface of my table speaks sense to me. Who cares anymore? "Put down paper towel first," I tell her.

When they arrive, Ava flies toward Maggie while Tori lingers in the doorway. "Don't worry," I assure her. "If she wants to come home for any reason, I'll call you."

"I know I'm being ridiculous."

"You're reacting like any mom would. But they'll have fun. Really."

She nods. "This is a good thing, her wanting to be here. I wonder if she'll say anything when she sees John."

"He's out, but he should be back soon." I can't tell if she's disappointed or if I'm imagining it. "You know, he doesn't expect anything. Like for her to say anything at all about what happened."

"I know. He's a good guy. That's what she calls him *The Good Guy. The Good Guy* who caught *The Bad Guy*." She walks over to where the girls are separating the pinks from the purples and plants a kiss on Ava's head.

She's halfway down my front steps when she turns around. "Oh, by the way, Seth will be picking her up. In a couple of hours if that works."

"Sure."

"But if there are any problems before that, call me."

"I will."

When I pass the girls on my way to the basement, I see that Maggie has bestowed Ava with two of her treasured, press-on leopard print nails. An unmistakable sign of her adoration. They fan out their fingers and I tell them they look fabulous.

Some time later, John walks in with PVC pipe. "Sink's leaking," he says and lays on the floor to gain access under the kitchen sink.

From where she's sitting at the table, Ava's eyes never leave him. "What's he doing?" I hear her whisper.

"Oh, him? He's checking for raccoons."

"*Maggie!*" But I can't help laughing. "You're so full of stories. He's fixing a pipe, Ava."

Maggie drops the doll that's getting a manicure up to her knuckles, and rushes to the kitchen. "Can we help, Daddy? We want to help!"

I start folding towels, stacking them on the seat of a dining room chair, and watch Ava watch John. She's on the edge of her seat, deciding whether or not to join Maggie.

From underneath the sink, John tells Maggie to hand him a pipe wrench. Maggie could pick out a pipe wrench before she could say the word. She hands it over. As quiet as a shadow, Ava slips out of her chair and kneels beside Maggie.

"Now what Daddy?"

No response.

"*Now* what Daddy?"

"Honey, let him work," I tell her.

Maggie is quiet for a collective five seconds. "Now what do you need Daddy?"

"Paper towel," John says.

"Your turn Ava!" Maggie prompts. "You get it!"

Apprehension clouds Ava's features and for a moment she looks just like Seth did the day we met him in front of the courthouse. She looks to me for help. I smile and tip my head toward the roll of paper towels on the counter. She jumps up, rips off two sheets, and thrusts them under the sink.

"Do you need more Daddy?" Maggie asks.

"No. Two is perfect."

Ava beams.

"We're good plumbers, right Daddy?"

"Yep."

The girls giggle and take turns balancing the level on their heads. I hear John curse softly. After a minute, he emerges.

"All fixed Daddy?" Maggie asks.

"No. I need to run out for another part." He peers down at his flannel shirt and plucks off a tiny, leopard print nail. "Don't think this is mine."

Maggie fans out her hands to check her nails. "Must be Ava's. Check your nails, Ava."

Ava does. Alarm passes over her face as she discovers her defective pinky. John takes her hand and gently presses the nail back into place.

"Thank you." Her voice is just above a whisper.

John smiles. "You bet."

My throat begins to close. I turn away, turn back to my basket of towels.

John grunts to his feet. "I'll be back. Again."

I look at the clock. Seth will be here in a half an hour. "Could you pick up something for dinner while you're out? Frozen pizza or something. And milk."

He nods and grabs his keys. "I'm out of socks."

"Already in the washer."

Frozen pizza and dirty socks. That's what we've been reduced to.

The girls have moved on to Barbies when I hear a knock on the door. I open it to Seth and even though it's entirely the wrong time and place, the sight of him jolts me with exhilaration. I can't help it; I want to grab the lapels of his jacket and kiss him. Instead, I join him outside, out of earshot of the kids.

He looks past me to the house. "How'd she do?"

"Great. They played the afternoon away. In fact I heard them talking about a sleepover."

Seth rubs his forehead. "Oh, I don't know if she's ready for that…"

"I'm not saying she is, I just thought it was a good sign, that she's at least talking about it."

He nods. He's chewing gum and I can smell the peppermint.

I step a fraction closer. "How are *you* doing?"

"Busy, actually. Lots of new projects." His eyes roam everywhere, landing on everything but me.

"Did I tell you or what? It's that new razzle-dazzle website of yours."

He smiles.

"Any more loveseats waiting to be made over?"

"No. No upholstery job. But two companies in Madison have hired me to redesign their offices."

"Hey that's great."

He rubs the back of his neck. He seems to be examining the pitch of my roof. Suddenly it dawns on me why he's acting so edgy. "John's not here," I say.

"Oh. Well, I should get Ava."

"Oaky. In a minute." I briefly touch his hand. "I've missed you."

He closes his eyes.

"You have no idea how many times I've wanted to—"

He holds up his hand. "Holly."

"I know the timing's not right. I get it."

"I can't."

I smile, tuck my hair behind my ear. "Don't worry. I can wait."

"*No*. I mean, I can't do *this*," he gestures between the two of us. "Whatever *this* is. Not now. Not after what happened."

I search his face, determined to make him look me in the eye. "We don't have to rush anything, But I want you to know how much I've thought about us, how I've come to see that you're right. We *are* good for each other—"

"S*top*." His voice holds an edge I've never heard before. "What kind of man would I be if I had an *affair* with the wife of the man who *saved my daughter?*"

I take a breath. "Seth, the truth is, my marriage was crumbling *before* you stepped into the picture. It was dying. It's dead. And with you… I feel alive."

He's closed his eyes again. "I'm sorry, Holly. I didn't want to hurt you."

I stare at him for a moment. "You can't really mean this. I understand you're preoccupied, confused…"

"Don't," he says abruptly. "Just don't. I can't do this to John. I *won't* do this to John. I know what it's like to watch another man swoop in…" He stops, looks at his shoes, shakes his head. "I'm no saint but even I can see there's no way this can work."

"I thought…" I can't keep the desperation from my voice. "I thought you loved me."

He looks at me and neither confirms nor denies my accusation. "I wish you all the best, Holly."

Are we wrapping up a business meeting? Is he telling me goodbye? Because that's what this sounds like. As if he can simply step out of my life. *Un*-introduce himself. Make me fall *out* of love. His words, these words, the hidden venom behind these words worm their way into my comprehension and I clutch the railing so I don't lose my balance. "Please don't shut me out."

"For the record, I always thought John was a decent guy."

"*For the record?* Seth, it's me."

He closes his eyes. "I can't be the reason. Maybe you're right. Maybe the two of you aren't going to make it, but I can't be the reason. Not after—"

The girls burst through the front door. They run to the oak tree in front of the house and make a leap for a branch.

"He's a decent guy," Seth says again. Then he walks to his daughter and as if I'm any school mom acquaintance calls over his shoulder, "Thanks for having Ava." Then he leaves me, standing there, with more broken pieces.

That night, I don't make dinner. I don't even take pizzas out of the freezer or switch on the oven. They can figure it out, the three of them. I'm not feeling well I tell my family, and go to bed. Whatever spell I've been under has broken. Everything is broken, and I am, once again, alone.

Even though I don't see Seth during the next few days, not at school, not out jogging, not when I drive past his house, I can't expel him from my mind. Annalisa, on the other hand, I run into almost every day—pushing Jackson in the stroller to and from school, chatting with the other school moms in the hall, navigating the aisles in the grocery store. We exchange nods and stilted *hellos*. If she bothered talking to me she might, to her satisfaction, discover Seth is out of the picture. Seth has torn up the picture. But she continues to punish me with her silence so remains in ignorance.

In spite of me half wishing they wouldn't, the days click by. A wedding coordinator emails me about setting up a time for a website consultation but I can't bring myself to call her. There's plenty to do, plenty I *should* do, but I walk through the hours half awake, as if I'm coming out of anesthesia. I want to return to my dreamworld, escape this reality where every little movement feels sluggish and purposeless. I try to run. I do for a few days, but eventually my long runs dwindle to short runs and then three days slip by, then a week, and now I can't remember when I last stepped into my running shoes.

John stuns me by noticing. "You're not running anymore," he says one morning as he's lacing up his work boots.

I wait for it, his chastisement on how I never finish anything.

"You seemed to like it," he merely says.

"Winter's coming," I tell him. "I don't want to run in the cold and snow."

"You should get a membership to a gym."

His words strike hard. "What are you trying to say?"

"That you should get a membership to a gym. So you can run indoors."

"Why don't you just come out and say it. I've gained weight. I've stopped running. I don't finish what I start. You win."

I retreat to the bedroom and stare at the girl—who am I

kidding—woman in the full-length mirror with greasy, shoulder length, non-extraordinary hair. I disrobe and slip out of my lounge pants and scowl at my hopelessly flabby thighs. Why would someone like Seth ever be interested in me? For that matter, why would John?

Because John's a decent guy, or so I've been told. Non-communicative, dawdling, doesn't know the first thing about partnership or romance, but *decent*.

During the next few days, I try to remind myself of this. Bizarrely, Seth's assertion of John's decency joins forces with my mother's admonishment about being grateful for my employed, non-abusive husband and Annalisa's threat to withdraw her friendship. What choice do I have now? Seth has left me with no choice. Seth has left me.

John is here. The kids are here. Maybe that can be enough. Maybe I can make them enough. I can try, at least, to make this family work. I can *try*.

After weeks of takeout and frozen pizza and cold cut sandwiches, I make a legitimate supper: oven roasted chicken. Mashed potatoes. Salad with croutons. And when Maggie, in between bites, brags about being chosen to take a recess casualty to the school nurse for a Band-Aid, I smile and nod. I'm trying. I ask Ben about his day.

His shoulders jiggle up and down. "Okay."

"Any math homework?"

He stares at his chicken.

"Are you having trouble with it?"

He shrugs.

John's shoveling mashed potatoes into his mouth. I silently plead with him to take part. Engage. *Try*. I'm trying so he should try too, because we are the little family that could. "You don't want to get behind, Ben," I tell him. "You already had one late assignment this week."

John's head shoots up. "You turned in something late? What did you turn in late?"

"Math."

"Get your work in on time."

"I *hate* it."

"Doesn't matter. You still need to turn it in on time."

Ben slumps in his seat and rolls his eyes.

"*Hey*," John barks. "Sit up straight. Show some respect."

I give John what I hope is a withering look but he doesn't notice; he's gone back to his mashed potatoes, unaware apparently, that his son has turned to stone and his eyes have turned to beads of resentment. He is so blind, my husband. Utterly blind.

"I'll help you with it after supper," I say, still looking at John. "We'll figure it out. You just need someone to help you."

John helps himself to a chicken leg.

After the table is cleared, Ben and I sit side by side, crouched over his math book. We struggle over the problems for so long I convert to his way of thinking: he's never going to use this stuff. At eight o'clock I tell Maggie to get ready for bed. She does and requests a story. I yell at John who's bonding with the TV. He doesn't respond. Blind and deaf, he is.

"John," I call again. "Maggie wants a story."

Ben deliberately falls out of his chair. I pull him up by his shirt and tap his notebook. We still have a half a page to go. The chronic *thump thump* reverberating from the hall tells me Maggie is jumping on the bed.

"John."

"What?"

"Read her a story."

He doesn't respond for a while and then, "Can't you?"

I slam Ben's textbook shut, stand up and hunt for my keys. "Here's an idea," I say to my husband. "Try being the hero at home for once."

"We haven't finished," Ben whines, on the verge of panic. I hate deserting him but if I don't get out of here right now I'm going to shatter the TV with his father's beer bottle and beat the poor dog and set that math book on fire.

I find my keys under a stack of bills. "Dad will help you. He's great at helping people."

It's raining outside. I squeal out of the driveway and roam the neighborhood before giving into temptation. Slowly, I drive past his house. The living room lights are on. Is Ava with him? Is he with anybody? Are he and his artists friends sitting around sipping espressos, discussing existentialism and Van Gogh and the affects social media has on the art of conversation? Does he ever host parties like that? It strikes me how little I know about him.

I drive past Annalisa's house. The front door boasts an autumnal wreath and squat pumpkins line the walkway. Her house, as always, radiates charm, the ideal of what a middle-class family house should be.

There is nowhere for me to go.

I keep driving anyway, my wipers angry hands slapping away the storm. Somehow, out of habit I guess, I wind up at the grocery store. I park toward the back of the lot and switch off the wipers.

Rain pelts the windshield. Streams of water course down the windows, hiding me from the world outside. No one would notice the woman weeping in her messy, not-yet-paid-for van that carts around a family who might not make it.

By the time I get home the rain has stopped. The house is quiet. Even the TV is off. I step out of my wet shoes and leave them by the door. John sits at the table, hands hidden underneath.

I start for the hall. "I'm going to bed."

"Holly."

I breathe through my nose and exhale. "What?"

A droplet of water snakes down my back. The look in John's eyes is new, unreadable. I shiver.

"How long?" he says.

"How long what?"

He rests his hands on the table. "How long have you been seeing Seth?"

I've heard wrong. I've misunderstood. But then I see what he's clutching in between his hands, in a grip so tight his knuckles are red. He's holding my phone.

19

"What are you talking about?" My voice sounds small, false. Dread rises in my stomach and works its way up my throat. "Seth and I are friends. The *girls* are friends…"

"Do you think I'm blind?" He holds up my cell phone, the phone I always tuck away in my purse or pocket, the phone I take with me everywhere. Except for tonight.

I move toward him, take the phone, skim the text from Seth that came in minutes ago.

Don't think I don't miss you. We just can't do this anymore.

I close my eyes. "It's not what you think…"

"The hell it's not." He stands and goes to the kitchen. I hear the back door fling open and thud shut.

I rush after him, the backyard cold and soggy beneath my shoeless feet. "John, wait…"

"How long?" He demands.

My heart is a bird, thrashing inside a cage. "I don't know how to answer that."

"Did you sleep with him?"

"John, how can you even ask that?" But the mortification in

my voice shames me. That morning I walked to his house, bathed and perfumed. That ripe with possibilities morning. But I wouldn't have actually done it, would I? That morning when Ben forgot his gym shoes, when everything changed. "I promise you. Whatever was going on between us, it's over." I wet my lips, take a breath. "And no. I didn't sleep with him."

He paces the length of the yard then comes back. "What *did* you do with him?"

I lower my head.

He comes at me swiftly, so quickly I fear—for the first time in my life—that he may strike. He brings his face inches away from mine. "What, Holly. What *did* you do." This is a demand, not a question.

What do I tell him? About our conversations? About the love seat? Our runs together? The kiss by his door? When, exactly, did I cross the line? I don't even know. The whole thing, the flirting, the texting, the sneaking around, suddenly seems absurd. Juvenile. As if someone else, a different Holly, acted in my place. Not me. Not Holly, wife of John. It couldn't have been me. Oh God, how could it have been me?

I begin to cry, surprised I have any tears left. "I'm sorry. It's over now. I promise."

"You *promise*. Like that means anything." He snatches my phone from my hand. "This can't be the only one." He scrolls through my texts.

"I deleted them," I tell him quietly.

He locks his jaw and breathes noisily through his nostrils. It happens so fast. He raises his arm and pitches my phone across the yard. It smacks into the back fence then falls to the wet grass. He heads to his truck. I follow. "John, please don't leave like this."

No response.

"Where are you going?"

He jumps in his truck, slams the door, and screeches out in reverse. I watch him barrel down the street, the soggy ground seeping into my socks. I don't know how long I stand there, sinking into the quagmire of our yard, my feet turning to ice, watching in vain for the lights of his truck to shine on our driveway.

It begins to drizzle. I dislodge myself from the mud, return to the house. I can't stop shivering. My fingers, tingling from numbness, peel off my saturated socks. I can't feel my feet. I can't feel much of anything.

The following morning, Ben bursts into my room. We're supposed to go to the cranberry marsh he reminds me, for the harvest. A few more minutes, I beg. Mom didn't sleep so well. Mom didn't sleep much at all, but guess what? There's a new box of Pop-Tarts in the pantry. He races out.

John never came to bed. Maybe John didn't come home at all.

I bury myself under the blankets until Maggie jumps on me, her fingers sticky with red Pop-Tart filling. I force myself to get up and get dressed.

In the kitchen, coffee floats in the pot. He's home. I don't deserve any, but I pour myself a mug and head outside to throw out the trash Bernice won't leave alone. I find John in the garage seated on an overturned plastic paint pail. He glances at me then ducks his head, goes back to whatever tool or part he's cleaning with a rag.

I toss the garbage into the bin. "I promised the kids I'd take them to Laura's. They've flooded the beds."

Bernice sits by his feet, waiting for his attention.

"We'll be home for supper," I say. "I mean, I'll be home to make supper."

Will he? Be home? With bags packed? With my bags packed? All night long, the words *I'm sorry, I'm sorry, I'm sorry* circled my mind, but voicing them now would accomplish nothing.

I haven't the right, but I want to know where he went last night. A bar? A woman? Does he hold his own secrets? I want to interrogate him, pry open his mind, his heart, his mouth, but I open mine and say, "I'll make meatloaf."

The fall colors must be breathtaking. From the backseat, my children, forced to leave their screens at home, produce a litany of exclamations as we make our way to Laura's.

"Look at that one!"

"That tree's on fire!"

"Whoa, it's so *orange*!"

Yet nature's brilliance is lost on me. I see it of course, but the colors don't register. A filmy, grey haze—a cataract—has shrouded the world. Red, orange, yellow. It's all there. But nothing penetrates. My favorite season has failed me.

We arrive at the marsh and the kids join TJ jumping in a pile of leaves. Laura meets me on the porch and I hand her the latte I picked up on the way over. "You remembered!" she says. "You're the best."

"Sorry if it's cooled off."

She takes a sip. "Perfect." She takes another, then lowers her cup and looks at me. "What's wrong?"

"What do you mean?"

"You seem down."

I shrug. "Didn't sleep last night."

"Come on in and sit down. I have cranberry bread in the oven."

Over the past few weeks, Laura has added her own touches to the house—new curtains, a runner on the table, a shelf housing her inherited Hummel collection I've always found vaguely creepy. But that high and mighty rooster still glares down at the world. Why hasn't she made Phil get rid of that thing?

Laura pulls a loaf pan from the oven and sets it on a cooling rack. "You wouldn't believe how much baking I've done since moving out here. Me. *Baking*."

"Must be something about that fresh country air," I suggest.

"Must be," she says and slides a knife around the perimeter of the loaf pan before flipping the bread over. "So, no John? Or Annalisa?"

"You're stuck with just me today."

"I'm thrilled to be stuck with just you. I just want to make sure that you and Anna have made up."

I take a sip of my Americano.

She carries the used loaf pan to the sink and fills it with water. "I take it that's a no."

"Just a misunderstanding."

"Yeah, right."

"Why? What has she told you?"

"Nothing. Anytime I ask her about it she tells me I should ask you, that *you* should tell me. So I'm asking you. What's going on?"

"A lot." I despise the tremor in my voice.

She studies me then sits down across from me, her gaze intent. "You're kind of at the bottom, aren't you?"

"What?"

"Of the pit. You're at the bottom of the pit, or close to it. I've spent enough time there to recognize it in someone else."

My eyes burn and my nose starts to run. I grab a napkin from the center basket and dab my face.

"Listen, you don't have to tell me everything if you don't want. But keep in mind, even if it may feel like there's no way out, there is."

My face is leaking uncontrollably. She leaves and returns with a Kleenex box. I blow my nose and then blurt out, "Do you blame me for Jake's death?"

"What?"

"Do you think Jake's death is partly my fault?"

Her eyebrows wrinkle together. "Are you serious? Is that what this is all about?"

"I don't know. Not really. But I have wondered."

"Why would I blame you for Jake's death?"

"I took you to see *Wicked*. If I hadn't bought the tickets and talked you into going Jake might have… he might have…"

"Died anyway?"

"But you would have been with him. You would have known

how bad he was and..."

She touches my arm. "Holly, he had an *aneurysm*. He would have had an aneurysm whether or not I went to *Wicked*."

From outside, Maggie shrieks. I glance out the window and watch Ben and TJ chase her around a tree, throwing handfuls of leaves. The question hangs between us and right now I desperately need to hear the answer. "But do you *blame* me?"

She sighs, leans back in her chair. "At first I blamed everyone, I think. The EMT's for not fixing him. The ambulance driver for not getting there fast enough. His doctor for not catching something at his last physical. Myself for not having some kind of lover's intuition. God for letting it all happen. My mother for..." she shrugs. "Who knows? Mothers are easy to blame. So, yes. I'm sure at some point or another you were included in that mix. But I wasn't thinking clearly. I wasn't *capable* of thinking clearly. I didn't even know I was blaming everyone and everything. Of course I don't blame you. I don't blame *anyone*. It just... happened."

A leftover sob escapes me.

"Holly, how long has this been bothering you?"

"I don't know. Since forever."

"Listen. You didn't drag me to *Wicked*, I wanted to go. Jake wanted me to go. Did I ever tell you his last words to me, before I left? *Have fun without me.* It's crazy but I feel like that was his blessing, his permission to live a life without him. To be happy. Even marry again if that was in the plan. I never expected to be a widow at the age of thirty-eight, not in a million years, but it happened. And it dropped me straight down to the bottom of the pit. But you can't live there. You can't build a life there. You have to keep moving, keep living. Even when you're at the bottom you're still living your life."

"So how do you get out?"

"You pray. You let others reach in and pull you out. You examine everything you believe, everything you've been taught. Especially all the stuff you learned in Sunday school about heaven and about people dying and coming back to life. *God himself* dying and coming back to life. And eventually you realize we're not meant to live here on earth forever. None of us. I mean, life is a gift but in the end we all die."

"Dead is dead."

She shakes her head and smiles. "No. Death brings life."

I don't have the energy to follow this rabbit trail right now. "I've made such a mess of things. With Annalisa. With John. With everything."

"Oh. So this is about you and John."

I grew up Lutheran. I've never been to confession. But sitting here with Laura may be the next closest thing. "Can I tell you something else?"

"Anything."

I search her face, wondering if I should actually release the words. She's looking at me so calmly, so expectantly, I figure I have nothing to lose. "I was jealous. Of you and Phil. Don't get me wrong, I was happy for you, *am* happy for you, but watching the two of you build a new life together, start from scratch, I don't know... leaves me a little envious. Of the new beginning. Not what you've gone through to get there. It's completely absurd. I'm sorry."

She doesn't speak for a minute. "Jake and I were married for over ten years. I understand how flat marriage can get. And it's not like things with Phil are going to stay fresh forever. They both have their strengths, Jake and Phil, and they both have their faults. Love helps you overlook the faults."

"And if there's no love?" I ask quietly.

She raises her eyebrows, waiting for me to elaborate. I've come this far and she hasn't kicked me out.

"I don't love John anymore and I'm pretty sure he doesn't love me."

She sits back in her chair. "You can work around that."

"I'm sorry, what?"

"Not loving each other. You can work around that. There was a time when I didn't love Jake and I'm sure there were more than a few moments when he didn't care all that much for me."

"What?"

"You can still love someone and not love them."

"*What?*"

"You can *love* someone, do what's best for them, put them first, *love* them, without *feeling* like you love them at all. You don't even have to like someone to *love* them."

"Well that sounds like hell."

"Or it could turn the whole ship around. Love when it feels impossible, when it's the last thing you feel like doing. Yes, when it feels like hell, when it feels forced. Love with actions. Die to yourself. Let death bring life."

To my knowledge, she knows nothing of Seth. "What if I'm stuck with the wrong person? What if my soul mate is.... is out there and I'm missing out?"

"I loved Jake and now I love Phil. Jake drove me nuts and guess what? So can Phil. Already. The point is, *make* John the right person. *Make* him your soul mate."

"But that takes two people, doesn't it? Two people communicating with each other. Two people trying to make it work."

"That does make it easier," she concedes. "But sometimes if one person changes, the other follows. Not always, but sometimes. It's worth a try. But Holly, there is no single, right person. They made up that notion to sell movies. Those are fairy tales. Fairies don't actually exist, neither do their tales."

"Wow. Don't ever work for Hollywood."

"Look, it's all fun, all those rom-coms, but they're not *real*. My question is, do you *want* to make it work with John?"

"I don't know. I guess." I look out the window again. Ben's reclining in a metal red wagon as Maggie plays horse, pulling him around. What would it be like to sit my children down and tell them their dad and I are splitting up? Serve them their own blueberry pancake morning? Logistically, realistically, how would I manage the whole single parent thing? The back and forth, trading and dividing holidays and weekends?

The truth is, what I'm leaving out of this confession is that it's no longer up to me. Now it's up to John. Does *he* want to make it work, or is he planning his escape? "I think it's too late for us," I say.

"It's never too late." She gets up and throws away her paper cup. "Come on. I want to show you the bog."

The flooding started a couple nights ago, Laura explains as we walk along the gravel road toward the cranberry beds, our three children trailing. As we draw nearer, brilliant blue water meets red berries, all cloistered together from the wind. Maybe my conversation with Laura proved cathartic, washed the film from my eyes, because these colors penetrate. Blue, red, green, and blue again. Water, berries, land, and sky. Crisp and distinct, like a clearly defined map.

We continue down the road, past beds that have yet to be flooded, beds currently being flooded, and flooded beds undergoing harvest. We pass trucks and machines and men in waders.

"Those beaters," Laura says, pointing to a tractor-like machine rumbling through the water, "are stirring up the berries, knocking them from the vine."

In the machine's quake, liberated berries rise to the surface of the water. We walk to where men in waders stand thigh deep in water, corralling berries with special looking rakes. A machine with some kind of tube appears to be sucking berries and shooting them into the back of a truck. One of the men approaches. TJ runs out to meet him. "Welcome, Holly," Phil says when he sees me.

"This is something," I say, watching the tube shoot berries into the back of a truck.

"Want to go in?" He hooks his thumb toward a flooded bed.

"In?"

"We'll put you in waders."

"I want to go in!" Maggie pipes up. "I'll go! I'll go!"

"You kids will all get a chance," Phil says, "but first Holly."

The rubber waders wear like suspenders and rise above my waist. I take Phil's proffered hand and ease down the slope into the water.

"You've got this Holly," Laura cheers from the sidelines as if I'm on some reality TV sports show.

It takes a second to find my balance. Then I let go of Phil's hand and follow him further into the bog, the water making a gentle swooshing sound against our rubber legs. Blue gives way to red and soon I'm surrounded by tiny, crimson spheres. I scoop up a handful and let them dribble back into the water one by one. *Plop plop plop.* Here I am, standing in the middle of a thousand cheery little balls, bobbing along, clamoring against my thighs. I laugh, the sensation so foreign after these past few days. "They're beautiful," I say to Phil. "Just beautiful."

He grins, the pride evident on his face. This is a man in love with his land. He scans his crop. "They are. All the work comes down to this harvest."

"Will it be a good harvest?" To my untrained eyes there looks to be enough cranberries to feed the whole country.

"Yes. As long as the weather cooperates."

"What do you mean?"

"A hard frost can wipe out the berries, be the difference between a good harvest and a bumper crop."

"What do you do if there's a frost?"

"Irrigate. Keep flooding the beds to keep the berries from freezing. And pray. "

"If a hard frost could kill them now, in the fall, how do you protect the plants in the winter?"

"Same thing. Flood the vines. Gotta protect the vines. No vines, no berries."

I consider the tangle of hidden vines under my feet that produced this fruit. I pluck out a single berry and hold it to the sun. It's not entirely red, I realize, but flecked with brown and even green. Ever since I was a kid, cranberry sauce garnishes our table every Thanksgiving and cylinders of concentrated cranberry juice line my freezer door. But I've never thought about how it all happens, how they grow, how they need to be protected, how they're harvested when the time is right. "So much work," I murmur holding the berry in between my thumb and forefinger.

"Sure. But it's worth it."

As far as my eyes can see, I see nothing but silent berries nodding in the sun. I close my palm around the single sphere. "Thank you for bringing me here."

He smiles and, like the gentleman he is, tips his hat.

20

I am terrified to run.

My Nikes, with their electric blue laces, taunt me from where they sit by the back door. Twice I've spotted Seth on school grounds. Twice I've changed directions. The thought of running into him fills me with such anxiety I mostly stay inside, even though the air is perfectly crisp and the sidewalks are covered with leaves just waiting to be crunched under foot. But I can't risk facing him so I huddle inside my house and miss these favored, golden days of fall.

John and I adopt the type of cold politeness that exists between strangers. We only exchange words necessary for living with two dependents. *Can you pick up Ben at three? Running to the store. Maggie threw up; no more sugar for her.* He's taken to sleeping on the futon in the basement while I wallow in my guilt alone in our bed.

I'm used to John's reticence, but this silence is different. This silence is heavy and thick, clinging to all of us like oppressive humidity. A part of me wishes for the storm, for him to burst and and let the words *divorce* or *separation* pour out so I can breathe again. But this dragged-out deliberation—will he stay, will he go, will he ask me to go—could last indefinitely. We could allow the weeks to turn to months to turn to years and never speak of the Seth episode, never speak of any of the factors that brought us to this point. The thought of carrying on the charade, propping up our withered marriage for the sake of children and friends and pretense, makes me want to run away. But I am afraid to run.

Yes, I was the unfaithful one, the obvious culprit, but John is not blameless. Laura's question has stumped me. *Do I want to make it work?* Depends on the day. Sometimes the hour. What I want, what I've wanted for months I think, is to start over. But how is that possible after fifteen years of marriage? How do you plant something new, let alone make it grow, when there's nothing but barren, desert ground? Dead isn't dead, so my friends like to tell me. If that's so, how do you resurrect the dead?

This morning I rise early. Perhaps subconsciously motivated by Laura's pep-talk, I make eggs and sausage while John's in the shower. When we were first married I used to do this all the time. But somewhere between work and kids and dogs and bills, cooking breakfast sausage lost priority. Right now, with the links sizzling in the pan and the aroma spreading through the house, I wonder why I didn't keep it at the top of the list.

John appears, his hair still wet. I hand him a plate with scrambled eggs and two links. He looks at me in surprise. "Thanks."

I nod and divide the remaining links for the kids.

He carries his plate to the table and sits down. When he's finished eating, he puts the plate and the fork in the dishwasher. Without exchanging a word, we assemble his lunch. Before he steps out the back door he turns to me. "Thanks for breakfast."

"You're welcome. Have a good day."

I wake up the kids by announcing there's breakfast sausage. Maggie eats hers in between two toaster waffles and asks if Ava can come over after school.

I take a sip of coffee and attempt to redirect her. "What about Jasmine?"

Recently, Maggie has fallen under the spell of Jasmine, the new girl from California. She's gorgeous, with waist-length jet-black hair and a clear desire to rule the world. I don't know why Maggie puts up with her.

"No. Ava. Ava hasn't been here in *forever*."

Secretly, I'd prefer Ava to Jasmine any day, but I'm up against a wall. "It just doesn't work."

Maggie wants to know why and of course and I have no sufficient answer. We argue, until I ultimately throw down the "because I said so" card, and she slams the door on her way out to school.

On Tuesday, John tells me he'll be working up north, leveling a parking lot. He's not sure how long he'll be gone. *Will you come back?* I silently ask as he leaves.

On Wednesday, Maggie announces she won the class spelling bee and has the certificate to prove it.

On Thursday, after staying up past his bedtime to finish a science project, Ben rushes to where I'm paying bills at my desk. "Did you brush?" I ask without looking up.

"Bernice is breathing weird."

"She's probably just snoring."

"No. Something's wrong. Come on, Mom. Listen to her."

I look up from my checkbook. His furrowed brow and solemn blue eyes soften me. He takes me by the hand—a beautiful rarity these days—and leads me to where Bernice is laying on her pillow. Even before I step into the room I hear her. Ben's right; something is wrong. Her breathing is labored, desperate sounding, as if she can't get air into her body fast enough. Thankfully Maggie's already tucked in for the night, otherwise she'd be in hysterics.

I kneel down beside Bernice, my fingers sinking into her lush red fur like they've done hundreds of times before. Her heartbeat feels dangerously fast and she has a frantic look in her eyes.

"Should we take her to the vet?"

"The vet's closed," I tell him. "But maybe they have emergency hours or something. Go get my phone." But my phone's been destroyed. I haven't replaced it since John smashed it against the fence. Being demoted to the landline seems like an apt punishment. "Get the phone book."

"The what?"

"Never mind." I hurry to my laptop.

"I'll stay here with Bernice." He positions his face beside hers and says in a surprisingly calm tone, "Good girl. You're a good girl. It's okay, girl."

I tear my eyes away from the scene, type the name of my vet into my search engine. Bernice intakes a ragged breath.

"What if she's dying? What if she dies when Dad's not home?"

How I want to tell him that would never happen, but what do I know. Powerless to do anything else, I click open the website, click on *emergency*.

"I'm calling Dad." He jumps up, runs to the kitchen, and returns with the cordless. "Dad," he says, beside Bernice again. "It's me. Mom's okay and Maggie's okay and I'm okay but something's wrong with Bernice. She can't breathe." His voice cracks.

It dawns on me that I should be handling this. Me. The parent. I should be relaying the bad news to John.

"Listen." Ben holds the phone close to Bernice then brings it back to his ear. "See? What should we do?" He's quiet, listening to John. He nods, says "okay" a couple of times, hangs up, and turns to me. "Dad thinks we should take her to the vet."

I nod dumbly and head to the closet for a blanket. Isn't that what you're supposed to do? Don't they do that in the movies, wrap the dog in an old blanket? But she's sixty pounds. I'm not sure if I can lift her. Maybe, since she's not unconscious, I only need to click on her leash and lead her to the van.

I pass Maggie's room and stop short. *Maggie*. She's sleeping. I can't just leave her. Annalisa and I haven't talked in days, weeks, but this is an emergency. If I asked, she'd be here.

"Mom!" The fear in my son's voice prompts me to drop the blanket and run. I crouch down beside Bernice who's wheezing and stretched out in an unnatural way.

"Bernice, Bernice!" Ben lays his head on this creature that's been a part of his world since before he could remember. "I'm right here, girl. I'm right here."

He doesn't let go of her, doesn't shy away when her body grows still and the terrible wheezing stops. He doesn't look at me in question; he knows. We're paralyzed for a moment, him nuzzled up to Bernice, me nestled close to him, my hand on the back of my boy who's turning into a man right before my eyes.

John gets home late that night, shortly after I managed to pull Ben away from Bernice and get him into bed. He fell asleep crying while I sat on the edge of his bed, crying with him and rubbing his back.

John crouches down beside Bernice for a long time, stroking her head. I linger in the living room. He tells me he's going to place her in the bed of his truck. Then he wraps her in the blanket and carries her out. He's gone longer than what the task requires and when he returns his eyes are red.

He sinks down onto the couch. I give him the play-by-play while he unlaces his boots and peels off his socks. "Ben was amazing," I conclude. "So grownup, so mature."

He rubs his face with his hands. "Wish I would have been here."

I do too. I don't know how to voice this without it sounding like chastisement.

We sit in our quiet house on either ends of the couch, our kids in bed, our dog gone forever. I brush away a tear. John glances at me, then looks straight ahead. Seconds later, he stretches his arm, plants it on the back of the couch, and gives my shoulder a squeeze. One squeeze. Enough to prompt more tears. In spite of everything, everything I've done and everything he hasn't done, I want him to to pull me to him. To hold me and let me cry.

But he gives a little sniff, then stands and heads down to the basement. I can't move from the couch.

Bernice was just shy of two, not even out of the puppy stage, when we brought Ben home from the hospital. I feared she'd be jealous. Still topped by his hospital beanie, I placed the car seat, with Ben in it, in the center of the living room and pointed my finger at Bernice. "This is the new baby," I said. "You are no longer the baby. *He* is the baby. You are not the baby, you are the *protector*. Understand?" John chuckled, but to this day I'm convinced Bernice understood. She looked at her tiny, red-faced master and prostrated herself, nose on paws. I rubbed her head and told her she was a good girl, but things were different now and she was going to have to get used to it. Things were different. In all her years, she's never made a vicious move toward either of the children, even when they deserved it.

The next morning, all four of us drive to the marsh. As John and Ben dig the grave, Maggie, Laura, Phil, TJ and I stand and watch. After ten minutes of hollowing out the earth, Phil steps forward and offers to take over for Ben. Ben declines. John does as well.

When the ground is ready, John lifts one side of the blanket and looks to Ben to grab the other. Ben bursts into tears. "How can we do this? How can we put her down there?" He shields his face with his hands, ashamed to be crying in public. I want to wrap my arms around him and hold him forever.

I place my hands on his shoulders, shoulders that seem to be gaining breadth by the day and pull him toward me. "Because she's gone, honey. She's dead. And when someone is dead this is what you do. You bury them. You tell them you love them, you remember them, and you put them in the ground and let them go."

Phil grabs the other end of the blanket. He and John drop Bernice into the gaping earth, the weight of her body making a heartrending thud. Maggie wails. I tuck her close to my side and wonder if having the kids witness this was a good idea. But across from me stands TJ and I know it's not excessive, it's necessary. Death has confronted my children and there's no easing the blow.

I hand Maggie a tissue and spot two figures walking toward us from the direction of the house. They crest the hill and three smaller ones follow. I look to John. "Did you call them?"

"*I* called them," Ben snaps. "They loved Bernice too. Antonio would want to be here, so *I* called them."

John rests his hand on Ben's head for a moment. "Good thinking, son."

In silence, Annalisa and her clan join our circle. The boys are holding handfuls of dried prairie grass, weeds mostly, they must have picked on the walk over, October's leftovers. When Annalisa passes behind me she touches me on my back.

We stand there, the twelve of us, and stare down into the dirt hole that holds my dog. Nobody speaks. Finally, Maggie pipes up. "I wrote a poem."

I smile at her. "Would you like to read it?"

She extracts a piece of notebook paper from her coat pocket. "To Bernice." She clears her throat and tosses her hair back. Even in genuine grief she's relishing the spotlight.

"Bernice is my dog who is really nice.

She likes to play and doesn't bite.

She sleeps on a pillow and rests her head.

But now she won't because she's dead."

I squeeze my eyes shut. John, beside me, makes a low, throaty sound. I chance a peek at Annalisa who's covering her mouth with a tissue. "Thank you, Maggie," I manage. "That was... very sweet."

"It took me a long time to think of a word that rhymes with *dead*."

Laura is the first to break. "Oh Maggie, you're a gem. We needed to hear your poem. Thank you for sharing it." She wipes her eyes with the back of her hands and laughs without shame.

The sky rumbles.

"We should get on with this," John says and picks up a shovel.

I take in Ben's stony face. "Do you want to say anything, Ben?"

He rubs his nose then shoves his hands into the front pocket of his sweatshirt. "Bernice was a real good dog. She always listened to me. She's the one I talk to when I get angry or something. Like if I got a bad grade or something. I'd talk to her. Or if mom and dad were fighting. She was the one I'd talk to."

A drop of rain lands on the back of my neck. I close my eyes. I want to disappear, sink into the ground with Bernice. I tuck my hands into my jacket pockets and feel, of all things, a dog treat.

"Thanks Ben," John says. "We better beat the storm." He and Phil begin to cover Bernice with dirt. Surprisingly, the children don't cry again.

After she's buried, and after Ben and Maggie position the rock they've drawn on with Sharpies to mark her grave, Annalisa and Laura and their families start off for the house, giving the four of us the opportunity to linger. We circle Bernice's grave. Maggie is the first to verbalize her goodbye. Softly, we all follow her lead.

John turns to leave. Maggie joins him and slides her hand into his. Ben sniffles and follows. From my pocket, I extract the dog treat I've been rubbing in-between my thumb and forefinger, dust off the lint, and lay it next to the stone. "Good dog," I say, "Good dog, Bernice."

I turn to follow my family.

And then I realize where I am, where we've been standing all this time. The curve in the dirt path and the boulder on my right confirms it. My dead dog lies beneath the ground where I once sat in the darkness and listened to crickets and frogs. Where I offered pieces of my heart to another man.

I double my pace and catch up to my family.

At the house, we gather around the table with mugs of coffee and hot chocolate. I catch Annalisa glancing at me and I can't help but wonder, again, what she's told Marco. Paranoia has become my frequent companion. What do they know? What, if anything, has Annalisa told them?

Phil turns to John. "How long did you have Bernice?"

"Thirteen years. Almost as long as we've been married."

My head shoots up, surprised he included this detail.

"Wasn't she a gift, Holly?" Laura asks. "For your birthday or Christmas?"

I nod, wanting that to be the end of it. Maggie however, who's been playing with a rocking horse in the living room, rushes to my side. "Tell the story! Tell the story!"

I do not want to tell the story. I do not want to sit here and fall apart from grief or guilt or both and narrate a story that showcases the wonderfulness of John.

"Maybe you should tell it," I tell her.

She's thrilled. She sits up and waits until she has everyone's full attention. "Daddy got Bernice when she was just a tiny little puppy," she says, cupping her hands around an invisible tennis ball, "and he put her in a box under the tree and on Christmas morning she popped out!" Her hands explode open. "And Daddy said they should name her Bernice because of her red hair. Because Bernice is my mom's favorite aunt and *she* had red hair, too. And she'd just died. So they named Bernice *Bernice* because of *Aunt* Bernice. She's the aunt Mom lived with for a whole summer after Grandma and Grandpa got the divorce a long, long time ago—"

"Yes, Maggie," I cut in. "Bernice was named after my aunt Bernice. My favorite aunt."

Maggie sighs. "And now both Bernices are dead."

I reach over and smooth her hair.

"Both Bernices were very special," Annalisa, who met Aunt Bernice on several occasions, says.

Eventually the conversation picks up again, slipping into the comfortable, to things other than life and death and divorce and marriage. From across the table I glance at John. He's staring into his mug as if it holds the answers to all of life's questions.

21

A day after we bury Bernice, the kids and I drive to the humane society to donate her food and leftover treats. Later on, when I'm alone at the grocery store and unintentionally find myself in the dog food aisle, I burst into tears. Later that night, Maggie wants to drag Bernice's pillow into her room and sleep on it. John tells her no. I agree. If we give in she'll never let the ratty thing go. I throw Bernice's favorite plush toy in the washer, tell Maggie she can have it after it dries, and hand Ben Bernice's dog tags.

Amputees reach out to scratch phantom itches. They forget that what used to be there—what has been there forever—no longer exists. That's what this feels like. That's what I find myself doing; reaching out to pet a dog no longer at my feet. Patting the couch at night. Grabbing the leash before I go for a run. A portion of our family has been hacked off. *Whack!* Like when John took an axe to a dead branch on our cherry blossom tree.

By the end of the week, both kids are asking when we we're getting another dog.

"I don't know," John tells them. "Let's wait and see."

Wait and see for what? the kids want to know.

But I know. Wait and see if we're going to make it, because families on the verge of tumbling over the edge don't get new dogs.

A couple of days before Halloween, Ben hands me a bright orange sheet of paper informing me I've been drafted to provide a healthy snack for the fifth grade party. I ask Ben what healthy Halloween snack he thinks his class might enjoy.

"Candy?"

I sigh. "Exactly."

We decide on dried fruit, mostly raisins and chopped dried apricots to keep with the black and orange theme, then rebelliously toss in handfuls of chocolate chips.

After dropping Maggie off at her classroom, I carry the ice cream bucket filled with our moderately healthy Halloween snack to Ben's classroom and set it on the counter at the back of the room. Annalisa enters with Jackson in the stroller and removes two jugs of apple juice from the stroller basket.

Jackson writhes and reaches out to me. "Ya yee!"

I wave at him. How many times have I simply reached out and scooped him up? Now I feel like I need a parental release form.

"You want to see Holly, don't you?" Annalisa says, unclasping his safety belt. "Do you mind?" she asks me.

I hold out my hands. "Are you kidding?"

She drops him in my arms and he hugs me around the neck.

"He's always loved you," she says.

It's true. I have no idea what I ever did to win this beautiful child's affections, but he's adored me from the very start. I ask him about the train he's holding and we converse for a few minutes. "He's talking so well now," I say to Annalisa.

"He'll be three next month."

"How can you be turning three?" I ask him over and over again until he giggles.

The first bell rings. Students flood into the classroom. I see Ben and wave goodbye. Annalisa tells Jackson it's time to get back into the stroller but he loudly objects.

"It's okay," I say as we step into the hall. "I've got him."

By the time we reach the main doors to the outside world, he's wriggling for freedom. I set him down.

"I wanted you to know," Annalisa says, taking his hand to cross the street. "I know John found out."

"Oh."

"I could just tell, by the look on his face, when he showed up at our house wanting to talk to Marco."

"When was that?"

"A couple of weeks ago," she says. "Before Bernice died. I'm glad you told him, Holly."

I ingest this information. The night he found out, the night he demolished my phone, John fled to Marco's. Not to a bar like I've been imagining. I pull my sweater tighter around myself. "I didn't tell him. He found out. He read one of my texts."

"Oh. Well, I wasn't in on the conversation. I only know he and Marco talked well into the night."

Jackson brings me a pinecone. I examine it, tell him it's a keeper. "And I should probably tell you, it's over. With Seth. We're not even talking."

I glance at her, see the relief relax her features. "How are you doing with it?"

I fix my eyes on the approaching stop sign. "Do you want me to tell you the truth, or what you want to hear?"

"The truth."

"I miss him. I know I shouldn't, but I do."

She remains quiet.

"And I'm not sure what to do about the girls. I can't make them stop being friends."

"I didn't even consider that. Do you know Ava's mom? Can you arrange play dates and things with her?"

"Yes, when Ava's with her but she's usually at Seth's."

"You need to stay away from him. Entirely."

"You make him sound like a rabid dog."

She stops walking and looks at me. "You almost left your husband because of him."

We continue on and wave to an older man raking his yard. "The thing is," I finally say, "I don't know what John wants. I'm not sure he wants to work it out between us."

"What do you mean? Of course he does."

I shake my head. "I'm not so sure."

"He's with you, isn't he?"

"Barely. He's sleeping in the basement. Most days I think he's forming his getaway plan. We haven't talked about anything."

"You haven't?"

"No. Not a word since he found out. I'm not sure if I'm supposed to bring it up or what."

"You have to talk about it. If you want to get through it together, you're going to have to talk about it."

"I know that. Tell it to John. That's the problem. We don't talk. Not just about Seth but he doesn't want to talk about much of anything. And I know you don't want to hear it but I can't go on like this. And please don't lecture me. Please don't tell me you'll pray. You're not walking in my shoes."

"You're right. I'm not walking in your shoes." She's silent for a minute. "Why do you think that is?"

"What?"

"John. Not wanting to talk."

"I don't know. I think it has a lot to do with his Dad and how he didn't talk. Repressed emotions and all that stuff."

"Stuff a counselor could help him work through."

"Gee, Anna. What a great idea."

"I'm sorry. I'm not trying to sound like I have all the answers. But can I at least tell you how proud I am of you for breaking it off?"

I nod, not about to tell her I had zero choice in the matter.

The first Saturday in November it snows. Only a fine powder covers the lawn but the kids dig out their winter gear and find the sleds and go outside and roll around. I check emails at my desk and now and again glimpse them from the window, their laughter brightening this otherwise grey, mundane day.

John appears and stands at the window. He's looking at the children, but he doesn't appear to be watching them. "I've been thinking."

I fix my eyes on my computer screen. Today. It's all crashing down today.

He picks up my stapler, spins it around in his hand. "Maybe… you and I…"

From my periphery, I catch the bright pink flash of Maggie's snow pants as she dashes across the yard. The last thing I want to do today is bust up this limping little family. Maybe John and I screw up eighty percent of the time, but we two, as defective as we might be, are the only parents those kids have. They're laughing in the yard. Where will they be ten minutes from now, when they topple through the door asking for hot chocolate? What will they find? That life as they know it is careening toward a cliff? I've been trying. Why can't John try? Why can't John fight for us? Stop stringing me along, I want to scream. Put me out of my misery already. "What, John? What do you want to say?"

He stops twirling the stapler. "Forget it."

I can't walk this minefield any longer. "No. Just tell me."

He slams the stapler down on my desk. "Do you want to go out for dinner."

"Dinner?"

"Yes."

"You mean the two of us?"

"Yes."

Nothing could have prepared me for this. "Oh."

"Look, do you want to or not?"

"Tonight?"

"Tonight."

From outside, Maggie squeals. Ben's trying to stuff snow down her back. "Okay," I say, turning back to face him. "Sure."

"Be ready at six."

"Six."

He nods and walks away. I turn back to my computer screen and position my hands over the keyboard but they're trembling too much to type.

I spring from my chair. Head to the kitchen. Grip the counter and try to slow my heartbeat. He didn't ask me for a divorce. I think he just asked me out.

At lunchtime, when I'm feeding the kids tomato soup and grilled cheese, I wonder if John thought to arrange a babysitter. Ben is eleven, old enough to stay home with Maggie for an hour or so, but does John realize he doesn't like being home alone after dark? Should I ask about the plan? No. This was John's idea. He can arrange the details, or let the whole thing sink.

At a quarter to six I hear a knock on my door before Annalisa lets herself in. "Who wants to go to my house for pizza and a Wii tournament?" she calls out.

Maggie and Ben stare at her with eager eyes.

"Grab your coats and let's go!" she says.

The kids whoop and run off.

I shake my head. "You. You arranged all this."

"I arranged nothing. John merely asked me if I'd take the kids tonight." She gives me the once over and scowls. "Is that what you're wearing?"

I peer down at my jeans and black sweater. "I was going to put on a scarf."

She rolls her eyes. "Come on, Holly. This is a *date*. Go put on that blue dress."

"It's sleeveless. I'll freeze to death."

She heaves a sigh, takes me by the hand, and drags me down the hall to my room. "Make yourself at home," I mutter. Yet I can't help grinning. This feels like *before*.

She combs through the contents of my closet until she finds the navy dress. Then she flips through hangers again, holds up my red cardigan, drapes it over the dress, puts it back. She pulls out my long brown wrap, scrutinizes it, puts it back. When her hand hits my faded, fitted denim jacket she smiles. She drapes the jacket over the dress and then kneels down and starts rummaging through my shoes. After a minute she tosses out my chestnut slouch boots. "You have tights, right?"

Not waiting for an answer, she makes a beeline for my dresser. "This," she says, holding out a long silver chain with the turquoise pendant, "and this." She holds out the charm bracelet, the one with the dangly crystals. I take it from her and obediently fasten it around my wrist.

"There," she says, eyeing the ensemble on the bed. "A tad country chic but you can pull it off." She turns to me. "This is a date, Holly. A *date*." And she slips through my door, calls for my kids, and I'm left with nothing to do but change clothes.

Although I've passed it a number of times, I've never set foot in the Italian bistro that opened downtown last year. As soon as we step inside, I'm glad Annalisa forced me to change. "Nice," I say taking in the candlelit tables. "Swanky."

"Marco recommended it."

"Then we know it'll be good."

We're seated at a corner table. We study the menu, order, and are left alone with a basket of bread. Wordlessly, we dip pieces of bread into seasoned olive oil and examine the photographs of Venice and Rome lining the walls. We glance at the people around us. We take note of the food the waiters carry.

When the bread basket is empty, John clears his throat. "How is work?"

He's trying. I'll give him that. "Fine. I finished the gymnastics site, thank God."

"And they like it?"

"Finally. The owner is this finicky little cat of a woman. Nitpicky about colors and font sizes and things she knows nothing about. How about you?"

He shrugs. "Work is work."

I nod. We stare at the empty bread basket.

"So, do you still plan to go through with it?" he asks.

I stiffen. We've only just arrived. We've only just finished our bread and already he's questioning if things are truly over with Seth.

"The half marathon," he says.

"Oh." I take a sip of water. "I don't know. I probably shouldn't have signed up in the first place."

He brushes a crumb from the table. "I think you should do it."

"So we're not out the registration fee. Yeah, I know."

"No. Because you wanted to do it. You trained. You ran your butt off. You should do it."

"I can only do eight miles right now."

"When is it?"

"April."

He counts on his fingers. "That's five months. You could work up to thirteen miles in that time."

"You think so?"

"Yeah. Sure."

Our salads arrive and I spend a minute redistributing my dressing. "How do you think the kids are doing? Without Bernice I mean."

"They seem to be handling it okay."

"Ben tries not to cry at night."

He looks at me, evidently surprised. "He does?"

"Sometimes I hear him crying behind his closed door." I eradicate a red onion from my salad. "What do you think about their idea of getting another dog?"

He finishes chewing and takes a drink of water. "I'd be up for that."

"You would? Me too."

"What about for Christmas?"

I smile. A real, unforced smile. "I love that idea. We could put her in a box, like you did with Bernice. Can you imagine their faces? They'd have so much fun with a puppy."

"A puppy?" he says. "Who said anything about a puppy?"

"Oh come on. Can't you imagine Maggie with a puppy?"

"Puppies pee. All over the place."

"But they're so sweet."

"So much work."

"I know, but the kids are old enough to do the work. And it's not like they don't know how to take care of a dog after all of their years with Bernice. That reminds me, Ben asked an interesting question the other day. He wanted to know what happened to Bernice, like if she had a soul. He wanted to know if she'd go to heaven or be reincarnated or if she was she just gone."

"Huh."

"Yeah, I said I wasn't sure. And then he asked about people, if they went to heaven when they die.'" I pop a colossal crouton in my mouth and chomp it as quietly as I can.

"What did you tell him?"

"I told him I wasn't sure about that either. A lot of people think there's a heaven, but I told him I didn't know, there was no way of knowing for sure."

John looks at me for a second and then starts sifting through his salad.

The waiter stops by and tops off our water glasses. "This dressing is amazing," I say to John after the waiter leaves. "I think it has fresh basil in it."

"So, what *do* you think?"

I take another bite. "Yep. Basil."

"No, about heaven."

"What do I think about heaven?"

"Yeah."

"Oh. I don't know. It's a nice concept. I'd like to *think* there's a heaven, I'd like to think Aunt Bernice is up there, wherever *up there* is, but who knows? There's no way to prove it so I'm not sure how strongly we should sell it to the kids. Annalisa has bought into the notion hook line and sinker but that's her, at least ever since she's joined the whole Jesus-is-the-only-way club."

"Marco believes the same thing. And about hell, too."

"Doesn't that seem a little arrogant? I mean, how do they know? And how can they say Jesus is the only way to heaven, *if* there is a heaven? I love them to pieces but sometimes they come across as a little smug."

"Yeah. But I wonder sometimes. Maybe they're right. Laura and Phil too. They basically believe the same thing."

"How did the two of us get mixed up with such a religious bunch?"

He smiles.

"They're all probably waiting for us to *see the light*," I drawl in my best southern Baptist impersonation. "Hear from the *Lawd*."

His eyes dart around the room.

"Sorry. Didn't mean for my fire and brimstone to get so loud."

The waiter presents us with our entrées. I poke my fork into a tortellini. I savor a bite and insist John try the cream sauce.

"The other night," John says after laying a sample portion of his lasagna on my bread plate, "Marco asked me if I wanted to go. To church."

"Annalisa used to ask me all the time. I think she's kinda given up. Now it's only once every few months. Of course she says she prays for me all the time, but I don't mind that."

"Maybe we should go."

"To church? You mean at Christmas."

He shrugs. "Or before."

I stare at him, dumbfounded. "You want to go to church?"

"Might be good for the kids. Ben's asking all of these questions anyway. Can't hurt. Seems like we need to do *something*." Just like that the mood shifts. Jaw set, he peers at his plate. How close to the surface does his rage lie?

I stir my tortellini. Of course he wants to get me inside of a church. What else is he supposed to do with his wayward wife? Yet I know he's right; we need to do *something*. In all our years of marriage it's always been me, not him, that's dragged the four of us to church, me who signs up the kids for the weeklong summer program at Annalisa's church, me who makes everyone quiet down and listen to Linus read the Christmas story. This is what I've wanted all along, for John to engage. Take part. Try. As awkward and bumbling as this feels, this is him trying.

"John," I say, waiting until he looks me in the eye, "you're right. Let's do it. We'll just show up without telling any of them. Won't that throw them off?"

He grins, and the tension holding us loses its grip.

On the drive home he misses the turn for Annalisa's street. "They're staying the night," he tells me when I point this out.

"Oh. Okay."

We approach Hoover Elementary. I glance down the dark alley where it happened and notice John does the same. "Has the trial date been set yet?"

"Probably won't be until after the new year."

Whenever it's scheduled for, John will have to testify, an event I'm sure he's dreading. I've long stopped milking him for information, even though so many questions about the whole incident niggle at the back of my mind. Tonight's conversation flowed smoother and deeper than it has in months so I decide to try my luck. "Can I ask you something about that morning?"

I take his silence as a yes.

"Why'd you bring Ben his shoes? I mean, don't get me wrong, thank God you did, but we both know it's not the first time the kid's forgotten something. Your standard response is 'deal with it'. So why was this time different?"

"At first I told him to deal with it. I told him he needed to be more responsible."

"But you brought the shoes."

He drives another block without a word. I stare out the

window and determine that even if the conversation ends here, tonight edged on a miracle. He's here beside me, driving me home from dinner. Trying to nudge us forward. This can be enough. This can be a start.

He pulls into our driveway and shifts into park. I move to get out of the truck but he says, "I couldn't get back to work. I couldn't do anything until I dropped off those stupid shoes."

The moment is precarious, thin. If I utter the wrong word, the conversation might disintegrate. I say nothing, ask nothing, only give him my attention.

He rubs his chin with his fingers. "It was like something, or somebody, told me to go. *Now*. To get in the truck. So I did. And I don't know why but when I was heading toward the school I just happened to look down the alley and saw the van. Something didn't feel right. And then I saw him, yanking her by the arms. Everything happened so fast. I got out. He saw me. He let go of her. I grabbed him by the back of his shirt, he turned around and kneed me in the gut—"

"He kneed you in the gut?"

"Knocked the wind out of me."

"And then you got in the truck? Chased after him?"

"Took a second to get my breath back but yeah. I only had an eighth of a tank of gas, maybe not even that. I followed him to highway 29, kept glancing at the gauge, hoping there'd be enough. I'd run the thing dry until the police came."

I can see it. I see the knee in his gut. I see him stumbling into his truck, foot slamming the pedal, eyes darting to the fuel gauge as he tears through town. "When the police came, what'd you do?"

"Two squad cars came racing up from behind us. The guy had nowhere to go. He pulled over and I pulled over behind him. I got out of the truck but an officer told me to get back in. So I just sat there, watching the guy get cuffed." His jaw locks in place again as he stares at our closed garage door. "He almost had her in his van."

The thought makes my skin crawl. We sit in silence, warm air wafting steadily through the vents. "If you had caught him before the police did," I venture, "what would you have done?"

He tightens his grip on the steering wheel. "The whole time I was chasing him, I kept thinking of Maggie." He turns to look at me. "I might be facing my own criminal charges, I guess. What I keep wondering is, what if I had never brought the shoes?"

I touch his arm. "But you did. You *did* bring the shoes."

"I wasn't going to at first. I had a lot going on that day."

I have to look away. I had a lot going on that day too. Or so I thought.

He clicks off the heat but I don't want to leave the truck. I don't want to give up this moment. I turn to him again. "So this voice you heard..."

"It wasn't a voice."

"Okay, this... whatever it was. What was that all about?"

He rests his elbow on his side window and turns to look at our dim house, the house I intermittently love and hate. I hate the drafty windows and small, outdated kitchen but I love the original wood floors and flower boxes and how it looks draped with Christmas lights.

Evidently John has taken my question as rhetorical. I feel for the door handle.

"Holly?"

I sit back. "Yes?"

Even in the darkness I can see he's wrestling internally, trying to line up his words just so. "That voice, or whatever it was...."

"Yes?"

Something tells me not to move, not to disturb the connection, as thin as a spider web, forming between us. Finally, he looks at me. "I think it was God."

I nod. Turn back to face the garage.

I hear him exhale, as if this conversation, this admission, perhaps this whole night, has drained him dry.

"I believe you," I say. John has his faults, but he's no liar.

He exits the truck and I follow him to the back door of our house, the heels on my boots clicking along the cement path. As I follow him, my breath visible in the cold, the story plays again in my mind: him taking a knee in the stomach, racing through town, running out the gas tank to protect Ava—and therefore Maggie. Chasing evil until it's captured.

I stop in my tracks. Dear God. This man is a hero.

He's fitting the key into the door when I step up behind him, rest my head on his back, the leather of his jacket cool against my cheek. I know this scent so well. I inhale, drink it in, and he seems to stiffen. I slip my right hand inside his unzipped jacket and press my palm against his chest until I can feel his heartbeat. I have no idea if this okay, if he wants me to touch him at all, but he brings his hand inside his coat and covers mine. I stand on my tiptoes and softly kiss the back of his neck.

Snow begins to fall. The crystals touching my face provide a tantalizing contrast to the heat I can hardly believe is catching between us. "I'm sorry," I whisper. "I'm so sorry."

He turns around, sweeps his hand underneath my hair that now falls just to my shoulders.

I close my eyes for a moment. "And I'm sorry about my hair."

He tugs on the ends and smirks. "I kinda like your hair."

Before I can talk myself out of it, before I let my mind race down the treacherous path of past hurts and future uncertainties, I grab his coat, pull him to me, and kiss him. Snowflakes land on my cheek and our kissing grows slower, deeper, better. "Let's," I murmur in the in-between, "go inside."

He opens the door and ushers me in, his hand steady on the small of my back as he guides me through our warm, waiting house.

22

Tori's condo is spotless. Even the color scheme, white and grey, feels crisp and calculating, like the room is just waiting to call foul on a pair of muddy sneakers. Where does Ava keep her toys? I wipe my feet on the welcome mat then pull off my boots anyway and gesture for Maggie to do the same.

"Thanks for coming today Maggie!" Tori says with too much enthusiasm.

"You're welcome."

I help Maggie out of her coat. At some point I should explain that the appropriate response is something along the lines of *thanks for inviting me* but I kind of like her youthful literalness. When Tori opens the front closet to hang up Maggie's coat, I steal a peek. Organized. Freakishly so. Beige, cloth-covered boxes with nothing hanging out line the top shelves. Hangers evenly spaced. Two pairs of boots positioned on a mat on the gleaming tile floor. It's November; the plows have already been out. The floor should at least show traces of sand.

Ava prances into the living room holding two safety suckers still wearing their plastic sheaths and hands the purple one to

Maggie. "Not in here," Tori says. "In the kitchen, peanut."

At my house her daughter hacks the hair off dolls with tattooed rear-ends and eats popsicles on Maggie's bed, and she kind of seems to like it. "Does five work?" I ask.

"Perfect."

We stand in the entryway, smiling at each other, and my old foe Paranoia sweeps in. For all I know, Seth could have told her everything. I force myself to focus on the girls, now at the kitchen table, suckers inserted. Ava's procured a plastic container of Little Ponies and she and Maggie are arranging them on the table. Anxiety is rising—what does Tori know?—but I transfer my attention to Ava. "How is she doing?"

"Better all the time. We've been taking her to a psychologist to help her process the whole thing. Some of the things that come out..." She studies me, as if she's trying to decide something. "Hold on a minute. Let me show you." She disappears for a moment and returns with a piece of paper. She steps into the living room, out of sight of the girls, and beckons me to do the same. Would she have invited me on the white carpet had I stayed in my boots?

"One of her drawings," she says and hands me the paper.

It consists of a crayon-drawn rectangle with wheels—a van I assume—with three figures beside it. The smallest figure, in the middle of the other two, bears a frowny face and brown hair. The figure closest to the van, with angry, downturned slashes for eyes, stretches his disproportionately long arms toward the smallest figure. The third figure, with yellow dots for hair and a bright red smile, stands the tallest by far. His stick arm just touches the arm of the girl.

"Dr. Korten says this is a good sign," Tori explains, "that she made John the biggest, bigger than The Bad Guy. Ava sees John as her helper. Dr. Korten always comes back to that, how there are bad people in the world but there are also good people, people who will help you, people you can trust."

I study this simple depiction of my husband. "This is lovely."

"I cry every time I look at it."

I nod and hand it back to her.

"Would you like to keep it? Show it to John?"

"Oh no, I wouldn't dream of taking this from you."

"Trust me, I have four others. John's the big smiling hero in every single one. Keep it. Maybe it'll help him process everything too."

"Thank you."

We walk back to the entryway. The girls have abandoned the ponies and I wonder if Tori is the kind of mom who will call them back to clean up before they go on to their next, sanctioned activity.

"So you probably know that Ava will be with me for a while," she says, running a finger across the top of the half wall that separates the living space from the entryway, as if checking for dust. "Seth needs to figure things out."

I shove one foot into my boot. "What do you mean?"

"Oh, I thought you knew."

I thrust in the other foot. "I'm not sure what you're talking about."

"About the house? Sorry. I assumed Seth would have mentioned it to you, or that you saw the sign in his yard."

"He's moving?"

"Not by choice."

The pieces aren't fitting together. "So... is he moving to Madison?"

She laughs. "Hardly. Don't think he could afford Madison. He's hoping to find an apartment in the area. He should have sold the house years ago but Seth's not one to live in reality."

I take a stab. "The starving artist thing."

"It was charming for about a year. Until the bills piled up."

I nod as if I understand more than I do.

"Believe it or not I want the best for him, but he needs to get his act together." The girls are nowhere in sight but she lowers her voice. "If he wants shared custody with Ava, which he does, he needs to find a two bedroom which means he might need to find a steady job that gives him a steady paycheck."

"He'll lose his studio," I realize out loud.

"Yeah. It's sad, but this is nothing new. The phrase 'he's not good with money' doesn't even come close. It's more like he refuses to accept reality. I mean you can only sweet-talk the bank so many times before they slam you with a foreclosure notice. He's always been like that. When Ava was a baby, when we were barely making ends meet, you know what he did? He bought an oil painting done by one of his college buddies for fifteen hundred dollars. *Fifteen hundred dollars.* We didn't have rent money. It never even crossed his mind that we might need things like food or diapers." She waves her hand in the air as if she can erase this last anecdote. "Anyway, I assumed you knew about the house. Or if you didn't, I thought you should know."

Because I'm Maggie's mom and it'll affect play dates? Or is she warning me on a more personal level? "Sure. Thanks."

I call out a goodbye to Maggie and Tori sees me out the door.

When I pull into my driveway, I find John on a ladder by the basketball hoop cranking on a socket wrench. "Didn't want the thing to come crashing down," he says when he sees me.

"Thanks." I watch him work and wait until he climbs down. "I want to show you something."

I hand him Ava's drawing and recap the psychologist's interpretation. He nods and I can't tell if he's touched or indifferent. He gives the paper back to me, collapses the ladder, and drags it into the garage. "So the girls are still friends."

"Yeah, they get along really well. They saw a lot of each other over the summer..." The implication of my words silences me. "Ava's at Tori's. She'll be at Tori's place more often than... than at her dad's. I'll pick Maggie up from Tori's this afternoon," I clarify yet again.

John crouches down, snaps the socket wrench back into its case, then straightens and stares at the shelves in the garage.

"John, can we talk?"

"We are."

"Yes, but can we… *talk*."

He comes out of the garage holding a jug of windshield washer fluid and pops open the hood to the van. "Shoot."

I haul out a lawn chair from the garage, unfold it next to the van, and sit down. As he works, John repositions himself until his rear faces me. In my musings, the framework for this conversation has always looked differently; maybe we'd be on the couch, or talking over coffee, eye to eye. Yet all of our significant discussions, it seems, are fated to happen on the driveway. The tension has eased ever since our dinner out—and the subsequent interlude in the bedroom—but the bond between us, if it can even be called that, is thin. I'm walking across what I hope is a frozen lake. I'm feeling my way toward him with careful, tentative steps. One wrong move, one wrong step, and the whole thing may give underneath our feet and down I'll go. We'll go.

"John," I try again. "Can you stop for a minute?"

"Need to get this done. Might snow tonight."

"But I really feel like we should talk."

He chuckles a little. "Okay let's talk."

But where do I start? How do I sift through twelve years of marriage and pick out the grains of hurt that accumulated into resentment? In our tangled marriage, Seth is one of many knots, albeit a big one. How do I show I'm sorry while insisting on change? "I want you to know I'll be arranging play-dates and things with Ava's mom from now on."

"So you've said."

"What I mean is, I won't be seeing him anymore. That's what I want you to know."

He says nothing, his head hidden in the open mouth of the van.

"I never meant for any of it to happen. I never meant for a friendship to… to go too far."

He's pouring blue fluid in my van, so I can see through the snow and get home safely.

"I'm not trying to make excuses for myself but, so often, I feel like you and I are strangers. Sometimes I don't feel any connection with you at all."

"But you did with him."

Now I'm relieved we're not face to face. "Yes. But I want us to make it. I hope we can move past this."

He twists the cap back on the jug. "Did you kiss him?"

I look down at my hands in my lap. "Yes."

He's turned away.

"I'm sorry." I've used up the word, squeezed out every last drop of its meaning.

He carries the blue jug to the garage.

"It's not an excuse, but I just get so lonely."

"And everything's just perfect for me."

"What do you mean?"

He spins around, slams the jug on his workbench. "Damn it Holly. You act like…" He shakes his head.

"I act like what?"

"Like you're the only one who has ever wanted *out*. You don't think I've wanted out? You don't think I've had my opportunities?"

My throat goes dry. "Then I guess we need to talk more. I don't know what you're thinking or what you're dealing with because you never *talk* to me. I'm always trying to get you to talk."

"And I'm the one toeing the line. While you're off running, God knows where, I *toe the line*."

I close my eyes. His words ignite a literal mental picture. I see him, head down, toe right where it should be, in front of the white line of a racetrack. And there's me, twenty feet ahead. Running like a madwoman. Running after Seth. "I know. I know you have. I guess you're stronger than me."

He laughs. One angry bleat. "You think so? That's what you think?" He goes back to the van.

The thought, the image, of John with another woman, saying or doing the things I said or did with Seth… for a moment I can't breathe. If it had been John instead of me, where would I be? At my mother's? Annalisa's? Not here fixing basketball hoops or winterizing the van. Not cleaning up dishes or doing anybody's laundry.

I stand, go to him. "I want us to work. I don't want you to leave. Please don't leave me."

He doesn't say anything. He turns and drifts back into the garage. After a minute I fold up the chair and put it away and head back to the house.

I'm opening the back door when I hear him. "I'm not planning on it."

That afternoon, before the sun disappears, I go for a run. The air is chilly but the sun is bright. I run downtown, past the antique shop where we found Laura's dress. Past the gymnastics place whose website took me forever to finish. Past the bistro where John and I dunked bread into olive oil and contemplated heaven.

On the way back, I run down Cherry Street. I want to see the sign in the yard for myself. His studio lights are on and his car is in the driveway. I dash across the street and run home.

23

"I'm sick of being the only girl," Maggie grumbles a few days later. "And now I don't even have Bernice."

"Jana's a girl," I point out.

"She doesn't count," she says, collapsing face down on the living room floor. "She's the *babysitter*."

I step over her and she makes a grab for my ankle but misses. I hurry to the kitchen to set out paper plates and napkins and check to see there's enough lemonade. Then I rush to my bedroom for earrings. John's changing into a green polo. "Black," I remind him. "Annalisa said wear all black."

He yanks the shirt over his head and stares into his closest. I thrust a silver hoop through my earlobe, go to his closet and pull out his dark grey fleece. "Close enough," I say handing it to him.

Our door flings opens. Still facedown on the floor, Maggie worms her way into the bedroom using only her arms.

I wiggle in the second earring. "Did you break your legs, Maggie?"

"Yes. *You* broke them. They're too sad to work."

"Pity."

"I want to go to Marco's birthday party. Why can't I go to Marco's party?"

"It's not really a party," I tell her. "It's just a dinner. For grownups. You'd be bored."

"Then why do all their dumb kids have to come here?"

"Because of the party. I mean *dinner*. And stop it, Maggie. You like playing with Lucas and TJ and taking care of Jackson."

"No I don't. I *hate* them."

"That's enough," John commands and she slithers out.

Minutes later the doorbell rings. Antonio, Lucas, Jackson, TJ, and Laura stumble in. Laura warns all the boys to behave themselves. She'll see me in five she says, and scoots out the door. When Jana The Babysitter arrives, I head to Maggie's bedroom. Three homemade signs, attached to her door with stickers, greet me:

No boys aloud
Boys are gross
If you're a boy go away cuz you stink

I knock on the door. "The last one's my favorite. Jana's here."

No reply.

"See you later Alligator."

I wait for her response but she only throws something innocuous sounding at the door, like a stuffed animal. I tell her goodbye and walk away.

In the living room, Jana the Babysitter is attempting—bless her heart—to get the boys started on a game of Payday. There are pizzas in the freezer, I tell her, apples in the fridge, and a snarly little Maggie in her room. I grab the gift Maggie helped me wrap with newspaper and duct tape and head out with John.

We shut ourselves into the welcome silence of the truck. John nods at the package in my lap. "What'd we get him?"

"A nose hair trimmer and five brochures to the best retirement homes in the country."

He smirks. "How thoughtful of us."

The inside of Annalisa's house sounds like the Haunted Mansion at Disneyland.

"Funeral dirges," Annalisa says, beaming. "I found it at the library. Isn't it great?" Even her fingernails are painted black.

"It's horrible," I say pushing past the black and grey streamers cascading from the entryway. "Nice touch."

On the table sits a cake topped with black icing and sturdy 4 and 0 candles. The man of the hour appears, looking like an assassin in head-to-toe black, and gives me a hug and pounds John on the back. We obligatorily razz him about how old he is and how terrible he looks.

Laura looks uncharacteristically sophisticated tonight. Apart from Jake's funeral, which hardly counts, I've never seen her dressed in all black. She's let her bangs grow out but she's kept up with the highlights. "Marriage suits you," I tell her as she and I follow Annalisa to the kitchen. "You look wonderful."

"Thank you," she says, and blushes slightly. "How's the running going?"

"I joined the Y to get me through winter. I've met another runner who's training for the same half. She's a single mom who's lost over seventy-five pounds in two years. So I figure if she can do it, I can too."

Annalisa, slicing bread at the counter, glances up at me and smiles.

Dinner consists of a bountiful spread of appetizers. I check on the artichoke dip I'm warming in the oven and turn up the heat.

"You coming to church tomorrow?" Annalisa asks, transferring the bread to a platter.

"If John wants to."

John wants to, I already know. What's even more surprising is I do, too. No lighting bolts or voices from God when we attended last Sunday, but being there felt right. Sometimes, when I remember to water my plants after a period of neglect, they perk right up. That's what it felt like, sitting in church as a family. Like we'd been watered.

Annalisa sets out wine glasses. I find her corkscrew, pop the cork, and begin to pour.

"Oh, none for me thanks," Laura says when I try to hand her a glass.

"But it's white." The fact that Laura prefers white wine drives Phil crazy.

She doesn't look up; she's overly focused on arranging her squares of pepper-jack cheese.

"Laura?" I try again.

"No thanks."

Annalisa stops chopping strawberries. We both watch her.

"What?" she finally says. "Can't a girl refuse a glass of wine?" She clicks her tongue in exasperation and exits the room. Annalisa and I look at each other for a second and follow.

The men are still in the living room, merrily jabbering over the funeral dirges. Phil places an arm around Laura. A *protective* arm.

"I'm pouring wine," I announce, holding up the bottle. "Who wants wine?"

All three men, plus Annalisa, give their assent.

"Laura?" I ask in mock innocence. "Wine?"

She's trying not to giggle and exchanges a look with Phil. "These two aren't going to leave me alone," she tells him.

Phil shrugs amicably.

Annalisa grabs a remote, clicks off the dismal piano chords, and looks at Laura expectantly.

Laura shakes her head. "This is Marco's night."

"We'll sing to him later," Annalisa promises. "You go first."

"Seeing as you two aren't going to drop it." Laura looks up at a beaming Phil. "Well, it looks like this coming fall we'll have more than a crop of cranberries to show off."

Marco, holding a bowl of nuts, pops an almond into his mouth. "You growing pumpkins too?"

Laura lets out a little laugh. "Just one, Marco. We're growing *one* little pumpkin. At least, I think there's only one."

She's hardly gotten the words out before Annalisa and I rush her. We wrap our arms around her and jump up and down. "We just found out," she says after we let her go. "We were planning on waiting a little while before telling anybody, a few weeks maybe. Or at least until after dinner. TJ doesn't even know so *no telling.*"

"Please," I say to Laura, "for Maggie's sake, please have a girl."

Laura throws her head back and laughs. "I'll do my best. Honestly, I never thought I'd be here again." She's not even close to showing, but she rests a hand on her belly anyway. "I was beginning to think I was too old."

"Apparently not," I say.

TJ's conception took some doing and, before he died, Laura and Jake were trying again. In fact, she had just convinced Jake to see a fertility specialist. A few weeks after the funeral, someone from their clinic called and asked Laura if she'd like to reschedule her missed appointment. Laura never told me how she handled it. Maybe she erupted into tears or slammed down the phone or screamed profanities or simply said *that won't be necessary.* So many of her dreams died right along with Jake, she once said. Having more children was at the top of the list.

I watch her now—so animated, so pretty—and marvel at what can happen in two years. In the grand timeline of life, two years is nothing. Yet here she is, her dream resurrected. Alive and soon to be kicking in fact. Dead isn't always dead.

Annalisa mixes a kiddy cocktail for Laura before we gather at the table. Marco hoists his glass. "To Phil and Laura's new life together, and to their new little life."

I glance at the faces surrounding me. What if I had missed this? I slip my hand under the table and rest it on John's knee. Briefly, his hand finds mine. Then we pass food and swap stories and dream of the future with our friends.

When we return home, Jana the Babysitter meets us at the door. "She's locked herself in her room and I can't get her to come out."

Laura, who's followed me over to collect the children that

aren't mine, gives me cash for Jana and a *have fun with that* look.

"She came out for pizza and for part of the movie," Jana continues as we start down the hall, "and then I don't know what happened but she locked herself in her room and won't come out. I tried everything… ice cream, games, I told her we could play Barbies. Nothing worked."

At Maggie's door, I rap lightly and then try the knob. The door opens.

Jana's eyes double in size. "It was locked. I swear it was locked."

"Oh trust me, I believe you." I slip her her due payment, apologize for Maggie, and as she spins on her heel to go home to her tranquil, single life, wonder if I'll ever see her again.

I push on Maggie's door but it won't open any further. I nudge it until I'm able to squeeze through. A jumbled barricade of books and toys and stuffed animals meets me. "Maggie?"

The still made bed holds no conspicuous lumps. A rustling sound comes from the closet. I open the door and spot a big toe. Part of me wants to grab it and haul the little goblin out but I'm not ready to give up my euphoria just yet. "So, my darling. How was your night? Good, I hope?"

A folded up piece of paper comes sailing toward me. *TO MOM* is written on the front in all caps. I open it.

Dear Mom,
    I hate Ben. I'm not talking to him again. Don't make me. You can't make me. I'm not talking to him for forever.
Love,
Margaret Anne Lewis

Full signature and everything. She's not monkeying around. "Bad night, huh?"

"I hate him."

"Maggie. You have to stop saying that. You can't say you hate somebody just because you're mad. No more saying *hate*."

She thrusts her legs out straight toward me, two angry skinny sticks. The rest of her body remains hidden behind dresses.

"When Jana told you to unlock the door and come out, you needed to come out. You have to listen to the babysitter. You know that."

"She doesn't know anything. She didn't stop them when they were mean, when they called me Baggy Maggie. And Ben started calling me Gaggy Maggie. He said, 'Maggie you make me gaggie and they all laughed."

"That wasn't nice. He shouldn't have done that. I'll talk to him."

"I *hate* my name."

I sigh. "I suppose we could start calling you Margaret. I doubt they'll be able to find anything to rhyme with that." I examine her note. "Your cursive is getting really good."

Her toes wiggle.

"Did I ever tell you why we named you Margaret?"

"Because you'd already used up Bernice?"

I swallow a laugh. "No. That's not why. Have you ever heard of Margaret Thatcher?"

"She was at the wax museum."

I part the sea of dresses so I can see her. "Oh, so you've *met* Margaret Thatcher. I never knew how famous you were. So you may remember that Margaret Thatcher was the prime minister—the leader—of England. Long before I was pregnant with you, when I was in college, I did a big paper on Margaret Thatcher and I kind of fell in love with her. You know why? Because she was the first woman prime minister *ever*. She was the only lady in this great big group of men. But you don't know what that's like, right? Being the only girl with a bunch of boys?"

She glares at me. "It sucks."

"Maggie. Please don't use that word. Anyway, Margaret Thatcher had a nickname."

"Baggie Maggie?"

"No. People called her the Iron lady."

She inches forward, her eyebrows slanted together. "Why?"

"Because when she made up her mind about something, that was it. She wouldn't change her mind. She kept her promises and she didn't let people talk her out of what she believed to be right and she led her country through some really hard times. So they called her the Iron Lady because she was strong in her beliefs, strong like iron. You know the bars you like to twirl on at recess? Those are made of iron. You can't bend them, right? That was Margaret Thatcher. She wouldn't bend. She was strong."

"So I was strong when I was born?"

I smile at this breathtaking creature, and at the secret little life nestled deep inside of Laura. "In a way, yes. Strong set of lungs, that's for sure. That's what the nurses said. When Daddy and I first got to the hospital, before you were born, we were still deciding on a name for you. Olivia or Margaret. You were either going to be Olivia or Margaret. Then you came out, screaming your head off, even after the nurses cleaned you up and laid you on my chest you just went right on screaming. Daddy and I looked at each other and said, 'Margaret'."

Maggie giggles and crawls into my lap. Her hair is sticking up all over from static. I smooth down the strands. "Our Maggie. And just like Margaret Thatcher, when you decide to do something, you do it. When you make up your mind, there's no stopping you. And that's a really good thing. Most of the time. But *sometimes*, when we realize we've done a wrong thing, or said the wrong thing, we have to change."

She rolls her eyes. "You're gonna say I have to talk to Ben."

"Well, not tonight. He hurt your feelings and he needs to apologize. You don't have to talk to him tonight."

"Not tomorrow either."

"Fine, not tomorrow. But forever? That's a long time, don't you think?"

"No," she says jutting out her chin. "I could do it."

I kiss her head. "I'm sure you could."

From where I'm sitting on the floor, I pull open her top

dresser drawer and feel around for a clean set of pajamas. She peels off her shirt and I tug the pajama top over her head, her hair fanning out like the sun again.

"Mom," she says, looking at me with those rich chocolate eyes, "I bet Margaret Thatcher had to put 'no boys allowed signs' all over her door too."

24

After the hubbub of Thanksgiving, winter rages in full force. In the mornings, with the temperatures lingering in the single digits, I tout the benefits of long underwear and knee-high socks but my kids defy me, leaving me no choice but to mummify them with scarves on their way out the door.

Laura is throwing up twice a day now. The only thing that tastes good, she says, are lemon flavored Starbursts. "And I can't live on those," she laments over the phone.

"Must be a girl," I tell her.

"Maybe. I only threw up once with TJ and that was because I was so hungry all the time I ate everything in sight." I ask when she'll find out the gender and she says in another month or so. "And if it is a girl we're painting the room pale pink. If Philip lets me get near paint, that is. That man has gone paranoid."

"He's a new daddy. It's sweet."

"Yes, but someone needs to tell him the heat from the oven is not going to burn the baby."

I check my casserole browning in the oven. "I don't know, Laura. I think you're missing an opportunity here. I'd go with it.

And I'd tell him that throwing clothes into the washing machine leaves you nauseated."

Laura laughs. "You're good, Holly. Really good."

Maggie gets to play Mrs. Claus in the second and third grade holiday program. The morning of the performance, I do my best to knot her sleek hair into a bun and promise to be in the audience at two o'clock. Like many working parents, John can't make it. Part of me wishes I had an easy out too, but I can't *not* attend.

Maybe sensing my anxiety, Annalisa offers to pick me up. We shuffle into the school cafeteria with other parents and younger siblings and find vacant folding chairs in the fourth row.

Maggie delivers her lines with confidence and flair. Lucas plays a reindeer and Ava is an elf. Before she recites her line into the microphone, Ava smiles shyly at the audience. "Hurry, Santa, Hurry," she says, still grinning. "It's almost Christmas Eve!"

A couple rows in front of me, over to my right, I spy Seth. A charcoal scarf wraps his neck and he's sporting a new haircut.

After the performance, we squish into one of the classrooms for cookies and punch. I've just bitten off the foot from a store-bought gingerbread man when I catch Seth's eye. He smiles, tips his head slightly, then gives me his profile.

Beside me, Annalisa clears her throat. "All set?"

I watch Seth disappear into a group of parents.

I zip up my coat and scan the room for Maggie. "All set," I tell her and smile.

On Christmas morning, I reach out my hand to find John's side of the bed empty. It's still dark, just after six, and miraculously the kids are still sleeping. It was after one in the morning by the time I crawled into bed, but the stockings are stuffed and the presents are wrapped and waiting under the tree. All but one. I push the covers aside, the cold air bites my bare feet.

John creeps into the dark room. "No, no," he whispers. "Back in bed."

"Get back in bed?"

"Yes. Back in bed."

"John. Seriously, we don't have time…" But I see that he's holding something, a mug with steam rising.

Happily, I climb under the covers again. He waits until I'm propped up with pillows before handing me the mug. I bring it close to my face, the steam bathes my cheeks, the rich, reassuring aroma permeates the room. Coffee in bed on Christmas morning. Just like when we were first married. Just like when the kids were babies. "Christmas coffee," I whisper. "I can't believe you remembered."

He sits on the edge of the bed. "I missed a few years but I thought it was time to reinstate the tradition."

I run my hand over the side of his face, his stubble tickling my palm. "Thank you." I pat his side of the bed. "Join me."

"But we have to—"

"I know. We will. But first, sit with me."

He walks around the other side of the bed, opens the window blinds, and gets in. I hand him the mug. He takes a sip and hands it back to me. I sip and then whisper, "You make good coffee."

"I do make good coffee."

The horizon outside is tinged a deep purple, heralding the dawn. I nestle closer to him, clutching the coffee close to my chest. "Are we ready for this?"

He chuckles. "Too late now."

"When are we supposed to get her from Marco's?"

"Anytime. He said come anytime after six."

"The kids are going to flip."

"You don't think they suspect?"

"No," I say. "No clue. Maggie's going to scream her head off."

He reaches for the mug and takes another drink. "Do you think they'll want to keep the name Tootsie?"

"I don't know," I say. "I kinda like it. But we can let them decide. After all, she'll be their dog."

"Theirs to walk, theirs to feed, theirs to clean up after."

"That's right."

We found Tootsie, a Beagle/Lab mix puppy, on Petfinder a couple of weeks ago. Her bio asserted she was "as sweet as her name" and I begged John to at least go meet her with me. The minute I laid eyes on the creature I wanted to wrap her in my coat and take her home. She's the Poky Little Puppy in the flesh. After I kissed and cuddled her I passed her to John. Tootsie worked her magic as she nuzzled her face into his neck and promptly fell asleep.

The shelter agreed to hold Tootsie for us until Christmas Eve day, as long as we signed all the papers and paid the adoption fee. Yesterday, I picked her up and brought her straight to Annalisa's for her one night hotel stay.

"Is the box ready?" John asks.

"Wrapped and ready to go. The lid is pretty light. Hopefully she'll just pop right out."

"After I get her from Marco's, I'll go through the back door and head straight for the basement."

"I'll tell the kids I forgot something and meet you down there. She may cry and give herself away. They might figure it out before we get the chance to get her under the tree."

He thinks for a moment. "Put on Christmas music. Loud Christmas music. Put on that stupid chipmunk song. The kids like that one. That'll drown her out."

"Good idea. I hate that song." I snuggle closer to him.

He takes another swig of coffee and hands me the mug. "I better go. The kids will be up soon."

"We won't start without you," I promise. He stands but I pull him back. "John." I have morning breath, he has morning breath, but I kiss him anyway. "Thank you."

He drags his fingers through my hair that once again falls just past my chin. Who knew he'd prefer it short? "Merry Christmas," he says and steals out.

I lean back against the pillows, lingering in what will most likely be the only quiet moment of the day. Soon wrapping paper will be flying and the kids will be bouncing and screaming and a puppy will be romping around, chewing and peeing on everything.

The lights from John's truck flash through the window. I watch him back out the last little way of our driveway and zoom down the street.

Coffee in hand, I tiptoe down the hall. Maggie's stirring in bed, coming out of sleep. Bring on the chaos.

I head to the family room, click on the Christmas tree lights, and cue up the chipmunk song. Outside, darkness wanes. I watch out the window as timid sunlight grows bolder, and wait for my husband to come home.

25

The kids can't get enough of Tootsie. Except at five o'clock in the morning when she whines to go outside. At that hour, no one but me seems to hear her. For as memorable as Christmas morning was, when I stand shivering in our backyard on cold, dark January mornings waiting for Tootsie to do her business, I wonder what possessed us to get a puppy in the dead of winter. But then she scampers across the room toward one of the kids, falling over her too-big paws, and I fall in love with her all over again.

Winter break winds down and school reconvenes. One afternoon, after the final bell, Ben's teacher beckons me into her classroom. Ben's math is declining, she says. It's important for him to keep up in math because the concepts he's learning now are the building blocks for algebra. As if this twenty-three year old fresh from the dormitory is telling me something new. Perhaps, she continues, her voice rising in an patronizing way, we should go ahead and formulate an IEP? I accept the packet of math sheets she's holding and tell her let's wait and see if a little more practice at home might help.

"You could help him every now and then you know," I tell

John later that night after dinner.

He sighs. "Holly, I get home pretty late most nights."

"And park yourself in front of the TV. And don't even tell the kids goodnight some nights."

He doesn't cast me a glance because his eyes are too fixated on that wretched screen.

I go back to the kitchen to deal with the supper dishes and holler for Ben to get out his math homework. Minutes later, I hear Ben's book thud on the table. Not long after that I hear pencils roll across the table then clatter to the floor. Soon after, he's on the floor.

I storm into the family room, find the remote, and click off the TV. "Time to tune in to the drama that's happening right here."

John pushes himself from his chair and joins Ben at the table. I'm wiping down the counter when I hear John bellow, "Come on. Everything you need to know is right here. Now solve the problem."

I peek around the corner. Ben's slouched in his chair, his eyes glazed.

"Sit up," John commands. "Read the problem again."

Ben grinds his elbows into the table and mumbles through the narrative of Pedro and the candy bars he needs to sell. Some with nuts, some without nuts. The same sad story problem that's been recycled down through the ages.

"Now use the formula," John says. "Plug in the numbers."

Ben rakes his fingers through his hair. "I don't *get* it."

"Use your brain. It tells you what to do right here."

"John," I say from the kitchen, "he doesn't get it."

"That's why I'm *helping*."

"You're not helping. You're yelling."

He glares at me. "We're doing fine."

I let out a brittle laugh. "This is fine?"

"Look. You wanted me to help, I'm helping."

I throw down my dish rag and walk into the dining room. "Help yes, not make it worse. You know what? Forget it. Just forget it." I motion for John to get out of his chair.

He doesn't move. "Holly, leave."

I stare at him. "Excuse me?"

"You're interfering. Get *out*."

"No. You're doing nothing but yelling."

"We were doing just fine until you butted in."

"You know that? Just go and watch your damn TV."

I move around the table to claim the other chair beside Ben, but John blocks me. I try to sidestep him, try to push past his arms, but he's an iron pillar. "It can't always be your way, Holly. Get out."

"Fine. You've got it all figured out, John. You know best. You know how to *patiently explain* to your son when he *doesn't understand*. I swear, sometimes you don't have a clue."

"Yeah, well sorry for not being Mr. Perfect."

I freeze.

"I'm sure *he'd* handle this just how you'd like. Maybe you should text him. Ask him what I should do.

"Stop it John."

"Maybe you can cry on his shoulder, tell him what a rotten husband you have."

"Ben," I say quietly, "go to your room."

"No," John commands. "Stay where you are."

Ben's eyes ping pong between these two idiotic people he has to call his parents.

"Fine," I say. "I'm leaving, all right? Happy?"

"Oh, so happy. Great. *Get out*."

Ben's bottom lip is quivering. I want to hug him, tell him this fight has nothing to do with him or Pedro and his stupid candy bars. I want to tell him I'm sorry for how nasty his dad is acting, for how I've yelled and fed into the madness. But John stands there, fists on hips, like a some kind of security guard.

Maggie creeps into the room, clutching her ratty baby blanket she keeps tucked under her bed until she needs it. "Mommy? Where are you going?" We've reduced her to *mommy*.

"Out, apparently. I'm going out." I grab my running shoes from underneath the coffee table.

Maggie follows me. "But you need to sign my permission slip. To go sing at the old people home."

I pull my laces tight. "Ask your dad. He'll take care of it. He'll take care of everything."

If I stay any longer, I'll break down. I'll stay. I'll gather them both in my arms and rush them into the bedroom and lock the door. But John's made it clear, he wants me *out*. So that's what he'll get. Let him deal with homework and tears and permission slips and bedtime.

I thrust my arms through my fleece, zip up, and step outside to Maggie's whines of *Mommy don't leave*.

My anger fuels me, and I feel little else. But by the time I reach the end of my driveway, it registers that arctic wind slices across my cheeks, my hands, any patch of exposed skin. I search my pockets for keys or gloves but find nothing. I can't go back. I won't allow myself to go back.

Even if John only meant for me to get out of the room, or take the van somewhere, this serves him right. Serves him right I'm out here in a blizzard. When he realizes what he's done, he'll be sorry.

Bare branches knock against each other above my head. The sky spits ice. As I run, the disparity between my internal temperature and the air around me leaves my lungs feeling like they'll burst. The insides of my nostrils are thoroughly frozen. I can't feel my fingers. But I keep running. Serves him right.

I run until I see his house. His lights are on. I have no intention of stopping; I only want to remember. To find strength maybe, or to feel something good.

I make out a figure wheeling a garbage can down the driveway. He positions it by the curb. Arm raised to shield himself from Mother Nature's fit, he squints at me. "Holly?"

I'm approaching the end of his driveway now.

"What are you doing out here?" he says. "You're crazy."

I nod. "Seth."

"Do you know we're under a winter storm warning?" He shouts over the wind. "Nobody runs in this kind of weather. Not even me."

"Guess I'm a real runner then." I can't keep my teeth from chattering.

"Let me at least get you a hat," he calls as I jog past. "A *hat*, Holly. Come in for a *hat*."

My ears burn from the cold. I stop, turn, and follow him up the driveway.

When I step into his house, heat prickles my flesh. He disappears into the next room and returns with a blanket which he throws over my shoulders. "People die in this kind of cold. I don't want to read about you in the paper tomorrow. At least you had enough sense not to drag poor Bernice out in this."

"Bernice died."

He stares at me for a moment. "Oh. I'm so sorry. When?"

"October."

He sighs. "I'm sure that was hard on you."

"It was hard on all of us." My children. My *husband*. I want to throttle him, but my *husband*. I cup my hands and blow into my palms. "You said something about a hat?"

He snaps his fingers. "That's right." He opens his front closet. A basketball and a yardstick spill out. He grabs a brown paper bag from the top shelf, rummages through it, casts it aside. He grabs a plastic bin from the floor, pushes past a hammer and a few roadmaps, and pulls out a brown stocking cap. He scavenges some more and extracts a pair of navy gloves. "You have to take the gloves, too. Can't let you leave without them."

"Okay. Thanks." I tug on the hat.

He grins. No doubt I look like Lucy Ricardo trapped in her meat freezer with icicles hanging off her eyelashes. "So you're still training?" he says.

I nod. "And I see you're moving?"

"Just across town, to an apartment above the bakery on Main. Although business in Madison continues to grow so I might move there yet."

Ava flashes to mind. How would she do with another change in schools? "Oh. Well, I should be—"

"Look. Holly. I just want to say, I'm sorry. For how things turned out. I never meant to hurt you."

"Oh. I know," I say as if he didn't hurt me at all.

"It was just that under the circumstances—"

"Of course. We were... wrong. It needed to stop."

"Yeah, I suppose so." His eyes rest steady on me. "But I gotta tell you, I miss you." He's looking at me with unequivocal yearning. To my alarm—and delight—something lifts within me. Even like this, red-nosed and soggy, he misses me. He *wants* me.

But John.

I take a step backward, pretend his words don't rouse me. Act like I don't recognize how his eyes glimmer with desire. I hold out my hand for the gloves. He opens one of the gloves and holds it out, like you do for a child, and waits for me to slide my hand inside. When I do his hand closes tight around mine.

"Holly. I don't know. Sometimes I think... maybe you and I..." He steps closer and I'm warmed to the core. "Man, I want to be with you."

His eyes are pulling me in, pulling me under, and everything in me wants to stay and swim in this warm loveliness. Curl up with him on the couch and cry and laugh and talk and kiss and who knows what else. I'm falling. I'm drowning, sinking fast, and I need to kick and fight until I break through the surface. I need to leave.

I need to make myself leave.

I look at my hand, held captive by a glove that probably once belonged to Tori. I pull away, so abruptly I yank my hand out of the glove, leaving Seth clutching the limp fingertips. "I have to go."

He tries to say something but I speak over his words. "No."

He's warning me about the cold, he can give me a ride home, he says.

"*No.*" The volume of my voice startles both of us. I sound just like Maggie. The mantra in my head is loud and steady. *Run*. I reach behind me for the doorknob and fall out the front door. I flee into the night.

I can finish what I started. I can show John I don't quit. I can go home.

But I'm running, I realize, in a different direction. I run until I reach Annalisa's house. I pound on the door with my red, raw fist.

"Holly," she says when she opens the door. "You're shivering. Get in here."

"Help. I need help."

I step inside and she begins to briskly rub my shoulders with the palms of her hands.

"I'm falling. I don't want to fall again..."

She stops rubbing. Her eyes scan my body for injury, for an explanation. "Honey, what are you talking about? Did you fall? Are you hurt?"

The tears I thought were frozen solid begin to drop. Annalisa grows still. Her features relax. She nods as comprehension replaces confusion.

She leads me through the family room, grabs a quilt from the rocking chair and bundles it around my shoulders. She leads me past a laundry basket of towels waiting to be folded and put away and used and washed again. She leads me through the dining room where, days ago, we toasted Laura's pregnancy. She leads me to her kitchen where she fills the kettle and positions it on the stove.

I sit at her table. Sleet scratches at the window like an intruder clawing to get in. I'm not out there. Thank God I'm not out there. I'm here, the warmth of Anna's house seeping into me, bringing me back to life. In a moment she'll set a mug of piping hot water in front of me and offer me her tea basket. Then she'll pull out a chair and sit across from me in this kitchen with walls as calm as the pale morning sky. I'll pour out the happenings of tonight. I won't gloss over or withhold details and I won't pretend I'm not scared.

Because I am. Scared. Scared at how quickly I fell under his spell. Scared at what may have happened had I stayed a minute longer. But it dawns on me, I'm not scared about John and me. We will move on. We'll work through the fight, somehow. The timing and context were all wrong but John has exposed his wounds, brought his fears to the light. Now it's out there and now, maybe with Marco and Annalisa, or maybe with a counselor, or maybe with just the two of us, we'll work through it. Stitch up the frayed seams of our marriage and go on.

Annalisa joins me at the table. She gives my hand a squeeze and waits for me to speak. She'll listen, until I've exhausted my words, and then I'll receive what she has to say. And when I'm ready, she'll drive me home.

26

Someone should have saved me from myself. Someone should have talked me out of this insanity. This crisp April morning, when the gunshot split the air, I set off voluntarily. *Smiling.* Now, sides splitting and shins screaming, all I can do is put one foot in front of the other, again and again.

Somewhere in the distance lies the finish line. I can't see it but I have to believe it exists, otherwise I'll crumple onto the new spring grass.

One more mile, I tell myself. But these miles before me, they don't end. The ten-mile mark has come and gone and I'm beginning to wonder if this is all a joke. If, like Alice, I've unwittingly joined a race that never ends.

Pass the man in the red tank.

Pass the willow tree.

Now the mailbox with the cardinals painted on the side.

I've trained. Lord knows I've trained, but will it be enough? Will I be enough? Even with this throbbing doubt, my legs keep undulating all on their own. My body has decided to go on, with or without my confidence.

A water station lies ahead. Make it to the water station. Someone hands me a paper cup. Drink. Splash.

Keep going! someone yells. *You can do it!*

I want to knock these people over, with their clean shirts and Starbucks coffee. How dare they tell me what to do? And yet they've stoked the embers. Maybe, just maybe, I can finish.

More groups of people appear along the sidelines. Looking at them makes me dizzy and the ground at my feet seems impossibly far away, so I look straight ahead.

I hear the finish line before I can see it. Clapping, shouting, whistling, cheering. Distant at first, but growing louder with each step I take, until the noise eclipses my raspy breathing. I round a corner and just like that, what I've been hoping for comes into sight. I can barely make out the finish line, but it's there. Thank God it's there.

Hundreds of people, maybe more, line both sides of the street now, the sound of their cheering like a roaring tidal wave. I scan the crowd. In time, my eyes land on Phil's trusty John Deere cap. Laura claps beside him, the hidden baby girl Maggie believes she prayed into existence swelling her stomach. I see Annalisa, grinning and bouncing next to Marco. And my kids. There are my kids waving at me, their faces enraptured. But where is John?

My feet stumble. I look straight ahead again and push on, my eyes glued to the finish line.

Then, above the roar of the crowd, I hear my name. I hear John.

He's up ahead, next to the finish line. Somehow he maneuvered his way through the crowd to meet me at the end. His arms stretch over his head as he applauds. His grin is wide, his face alive with pride. For me, he's cheering for me.

It's what I've wanted all along, all this time I've been running. For him to see me, chase me, and run to be with me at the very end.

ABOUT THE AUTHOR

Rachel Allord grew up as a pastor's kid, vowed never to marry a pastor, and has been contentedly married to her husband, a worship pastor, since 1995. She resides in Wisconsin where she avidly consumes coffee, sushi, and novels— preferably at the same time. Her stories and articles have appeared in MomSense, Chicken Soup for the Soul, as well as various other publications. Her previous novel, *Mother of My Son*, released in May 2013 through Pelican Book Group (Harbourlight).

Printed in Great Britain
by Amazon